LABORS OF LOVE

A novel by R.V. Cassill

LABORS OF LOVE

ARBOR HOUSE NEW YORK

For Jeffrey Holmes 1959–1978
"Then to the elements
Be free, and fare thou well!"
Shakespeare
The Tempest

Goodbye, my Fancy.
WALT WHITMAN

I

"**Y**OU ARE *not reading,* daddy."

"I am *reading.*" It was his best defense. Troy Slater was an editor. Reading was what editors were supposed to do, just as plumbers plumbed. The children were obliged to respect that. Not all children can have manually dexterous parents.

"You don't even have a book," his slip of a daughter said. Furtive as a chipmunk—and of course preparing to ask a favor —Ursula had come through the open glass doors onto the high deck and found him with his eyes fixed on the great blue emptiness of the Cape Cod sky.

"Nevertheless," he said.

Like her mother she knew when she had him cornered. "Since you're not doing anything, why can't you take me and Kevin up to Provincetown this afternoon?"

For today he could not use the excuse that their mother had

taken the Volvo around the Bay for her class at Harvard. Nancy had ridden to Cambridge with their summer neighbors, the Bronsteins. "I'll drive you to the beach," he offered Ursula. "I'll leave you and pick you up any time you like. You can each get a Fruito at Terry's wagon."

"Kevin says Provincetown. And to tell you we haven't been for nine days. It's a pity when we're this close."

"Why Provincetown? All the crowds!"

"To watch the queers," she said. That was just a joke to nudge him into better humor. It was also a father-daughter liberty, possible between the two of them. Her mother would not let her refer to gay people as queers. If the child grew up a bigot, it would be his fault, not Nancy's.

Admitting he had neither book nor manuscript in hand at that living moment, work was still his best defense. "Kid, I've got mountains of reading to take care of."

Her ten-year-old face twisted in pain. It hurt her to catch him at his lies.

"If you and Kevin will take your raft and go to the beach by yourself this afternoon, I promise we'll have a boat ride this evening before mother gets home for dinner. The tide will be just right then. Okay, how about taking your kites? Feel that breeze? Perfect for kites."

"You want I should go fly a kite?" Her comedienne touch of wit and woe might have won for her on a less catastrophic day.

"Aw honey," he pleaded. *"Honey. . .?"* He could only carry his points with the females of his family by sheer abjection, from the posture of a conditional surrender.

"All right," she agreed. "I'll tell Kevin. But you owe us Provincetown."

It was the story of Troy Slater's life that he was seldom forced to outright lies. In a manner of speaking—in his manner of speaking—he *had* been reading when Ursula pounced on him. Reading the signs of the times. A man reading the oracles of his life in hope of finding an exception in the small print needs more than paper in his hands. He draws from all quarters. The vacuum-cleaner principle.

After he had driven his children three miles to the ocean beach in their smoking Volvo, Troy went right back to the canvas chair on the deck where Ursula had found him supine. He continued to read.

Out there in the blue Atlantic sky was an angel. The angel had an enormous and terribly bright sword. From its angry blade came semaphores of reflected sunlight, a steady stream of messages with a uniform significance.

JUDGMENT DAY IS AT HAND. LABOR DAY AT THE LATEST.
THE CAKE YOU ATE IS ALL YOU HAD.
YOUR LAMP WAS DRY WHEN THE BRIDEGROOM CAME.

He knew exquisitely well what text must follow these headlines. And the alternative to lying helpless in the deck chair was to go from the deck to the basement directly below it, fitted out for his summer study and workroom, and write it all out in a novel with a pathetic ending. A fictional ending with decisive violence was all he could conceive as a resolution to the grim absurdity about to stifle him. If one of three people were to suffer sudden death . . . Neatness was the only thing that recommended such a conclusion to him.

Yet it might be just a little better to be caught by the Angel or his womenfolks down there facing his typewriter than up here not even trying to talk back. Writing was the other thing he was presumed to be doing with his summers in Truro. Every year when they came up here, Nancy told their friends he was going to "finish his novel." To those few with whom he could be candid he said he was going to *begin* it, because he always thought he would. Beyond argument, he owed it to Nancy to write one novel or another. When they married she had made unforgotten sacrifices to give him the free time he needed to go on from his first book of short stories and become an established writer. By no stretch of justice could it be said it was her fault that he had frittered away his chances, coming long ago to an alcoholic dead end, with two years back on Valium before there was enough security for her to get pregnant with Kevin.

Nancy's life was still geared to the assumption that he might chuck his unrewarding job as a text-book editor and go all out for the novel. At this very moment when he was immobilized in a sunny deckchair, she was in a Harvard classroom studying business administration. The push on the business frontier was her way of being realistic about their situation. She had run through a number of creative opportunities in preparation for once again becoming the main support of the family. One winter in New York she had worked as a seamstress, with a specialty in repairing and dressing antique dolls. Had been receptionist in an art gallery. Photographer. Ceramicist. Had been apprenticed to a cabinet maker. But now as her midlife crisis deepened and thickened she saw that money alone could truly satisfy her craving and her psychic need.

So far this summer Harvard had been good for her spirits. Each time she came back late in the evening she seemed in a euphoric state that suggested the School of Business provided drugs and mass orgies. But knowing Nancy he believed neither sex nor drugs could put such stars in her eyes. It was the incidental detail of business that acted on her central nervous system.

"Direct mail," she would say. "It's the way to go." She would give him instances and anecdotes of men and women "without half our imagination" who had borrowed five thousand dollars of front money to start a direct mail business from their own basements and become rich within two years.

"The thing is to *plan carefully*. That's what I'm getting from

6

class," she said. "Budget everything. Know thyself and budget it. Your time, your credit, your psyche, your advertising, your market, your employees."

"We don't have employees. What business are we going to plan?"

"You can hire high school kids for practically nothing to stuff envelopes."

"We have nothing to sell."

"Ha!" she said. "That's what's always been wrong with your thinking. There's always something to sell. Your thinking is nineteenth century and you can only think of selling hardware or sacks of flour. *Imagine* something to sell. Anyone with the imagination to write a novel can think of what to sell. T-shirts with witty slogans on them. Little kitchen appliances with a cute logo. Silk-screened barbecue aprons. Use your imagination on what we can sell and leave the business end to me."

"I haven't proved I have the imagination to write a novel."

"Then get busy and do it."

She often spoke as if he were holding something out on her by not advancing his career as a writer. He had published a book—a good book, she believed—before they were married. Why had he come up with nothing since?

Nancy drank martinis. As a controlled alcoholic, he rationed himself along on dilute bourbon. The different octane of their drinks might account for discrepancies in their notions of business realism and the uses of literature. When the crystal of a martini reflected the stars in her eyes, she cried, "Don't spoil my thinking by asking for details. CEO's don't *know* all the details."

"What is a CEO?"

"See? You don't even know that, so how can you argue with me? Chief Executive Officers." He began to see that Harvard trained nothing lower than that. "Junk jewelry with sex innuendoes. Pamphlets on how you save on the cost of fuel.

America's at the brink. There'll be political consequences unless someone gets a hold on it. Something that gets better mileage for the car. The Volvo is burning oil badly and I'm going to get bids on repairs before I let any of the scalpers out here on the Cape touch it. It's just a mockery that garage mechanics have more business sense than people like us."

"Yes. All right," he said. "If direct mail is the way to go, I can always lick stamps. We'll harness the energy of my tongue and save America from a recession."

"It's so you can shuck off this job you hate so much and have time for your writing."

Like the other woman closing in on him, she clinched all arguments by invoking his wish to write a novel. Margaret Gill said, "When we're settled in Ibiza (or Greece, or Sicily) I'll lie there patiently while you're typing, and when you get tired you can roll over and fuck me."

So you found that droll, did you? said the Angel stationed in the blue sky above Truro. It amused you that the women who cared most for you respected your talents more than you did, is that it?

It seemed entirely logical that when the Angel appeared to announce that judgment was at hand, the Angel should be a male with no sympathy for Troy's "unique way of seeing things," or for the unwritten pages of the novel he had been pregnant with so long, or for the businesslike way he had budgeted marital energies to accommodate Nancy at home near the New York editorial offices of Stoke & Bywater, Inc. and Margaret Gill staked out near Stoke & Bywater's printing complex in Cincinnati.

The Angel dealt in factual commonplaces. He saw Troy's accomplishment as *de facto* bigamy and knew Troy wanted it to continue just that way—or at least was incapable of imagining a more desirable rearrangement. And the Angel who had watched the situation for two years with apparent nonchalance had always had time on his side—the kind of time that is said to "run out" with the banal, devastating indifference of a tide draining the marshes along the Pamet River, leaving boats, good intentions, loyalties and poignant memories high and dry.

Time had run out with Troy's morning mail. A letter from Margaret:

> The die is cast. I'm coming back to New York to live with Jan Savery to be near you until you have settled with Nancy.
>
> Jan was here on company business, and I hadn't realized how much I needed a savvy woman to talk things over with until she and I got to brass tacks. Though actually I'd been dreadfully shaken since mother and daddy came for a week's visit and were shocked by the way I'm living here. They know all about you and me. . . .

It was just at this point in his reading from Margaret's delicate blue stationery that the Angel had butted in, with the first of his editorial comments: *N.b.* Mother and Daddy *couldn't* know all about you, or how convenient it has been to have *de facto* wives on both ends of the Cincinnati-New York run, if young Margaret hadn't decided your time for waffling had run out.

Yes, but . . . Troy rubbed his balding temples, blinked and went on reading. There was no use arguing that Margaret had been (probably) happier and more content with her secret place in his juggled life than she could probably be as his wife. It was Margaret herself who had seen it as a traditional parceling between "sacred" and "profane" loves. "Sacred is fucking; profane is housekeeping," she said. She savored wit more than reality and, with reason, saw no future for herself as a housekeeper. And yet, underwriting her contentment had been

9

the knowledge that his legal marriage was inadequate for both him and Nancy.

Daddy was particularly sarcastic (Margaret wrote). I got nowhere explaining that my generation has scrapped the codes he lived by. With that Senior Officer's wit I've parodied for you, he kept slicing me up. Even though I told him you were going to your lawyer about the divorce right after Labor Day, he came back with, "Yes, but has he asked his wife?" He says it is more likely you are waiting for Nancy to die of old age—and that I may go before she does, if I'm not mugged by junkies in this ratty neighborhood. Mother is hooked on the idea that it "must be all sex," and of course it is impossible to talk to her about sex in the rarefied terms you and I understand so well. She thinks it is impossible to have a "good, interpersonal relationship" with a man of your age. Little does she know, my darling person.

We had stormy, poisonous scenes. You know I can't stand them and never do well with unsympathetic people. Things got said that probably can never be taken back. I promised (oath of the General's Daughter) to review the whole situation with true detachment.

But after they had gone, nothing came but migraines. Then True Blue Jan arrived. I knew she knew something about "us." Oh, she does. I was made to feel that we are very important in her scheme of things and she wants the best for us in all ways. I told her I wanted you to have your own sweet time in settling your family affairs, including the children. She came back that I must stand by you, be close, because it will be hard for you, you being the compassionate, caring person you are with everyone.

Jan has arranged for me to have my old job back at Stoke & Bywaters—except as her assistant instead of yours—starting after Labor Day. I'll come to New York to her apartment as soon as I can liquidate my lease here. In spite of migraine since the folks left (they are headed for Egypt and Sardinia; I think Daddy is hooked in with the CIA again or top secret for an oil company) I am faithfully keeping our shrine. Keith will take me to a rock concert tonight. Then I will come home and jack off for you in our bed with the candles burning and Brahms on the record player.

If it is too touchy for you to phone me soon, write me something wise and light to help me see what the real reality is. You know I don't always see it until you point it out.

Your Strange and Sacred Love,
Margaret

Leaning ominously over the hilt of his sword, the Angel said: *You* swindled her into living in a slum without any social life but dating homosexuals like Keith. A ripe, attractive girl like that! You taught her to masturbate to fill her sex needs between your visits to Cincinnati.

No, no, Troy said. She would rather go the auto-erotic route than soil the "sacred love" we consecrate together. I only taught her the term "jack off" as an expressive synonym for a banality of clinical language. She is very literary and delights in making our private language out of hearty American slang.

Now it seemed to him he could just make out the Angel's face, etched with a spider web line in the blue of the ocean sky. The Angel looked a lot like the photo of her father Margaret kept in a silver frame on top of a hi-fi speaker. General Gill, U.S. Army, Military Intelligence, retired. Horseman and Olympic fencer. The man with the blade to skewer all the happiness Troy and Margaret had shared in the last two years.

Before the blade came down, he would just like to say some things about Nancy that *he* had to take into account, whether Divine Justice did or not.

He would like the Angel to perceive Nancy just as he saw her now in his mind's eye, in the Harvard classroom. Her sharp pencil was poised above a yellow legal pad ready to spear any of the lecturer's tips instantly convertible into a boost in the family income, her eyes fixed on the lecturer himself as if sizing him up as a possible object of merchandise for direct mailing to cannibals or slave traders. Her powerful, restless, dancer's legs clenched in readiness to spring on any opportunity that would make her marriage what it had promised to be.

It was all right to sneer at Nancy for jabbering so much about "midlife crisis" and her "rights of personhood." That might be fashionable media jargon, but it was all the language Nancy had for the cankering discontents whose subtlety called for a good writer to express them in terms of finer discriminations. He was her writer as much as her husband. He had kept the watch with her, and to turn his back on the pathos he had shared with her would be equivalent to renouncing the sympathies that might yet give him the pride and confidence to write a book. He was not a consumer of women, picking them off the counter according to preference.

He said: If I were smart enough to choose between these women, I would have already done it. If I could divorce the marriage and keep what I love about Nancy and the children . . . Okay.

That is not an option, the Angel said.

Let it be noted that Troy Slater was a man who kept all the promises he could. When the tide was high in the Pamet River that evening, there he was in the stern of their dinky outboard motor boat, winding through the savage green of the marsh, taking his two children out past Depot Landing to the Bay.

In the bow spindle-shanked Kevin trailed an arm over the side. His fingers spelled something idle and profound in the brown-green water sliding by. Ursula swayed on the tin seat in the middle like a tropical princess riding a howdah on the back of a ridiculously merry elephant. The frailest wisp of a moon had risen in the violet air behind them.

Oh yes, the evening sunlight into which their little boat drove was tasty as warm country butter melting into toast. Surely, the doomed man thought, he had no option but to love every buoyant cupful of water in the river and the woman smells of the brine. Every upstanding blade of marsh grass and the blued sand on the shadow side of the dunes. Beyond right and wrong he loved the widening river with its generous reflections of everything that bordered it, the anchored boats in the cove and the bright bathing suits of the last swimmers lingering toward evening. Right or wrong, he loved himself for yielding to the caress of good times like this when they came. Hopelessly seductible, he loved his wife *and* Margaret Gill.

Modestly their little boat yielded right of way to a big cabin cruiser coming in between the boulders of the channel breakwater. Two magnificent women in bathing suits—they seemed magnificent in this setting—sat aloft in the fishing tower of the big boat, dangling their legs among struts while the bearded helmsman at the wheel drove straight up the channel at full power, nearly swamping Troy and the children with his wake.

Splashed and ignored, Troy nevertheless paid a tribute of envy to the bearded playboy in the bigger boat. It was the writer W.T. Bowman, national celebrity and a perennial topic of local summer gossip. Troy had been introduced to him two or three times at large Provincetown parties in years past, had been noticed if not remembered, had clucked over the gossip that filtered to him through Nancy. It was gossip of sex and politics, in both of which Bowman had a valiant track record. Seeing him now with two choice bimboes on board, Troy felt it only right to envy the man—if he hadn't envied he might have been sore at the carelessness of big league folk. And Kevin said, "Wow, that's a keen boat." Only Ursula glared.

Then the whole Bay, slick as a sun-paved dancing floor, opened before them with its illusion that they could steer where they pleased. Troy made a big wobbly circle and headed south along the beach. Two miles south of the breakwater he beached under a high, split dune the color of the sinking sun. All three of them swam, Troy swimming out just a little farther than the children dared or chose to go, like any good old sheepdog father.

While he smoked a cigarette and admitted only happy thoughts, Ursula and Kevin ran back among the dunes and explored the shallows. The biggest thing that happened to them on the excursion was that Kevin found a grotesque seaweed that had attached itself to a rock the size of his fist. He came running with it to his father, saying, "Looks like it should be in a horror movie, doesn't it?"

"Gruesome," Troy said. "Put it back before its soul gets in your body. Or vice versa."

"I'm going to take it home."

"As food? In the night it might eat us."

"No! To put it in our aquarium with the guppies."

"It's important to raise them in a good aesthetic environment," Troy agreed.

"Can I?"

It surprised Troy how unshadowed his own laughter sounded here. He grabbed Kevin's wrist and jerked it twice like a man pulling a bell rope. "Did you ever realize what a ridiculous family we are? Is there another family in the continental United States of America that when they go away for the summer take their guppies along? Sure. Bring it along to scare your mother, and let's go see if she's back from the Business College. I'll cook us something rare for supper."

He flicked the butt of his cigarette into the shallow lace of surf and thought in maudlin resentment he would die if he had to divorce any part of this. He was fastened to it, like the ugly seaweed to the stone.

The accusing Angel manifested herself under water, speaking this time in the gravelly voice of Jan Savery: If you know that much, you know you should have kept it in your pants.

2

DELICIOUS SMELL of seafood cookery—the aroma of his guilty conscience. Squid on rice, all inky black and ingeniously spiced, that was his specialty, and he concentrated all his devotion on cooking it right. His propitiatory offering to the visiting Angel, to Nancy, Margaret, Kevin, Ursula and himself.

He had iced crab cocktails to begin with, and everything was just ready to set on the table when he heard the car door slam in the Bronstein's driveway and Nancy calling, "Thanks. Thanks a heap," to the Bronsteins for giving her a ride. He could tell her mood by the abruptness of her step on the wooden stairs.

"Christ, you're not thinking of eating at this uncivilized hour?" She seemed to know exactly how little he had accomplished that day, if not why he had lavished so much care on his cookery. "I want to shower and have one drink in peace."

"I've got us a nice wine. *Soave.*"

"If you and the kids were starving, you should have nibbled on something. Is there no cheese left?"

She dropped her purse with a menacing clunk as she went past him. He listened hard for the sound of her shoes dropping in the bathroom. When he heard them fall, he began humming and put his rice back in the oven to keep warm.

She came out quickly, unshowered but barefoot. Kevin tried to interest her in the seaweed, which by this time had been planted in the gravel bottom of the aquarium teeming with their guppies.

"Get rid of that thing!" she said with a shudder of plump brown shoulders. "It's decayed. Dead for weeks."

"Daddy said . . ."

"Do what you want. No one in this family listens to me."

"That's why we are where we are today," Troy said.

On the possibility that might have a double meaning she declined to answer. She said, "Did anyone bother to turn on the TV to get the weather for tomorrow?" When everything else failed her, Nancy listened avidly to weather reports in hope of cheering news.

She made a display of fixing her own martini. Troy had moved in the direction of the bar shelf, still hoping to soothe her, but she cut in ahead of him and then danced across his path when he turned back to the refrigerator to get ice for her. With her jaw set she marched out on the deck that half surrounded their little house. She leaned on the rail, a captain on the fighting bridge of a ship of war, defying the barred, ruddy clouds of the sundown to mean that rain would keep her from the beach tomorrow.

By a perfectly natural progression of reason Troy understood that she was ripe and ready for talk of divorce—or with a minimal nudge from him she would be, letting all her dissatisfactions with him expand as the night went on from recrimination to recrimination.

The hitch was (wasn't it?) that they had talked divorce so often. Surely (if anyone were keeping count, and if count mattered) he and Nancy had talked about divorce a lot more often and at greater length than he and Margaret had. A ratio of ten to one, he supposed. And the result of all this was that the passions and reasons of their talk had been incorporated as a stabilizing element that propped the whole thing up.

Should he press matters tonight he would more likely than not find himself more sturdily built into the marriage than before. If and when he ever was brought to the point of confessing that, yes, there was another (and younger) woman to whom he had some—ah!—commitments, he would find the concrete hardening around his ankles with a density and speed that defied imagination. Like suicide, divorce was something that had to be done on a thoughtless impulse, full speed ahead.

Carrying his bourbon carefully as a glass of nitroglycerine, he meekly stepped outside to join his wife. She turned on him to say, "Anyone who thinks I'm going to end my days mail-ordering T-shirts has got another think coming, Buddy."

No gain in pointing out to her it had been her idea. "T-shirts!" he said with contempt. "As for T-shirts, let the servants mail-order them. If God had intended us for business people, we'd have been born with a basement full of T-shirts."

Wrong again. She was certainly not giving up on Business. The day had merely elevated her sights. "I had lunch with a woman my own age. She's mortgaged her house for thirty thou. Borrowed ten from another bank. Got herself a word-processing machine. She's into local publishing on her own and just doesn't give a damn if she goes broke by Christmas. Why can't we take the bull by the same horns and damn the torpedoes?

You're supposed to have the publishing know-how. I could take care of the business end."

"Her husband has . . . the know-how?"

"She divorced the sonofabitch."

"Ah!"

"What does that mean? 'Ah'?"

"It means 'good luck to the lady.' And to her uxorious husband."

"The way you stymied us was by always saying 'wait and see.' We could mortgage this place. Other people *make* their opportunities . . ."

"They go broke by Christmas. Besides it's already mortgaged."

". . . while we stagger on. With a mortgage."

He said, "If I'm the Denver Boot on the family, you can at least take it out on me. You might at least have listened to Kevin about his seaweed. He thought the damned thing looked dead, too. That was part of his joke. He expected you to laugh at it."

"I spoil everything. Is that what you're trying to get through to me, all of you? That it's my fault we've come to this dead end?" For a hot moment it looked as if her mood might splinter either way. She might have vaulted the deck rail and broken a leg to punish them and to protest the unfairness of the universe.

But then at the boiling point of her emotions, she suddenly embraced him with her left arm. He was shocked by the muscular thrust of her tongue into his ear.

The slick, moist burning went straight through to his central nervous system. She knew what she had done to him. Laughed. Let him go. "What's 'uxorious' mean? Hell, I'm not going to divorce you or get a second mortgage. You know I love you all, and Kevin's seaweed and our house we built to be carefree in.

Carefree! Oh, wow! I just need to know I'm making a contribution."

"You had a bad day," the uxorious man said. (Uxorious was what Jan Savery called him, meaning *henpecked*. "Cunt-struck and uxorious," she said, reminding him that Mencken had called Sinclair Lewis *cunt-struck*, a great handicap to a great writer. Jan was another who insisted on analyzing Troy in terms of other writers' faults and virtues.)

"Bad day?" Now she shrugged it off with regal nonchalance. And, as if his own bad day had prepared him for sympathetic insight, he saw her as a fully dimensional woman—troubled and troublesome, silly, headstrong, and gallant, with a very tangible, embraceable gallantry.

"Maybe we should have someone in," she said. Her light eyes scanned the dark foliage for artists and writers of stature, or the wealthy madcaps known to frequent Cape Cod in the summer. Part of the reason for building up here had been to have the company of such free and distinguished spirits.

"Hey," he said, "we saw W.T. Bowman when the kids and I were out in the boat. He was coming in from a day of fighting the giant marlin or tuna. He had a couple of sweet patooties decorating the boat. We could call him and invite him to bring them over to join the gaiety."

"Right!" Nancy said—but there was an implied sneer in her enthusiasm. Or else the grandeur of the evening was sneering at them both for being lightweights with heavyweight wishes. There was glamor not far off—glamor of beaches, ocean and sky and the glamor of wealthy and accomplished people—and here they squirmed in the frustration of getting so slight a share. Only a lick at the ice cream cone of the good life.

"Call him," she said, so dolefully he wanted to whip out a necklace of stars and a finished manuscript to cheer her up. He did not doubt that Nancy had been born to wear a giant's cloak or that she wanted one for him, too. He didn't expect one any more and she still did. That was the sinister difference that gnawed through their seasons together. They were roped in a pathos of falling short of the promises they had once and somewhere given each other. The pathos itched, but it bound them powerfully, face to face, resentment to resentment, belly to belly. It seemed neither escapable or tolerable. Now, as usual, he was kindled erotically by her undiminished greed for life. If she could have, she would have ripped the evening out of the sky and pulled it over them for a wedding sheet.

Too bad they didn't know Bowman or anyone in his league.

He said, "I guess we can yell over at the Bronsteins to come for a drink when we've eaten."

Her laugh was ghastly.

"Well, we can always screw," he offered. It might or might not be a loving offer, but whatever it was it was paltry. He might or might not have the wherewithal to make sex an act of love with this particular person, given his other commitments. Nevertheless, he wanted to honor her oceanic hungers and her deprivations. Too bad there was not a special and distinct organ of the body with which that honoring could be performed.

His dinner was no less successful for being postponed and kept on the warm while Nancy changed her mood. Her mood went up the string like a yo-yo that had gathered power in its plunge. Her laughter got more percussive as she recapped her day. The children, who might not understand how much she fictionalized, always delighted to hear her tear the world apart like a rodent's nest she had found in the closet.

Her Hah-vud professor had at last exposed himself as an egocentric dude who worked out his unconscious aggressions on the four females in the class. The other students—except for the woman she lunched with—were a bunch of losers. They had a few stale tricks to make them sound clever in the classroom. Just wait until *reality* got its teeth in them. The Bronsteins . . .

Well, the Bronsteins with whom she had ridden over and back and who had made her late for Troy's marvelous cookery were intolerable in the small space of a car, and now she saw them as undesirable neighbors. "He treats that dowdy woman like they were both a couple of Victorian ninnies. All the crudest clichés—'my bride' this, 'my bride' that, 'we'll have to stop downtown in Boston so my bride can get something for beauty's sake.' While *ogling* every little cutesypop who went by on the sidewalk. Which I'm sure she noticed as much as I. Call *him* a psychiatrist? I'll bet he can't tell her id from an igloo. I'm not even convinced they're Jews, since all the Jews I know are liberal." If she caught the Bronsteins' cat over on their property again abusing any chipmunks, she would break its back with Kevin's softball bat.

"He was at it again today," Ursula contributed. "He had one under the deck and the poor thing was just dancing and begging to be let go and making unhappy noises. Daddy was paying no attention . . ."

"I'm neutral in the cat-chipmunk war," daddy said.

"Your daddy has plenty on his mind besides chipmunks," Nancy said.

"Uxorious chipmunks," he said, seeing them dance in captivity before the Bronsteins' omnipotent cat.

". . . so Kevin and me pushed the cat with the broom and the chipmunk got away under the steps," Ursula said. She liked happy endings and saw no reason to belittle their effect by complaining that she had been cheated of a jaunt to Provincetown.

It was into this family armistice that the phone rang, and it was Jan Savery calling from New York. Nancy answered the phone, held it for Troy with a pantomime of extravagant questioning. It was not unusual for Jan to call, since she was another senior editor at Stoke & Bywaters, with an office next to Troy's. It was simply rare for her to call after dark, for the primary reason that she was nearly always soused after the sun went down.

Tonight was not an exception.

"Prrrrrmph, prrrrrrrmph, prrrrrrmph. Needa talk to you."

"I thought I'd hear from you."

"Prrrrrmph, prrrrrrmph. Margaret Gill."

"Understood. What about him?"

"Prrrrrmph, prrrrrmph, prrrrrmph."

"No." No there was no other extension in the house on which Nancy might be listening. Jan could speak freely, if he could not.

"Prrrrrmph, prrrrrmph, force the ishuh."

"Apparently you have. Something's going on I don't fully understand. Can you speak a little more into the phone, Jan. Can you hear me, Jan?"

"PRRRRRRMPH, PRRRRRMPH, PRRRRRRMPH. Die do right thing?"

A bright hope flashed through his mind. Just possibly Jan was having second thoughts about meddling in his business, and just possibly Margaret might be headed off from the folly of leaving Cincinnati. "I'd like to hear more specifics before I come down one way or the other," he said. "Can you call tomorrow from the office?"

"Prrrrrmph." Not good enough. Hungover tomorrow, Jan's stricter principles would dominate. She might lock into a position that tonight was still fluid.

"Tell you what. The best way to discuss it is if you come up here. We've been meaning to get you up for a weekend, anyway. Come on Friday. We'll meet you at the Provincetown airport. Okay?"

"Prrrrmph, prrrrmph. Genevieve?" He understood that Jan had agreed to come and was asking if she ought to bring Genevieve George along. Old Genevieve was another of his confederates at the office. Genevieve loved Cape Cod and no doubt at some profligate, boozy lunch he had promised to invite her up as well. "Prrrrmph, gulf?"

"Why not? Tell her to bring her golf bag. I'll dig up someone to play with her. You know I can't stand the game."

He came back to the dinner table as the children broke from it to watch TV. "Poor old Jan. Very low. Her mother's dying of cancer in Texas. I thought the least I could do . . ."

"I heard," Nancy said. "You asked her to bring Genevieve, too. Not exactly what I had in mind when I asked for lively company."

"I owe it to them. They're good old scouts. They keep me covered on everything at the office."

"She called about her mother's cancer?"

"Oh. About some dimwit author. Man named Dangleburn. In California. He's run into trouble about a book we're expecting. Hasn't delivered and shall we call back the contract? The world is full of writers who can't deliver."

"Ah now. Ah, *honey.*" She understood the abjectness of his plea. "I come home bitching about little things, and you have big things banging in your head."

She patted his crotch and laughed. As soon as she had her postponed shower and the children were settled, she would make everything all right.

As consolation for despair, he could have settled for what was at hand for the evening. But Jan's call had started him reviewing his cards, tricked him into hope. Now his mind was an accelerated metronome, whipping back and forth so fast it whistled audibly. He ambled past the open door of the bathroom just as Nancy stepped fresh and dripping from her shower. The corner of his eye registered the incurve of her flank cut by the blue edge of a towel. And . . .

. . . shouting that Jan had reminded him of business mail that must be on its way tonight, he ran from the sight. He galloped the Volvo down the hill to the post office, stopped in the little island of light around the glassed phone booth. He spread little piles of quarters, dimes and nickels on the shelf of the phone booth and dialed Margaret's number in Cincinnati.

He would tell himself later—oh, through most of the summer, because from here on in every minor circumstance would seem fateful as he endlessly, desperately, reviewed them all—that if she had answered on his first attempt to get through to her he might have escaped hanging for either a sheep or a lamb.

She did not answer.

The sheer loneliness of the phone ringing in an empty apartment where he had been so happy made it unthinkable that he should now return to his house and bed with Nancy.

He drove dolefully to the parking lot at Depot Landing. He took off his shoes and left them in the Volvo. Barefoot he walked down the faintly luminous slope of sand toward the edge of the receding tide. The pleasure boats at anchor rocked dimly and seemed to huddle closer to each other as the water went out. He lay down on the cool sand to watch Cassiopeia rising. And Andromeda following with what seemed indecent haste.

It occurred to him that he might have made a real mistake in inviting Jan Savery up for the weekend. He was well aware that she and Nancy disliked each other, that their dislike was absurdly rooted in some rivalry over him, the way they shared his time, his jokes, his intellectual sympathies. Whatever it was, Jan had transformed it into an uncompromising conviction that he ought to leave Nancy and grab Margaret.

"That woman will keep drinking your blood as long as

there's enough to float a corpuscle"—Jan's third martini assessment of Nancy. He remembered it from a lunch more than a year ago, the day he first talked openly with her about his "bigamous situation." From her pose as elder sister she declared, "One gamous is all any man is man enough to handle."

Jan said, "Fifteen years she's kept you from emerging. You were going strong as a writer until she put the bit and spurs to you. Some rider you got on your back, hoss."

"The truth is, I had a terrible, suicidal year before Nancy gathered me up and pasted the pieces together," Troy said. "Five weeks in Bellevue—which is not a joke I'd care to repeat. A shrink who saw me as a permanent meal ticket—if I had any way to raise the money for him, which I had not. Over eight thousand in debt to my parents. Getting to work and getting home on Valium, which my shrink dispensed like candy for the kiddies."

"So Nancy was a mattress to drop on. How many years do you owe her for that?"

"There's the marriage bond, Jan. The things you've been through together. It toughens even if it is not the same thing as love. We've got that and the kids. They depend on her as much as me."

"So! You admit you don't love her. Troy, be the steward of your talent as Scotty Fitzgerald said. Look what happena that poor bastard. And a woman put him there."

The lunch time martinis had made them both wise, so he said, "Jan, you know this fucking town is full of publishing lushes who believe they are Fitzgerald and keep repeating the Fitzgerald clichés. Let's be straight on one thing. I am not—repeat not—going to make much of anything as a writer. I'm a pretty damn good editor. I can not hack it as a writer. I'd hit the wall again if I tried. Or else I'd be cautious. That wouldn't work. I'll tell you what I want. I want things to go on as they are. I'm very lucky."

"Then," said Jan, lighting her cork-tipped cigarette with an old actress's flourish of contempt, "you're just another whore-hopping business pig with some young cunt stashed in Cincinnati. I have no respect for you. None. Never speak to me again."

She had actually lunged up drunkenly from the table in her indignation at his grossness. He caught her before she fell and led her to the door of the ladies' room. When she came out she was still eyeing him balefully, and as they walked back up Madison Avenue she kept saying, "Bind her to you with hoops of steel."

She said, "That Margaret's gotta *mind*, not just an orifice. Oh, frizzy. A mind like an Afro hairdo. Kind of weird, but a mind! Ultra literary. Bind her to you with hoops of steel."

"Troh-ee!" Margaret's glad voice penetrated his ear very much as Nancy's tongue had earlier. A maddening duplication of effects.

"Hope I didn't call after you'd gone to bed."

"Oh, I *am* in bed. Where else do I belong? Was it you who called about two hours ago? We were just coming in when I heard the phone ringing, and I couldn't get my key in the door fast enough. I knew it was you, so I brought the phone in by the bed to wait. I have our candles burning, Troh-ee. And now you're here with me."

" 'We'? When you and Keith came in?"

"No. Bob."

"A friend of Keith's?"

She laughed merrily. "Oh, not one bit. Bob has rented my apartment and bought most of my things, except what I'll bring along for us. He needed a place to live and he's already moved in."

"Oh."

"He's fast asleep on the couch, silly."

"But you've made the step. You've rented your apartment."
Her voice was small and grave. "Was I wrong?"

"It's just that I was startled. Having you back in New York
will be . . . It seemed the kind of decision we would have come
to together, after hashing it out."

She heard his rebuke and there was a down-swooping pause
with a quality of tears suppressed. Then gravely and quietly she
said, "Troy. I never, from the beginning, asked anything except
if you loved me, did I?"

"You had a right to expect . . ."

"Hush. Do you love me?"

"Yes. And at least your letter means it's time I faced some
things we didn't talk about directly."

"When have we not faced things? Do you mean I didn't go
into this with my eyes open? Oh yes I did. You know my life
wouldn't have any meaning without *us*. You came into my
strangeness and it was all there. We've come such a long way.
Left so much that was rotten and old behind us. When you
came along and said, 'Let's walk out of Sodom' I put my hand
in yours and I'm not going to be like Lot's wife and turn back.
Not even if you tell me to. Unless I've already done it by
writing that stupid, goddamn letter. I won't put any claims on
you except what you want of me."

"No," he said, because he admitted what he was hearing. It
was like being connected with the night itself, hearing its true
voice in hers, seductive with promises. The real Margaret, who
was never quite herself in daylight. "It's just that we have to
figure how to make it real."

"That's what I want," she said. Her voice stopped abruptly.
The dark kept on whispering around the phone booth, not
quite intelligibly. The wind coming up the marsh shook the
glass panes delicately.

"What?" he asked.

In the night wind he seemed to hear the rustle of her

bedding, the sub-sibilant whisk of a candle-lit sheet on her skin.

"What?" he asked again, his throat tightening.

"Troh-ee?"

"What?"

"Put your hand down inside your pants. Put your hand down and hold him warm for me and I'll tell you."

"Mmmmmm."

"Do you have hold of him? Warm and tight? So he'll swell up for me?"

"Mmmmmm." It was the exposure of being in a lighted glass booth that made him compromise, no doubt. He looked around the lot outside and saw a camper parked by the post office wall. So he put his hand in his pocket instead of inside his shorts.

"He's in me now," the voice of the night said. "From behind. Slow and powerful. Oh, he's touched it. Troh-ee?"

"What?"

"Troh-ee?" He could hear now the accelerated gulping of breath in her throat, saw the flicker on his eyelids of candlelight on white walls, the prance of shadows driven together.

"Troh-EEEE?" The silken scream, like a ribbon ripped by gale wind.

"What?"

"I love you. I love you-oo-ooo!"

"Yes."

"I love you-oo-oooo!"

The tapping on the glass of the booth was real enough. He jerked his head around, the instrument masking his bared teeth, to see two cheerily smiling faces confronting his from not more than a foot away, beyond the glass.

"Mister, you going to be using the phone much longer?"

"Two minutes."

"Cause we got to catch someone before they leave Provincetown or we won't have a ride to New York."

They were two ruddy, wholesome looking girls with back packs. Someone's daughters, young enough to be his—as Margaret Gill was, also. He raced past them when he left the booth, his hand in his pocket for the only disguise he needed.

At first he thought his shameful trembling came from having been surprised by the girls with back packs. When he tried to start the Volvo he could not get the ignition key inserted, and it seemed to him daylight might catch him there, still fumbling.

But when he had managed to get the motor running and the car in motion—it seemed to head for his house without his volition, without any need for a driver—he was at the mercy of some complex machinery that did not recognize or need him. Wires and wheels, wind and leaves and sea, pricks and cunts of incredible horsepower.

The spirit of annihilation rode beside him. The other bucket seat in the Volvo seemed no emptier than his own. He could not believe what he had heard on the telephone. Rather more precisely he could not choose what interpretation to give it. The words and sequence existed in perfect ambiguity, as if the needle on a compass would point at any given direction and call it North.

This was not the first time Margaret (if it *was* Margaret) had given him what she called a "telephone fuck." "It's part of my witchcraft," she liked to say, between solemnity and joking. "So talking to you when you're in New York or on the Cape and I'm here where I belong in Cincinnati won't be a substitute for anything. It will be the *real* thing." Call it a joke, it still tiptoed to the cliff edge of sanity when it worked.

Tonight something had gone past the edge. Out of her intended illusion a swarm of more menacing illusions multiplied, cats out of the bag, little bright firecrackers exploding in succession as the spark ran down the fuse. Illusions of an

29

unearthly creature between her legs when she shrieked his name like a battlecry—"TROH-ee!" Someone pounding her mattress who was Troy Slater, but was not himself. Or a champion sex-fiend who was himself, but was not Troy Slater. Man, animal, or demon there—then who was driving this unreliable Volvo on a road he seemed to remember?

He came to the Bronsteins' driveway and stopped the car there hesitantly, remembering Bronstein was a psychiatrist who might help him. It occurred to him that, as a psychiatrist, friendly Norman Bronstein would have to recommend castration for his difficulties. He drove on to a lane that swung in among the pines and told himself, "Troy Slater used to live here."

He left the car afraid of the sound he would make when he closed its door. He stood quaking in the dark, saying to himself (or maybe to Troy Slater), "You are going to be very sick."

He confessed that he had always been sick since he tried to be a writer instead of a husband, and the illusion that he had ever known a girl named Margaret Gill was the strongest symptom of that sickness. It came to him that if he opened the screen door of his house, he would find himself stepping back into the ward in Bellevue, which he had imagined leaving fourteen years ago. The faces in the ward would be exactly those he remembered and he would tell them again he was a writer of stories. The attendants would say, "Well, we all make up things. Nobody can tell where fiction begins."

He went in anyway, as quietly as possible, because there was something in the bathroom he had to have. Winter and summer he always took with him one capsule of Valium, as an alcoholic will carry an ounce bottle of whiskey through his years of sobriety. Talisman, memento, the last round of ammunition, saved for extremities.

30

Fortunately Nancy and the children were sleeping peacefully in the sweet night air. He had no accusers to face except those in his dreams, and after he took the Valium they turned out to be more sympathetic and curious than he had feared.

3

H IS DREAMS of that midsummer night ought to have given a chuckle to his neighbor, the psychiatrist Bronstein.

The first one was about Bronstein's cat. This animal, graceful and gross in the same movements, was down among the scrub oaks and hog cranberries by the Slaters' drive, stalking a bluejay.

Then it began to stalk Troy in a transformed guise—as a human figure in a white suit with an oversized tiger face, two dimensional as cardboard, fixed above the shoulders. This ridiculous figure came at a casual pace toward Marine Sgt. Slater as he huddled under the deck in an angle of the concrete block foundation. The tiger mask was incapable of a change of expression, a printed thing growing larger and larger in his field of vision.

But Sergeant Slater had a double-barreled shotgun with two

green shells locked in its barrel. Buckshot. He fired both barrels as the tiger mask disintegrated in an all-encompassing blaze of light.

You shouldn't have done that, said the tiger.

"What's the matter?" Nancy asked, waking beside him. She looked at her watch. "Where've you been all this time?"

"Muffler went bad on the Volvo," he said.

She felt for his cock, tugged it a couple of times like a marketer testing vegetables for texture, dropped it and said, "Well, you missed your turn, Buddy."

They both went back to sleep.

In his second dream he was flying home from Tokyo, after his tour of duty as a sergeant in the Marine's Communications Center.

How splendid the broad, keen wings were—overcoming the Pacific that lay under them half-silvered with the light of the rising sun! How he and his slant-eyed comrades flew like risen gods on a mission of vengeance and pacification! They were flying to attack Pearl Harbor again on a better Sunday morning, roll back the infidel to the California coast, and then make peace in the White House. Mr. President, you have nothing to fear from us. We have come to liberate you from the mistakes and corruption that began before Watergate.

As he left the White House lawn in a shower of white roses, Margaret Gill sprang from the crowd of onlookers cheering from the sidewalks. She knelt and kissed his left hand. Troy, your prick saved me from a meaningless life, she said. Proudly.

He woke from this second dream in a state of bliss. (He would not ordinarily have used the word *bliss* in assaying his own mental state. The dream had somehow compelled him to use it.) He felt forgiven and self-forgiven. So he went to sleep again.

In the third dream, Bronstein himself appeared. In a professional capacity. Bronstein had a handful of sharpened pencils and the kind of yellow legal pad Nancy favored for keeping her notes and her shopping lists.

"Let's discuss Margaret Gill's *strangeness*," Bronstein began briskly. Both of them giggled, man to man, over the *double entendre*. "Her *what?*" Marine Sergeant Slater asked. "You are simply not used to the way she handles language."

"Handles *what?*" Bronstein asked—and went off in a whinnying gale of snickers which, this time, Troy did not join.

As if he were lecturing or dictating to a stenographer, Troy said, "Miss Gill has the quaint habit of discussing her own strangeness with detachment, as we have heard ancient maiden ladies discussing their goiters, or as simple people justify their opinions by circumstances of their upbringing—as 'I was raised as a Campbellite in Northern Missouri, so I think . . .'—or as if her Strangeness might be a supernumerary orifice. Her Strangeness is like a pet dog, dear but demanding. She must take her Strangeness out for walks on a leash, as she herself so imaginatively puts it. Often she declares her Strangeness is like a foreign tongue which only I can translate. She insists—and I quote—'I'm stranger than what we are doing with our lives, Troy, though this love is what I was born for. I want you always to know that'."

Bronstein threw up his hands disdainfully. "Facts! Facts! Facts! Give me facts or . . ."

"I am trying to prepare for them with this preamble. Without it you may go astray, as I have gone myself."

". . . we will have to cut your peter off."

"Penis," Troy corrected him gravely. Bronstein seemed to accept the correction of nomenclature, for he erased something from his yellow pad and made a new entry.

Then he said: "I have someone here who will see to it that you stick to your story."

He called in Jan Savery, dressed in bright blue stockings and a severe black dress. At once she said, "The patient has always presented himself as a writer."

With a wink at her Bronstein said, "Well, he's going to write now, on pain of decapitulation."

"Give him the painful story, Troy," Jan said. "How you killed two birds with one stone."

Troy said, "I can't. That's why I'm here. Oh, I'm as able to give the facts as any man alive, and I can type at great speed if you'd prefer the facts written down. But I can't tell the story because the story can't be told. It may not be one story. It may be more than two stories, deviously interlinked, like several kangaroos in each other's pouches."

"I'll say," Bronstein interjected lewdly.

"Or, to make an analogy with which you may be familiar, it is like the famous double helix. You can't have one without the other and you can't have the other without the one and neither begins anywhere until after the other is started."

"That's the way all writers talk," Jan Savery said, "but some cut the Gordian knot."

"Or we'll cut it for him," Bronstein said. "We've unblocked writers before. I've never seen one yet who could stand up to my tiger."

"I'll try," Troy promised, "but as it comes out, little by little, you'll see that there is no guilt involved, because whatever I got from Margaret I brought home to Nancy. And vice versa."

"The gift of gifts for his bride!" Bronstein whooped.

"For blood-sucking Nancy," Jan Savery hissed. "It seems passing strange that you passed Margaret's poor little Strangeness along."

"That might well be my title," Troy said. *Passing Strange.*

In design and concept it is much like Gide's *The Counterfeiters.*"

"Facts, facts, facts," Bronstein shouted. "The truth, the truth, the truth. And make sure it is stranger than fiction."

"Then may I borrow some of your paper? I would be embarrassed to disclose it in my own voice in Miss Savery's presence. And style is not unimportant, as will be evident, though my writing hand is rusty and penmanship unremarkable."

Bronstein passed him two of the yellow pads and a handful of sharpened pencils. Then—Troy dreamed—he began to write with urgent concentration while Bronstein paced back and forth beside him like a proctor in a college examination, muttering rhythmically, "Facts, facts, facts. Truth, truth, truth."

H ERE ARE the facts of what Troy dreamed he wrote
that night:

The textbook house of Stoke & Bywater keeps its editorial
offices in Manhattan. The printing plants, most of the business
establishment and the distribution center of a vast national
combine are in Cincinnati. It is the practice of Management
to send senior editorial people like Slater to Cincinnati for
extensive consultation several times a year. Conversely, the
"hardware people"—those in production, accounting, sales
and graphics—are brought to New York for orientation in the
company's editorial practices. This applies particularly to ap-
prentices like Margaret Gill, who might some day aspire to
editorial jobs. Miss Gill majored in literature at Northwestern.
She came to New York for an eight-week training stint in

September, more than two years ago. There she was one day, sitting a little nervously waiting for Slater when he arrived at his office soon after ten.

"I thought editorial staff began work at nine," she said, more as an apology for her gauche punctuality than as a rebuke to him. It did not then, or thereafter, occur to her to rebuke him for anything at all, since, while she had waited she had found on the shelves beside his desk a copy of his one and only original production. A book of short stories published by a reputable house more than a decade before.

"You're a *writer*," she said. The intonation she gave the word foreshadowed all that was to follow.

Being hungover and grumpy that morning—and considering himself not so much a "writer" as a "failed writer"—he said, "And you're another kid who watches the Waltons on TV every week. I'm John Boy twenty-five years after. Look and despair."

"No," she said blushing. "I mean I glanced through *Vegetable Love* while I was waiting. Miss Savery didn't tell me anything else to do. She said not to mess up the permissions letters you have laid out."

"*Vegetable Loves*," he corrected, adding the *s* she had overlooked. He uncapped the orange juice he had grabbed from the stand by the elevator downstairs. Acid and sweet soothed his tongue and throat. "Though you're on track if you think the title derived from Marvell's poem."

" 'My vegetable love shall grow, vaster than empires and more slow,' " she quoted, starry-eyed. He thought she had a plain face, an ordinary college-girl face with a notable arch of bone in the forehead, but her eyes took on an amazing charge from her enthusiasms.

He said, "I was so young and innocent when I published it I didn't realize everyone would think I'd written a cookbook.

Love That Vegetable. In this business disillusion never ceases. Why are you getting into it?"

"Oh . . .!" Her eyes said *a sun, a watery main, the shadow of a magnitude* . . . When they said that, maybe he was gone already; maybe they were both gone. For the whole trip. (Though she would say later, "You don't remember, but you patted my head that first day. Maybe just being fatherly. When I felt your hand on my hair . . .")

"You're a writer, huh? John Boy's little sister."

"No!"

"I'll bet you're a writer. That's all we get, at least from the female side."

"I *wrote* [carefully in the past tense] some . . . quite a lot of . . . verse in college. Oh, and I keep a journal. Correspond a lot with friends. But, Mr. Slater, I have no illusions at all. I'm resigned to the way it is."

"Ha! Poets never give up. They only lie to themselves. They get into the publishing racket because—as you have no doubt put it—it's 'being near' literature. The path from that is downward all the way." He finished his orange juice and its flavor was ripe as the Mediterranean on his tongue as he glared at her and went on: "So let me give you the big warning before we proceed any farther with this business. Get out. Go home. Marry a lawyer, dentist, pre-med student. Have babies. Grow roses. Get out before it is too late."

She laughed crookedly, not knowing how much of this was theatrical jest, but she said, "It's already too late."

He had thought her face plain. It always seemed plain to him while she was clothed. When she lay naked to his gaze, her face was something else again. "I don't know what. Serpent of the Nile. Something on that order. Oh, hell, it *goes with* what else you've got."

"I believe so," she said with that curious, grave detachment that seemed so droll when she anatomized her "strangeness."

"The face seems to point at an angle to this. At another angle to this. And straight down to this."

"Yes," she said, "it does."

" 'Two hundred years to adore each breast. And thirty thousand to the rest,' " he speculated, semi-tumescent. Marvell's "To His Coy Mistress" had become their handbook—vastly more exciting than *The Joy of Sex* or the *Kama Sutra* with its suggestions of muddy Indians having at it in the Ganges amid floating pollutions.

"She's older than that," Margaret said of the part he was adoring with the tip of his ring finger. "She comes from Luxor on the Nile. Ever been there?"

"Huh-uh," he said, continuing his adoration.

"I have. Daddy's in the Army. A general, to tell the silly truth. So I've been everywhere. Northwestern was the longest I ever settled down anywhere. He took me to Luxor once when we were in Cairo. Well! The boats on the Nile in the early morning or just before sundown! Sails like big dirty wings. Or flowers. Shall I tell you what you can never, never believe?"

"Uh-huh."

"At Luxor I was possessed. That's where my strangeness began, anyhow, and I attribute it to being possessed. I was only thirteen and I used to think what happened was only that I was at an impressionable age. While you're doing this to me I know better. I know I was truly possessed. By the Nile. Somehow. I looked out on it from the hotel window, and I could feel what I belonged to. All of it. All the way back. You call it Serpent of the Nile. Yes, that's right. I realized it—*she*—belonged to the Serpent. Isn't that strange?"

"Uh!"

"And for years afterward I could never get the smell of the Nile out of my nose. I don't mean like the smell of incense that some of the pretentious kids at college used to burn. More like the smell of a snake. A very big snake that has been lying in the sun. Crawling very slow. Do you want to put your tongue in her now?"

"Uh-huh."

Margaret's first assignment for her training stint in the New York offices was to help Troy straighten out the mess of obtaining permissions for a textbook in American Civilization, intended for high school use. "It's not the kind of work I am supposed to have to do myself," he explained. "The secretaries bungled it." So Margaret applied the best of her intelligence to tracking down the holders of copyrights, sorting the correspondence with historians and archivists, and collating budgetary matters for the bookkeepers.

Her intelligence was first rate—when applied. After she moved over to Darcy Holbrook's office, she apparently quit applying it altogether. At a morning staff meeting Darcy wanted to fire her outright.

"She did excellent work for me, Darc," Troy found himself saying. He was known in the company for having a nasty tongue and he was afraid that now it might cut loose before he thought out the implications.

"She moons. She forgets things. I have to check over everything she does. I can't have a person like that on the other end of the wire in Cincinnati when she goes back."

"We're paid to check the work of people in training."

"Then you take her again."

Sleepy Dan Wiggs, first vice president, didn't know about that. Trainees should get the feel of all the departments in the New York office.

"Let her have the feel of Troy if he wants her," Darcy said.

"Is there some innuendo I'm missing in that?" Troy wanted to know. He could still—at that time—afford to challenge such

43

innuendoes, if they were intended. For—so help him God— he had never in the first weeks of knowing her even imagined there was going to be anything between them except an office friendship delicately colored by his pity for her innocence about the way publishing was really done.

When she did return to work for him, a few days after the staff meeting, she said, "Well, I managed that maneuver neatly, didn't I?"

"Maneuver? Maneuver?"

"Getting assigned back to you."

"Why on earth would you want that?"

Without batting an eye she gave him her reason. "William Blake says we must serve the best man."

She was not fooling. William Blake had spoken to her through the improbable medium of the printed page, telling her that the best men were artists, writers. Troy Slater had once published a wry collection of short stories called *Vegetable Loves.* Ergo, she would serve him.

"If you suppose," he said to her grimly, "that you can guide your life by what the poets say, you're headed for an early grave."

"But that's what I always do. It works fine."

He blew a tender raspberry. "It may work in that starry universe you inhabit. In the real world it will kill you."

"They haven't laid a glove on me yet."

"Where'd you get that expression?"

"I'm a magpie. I pick things up wherever I find them."

He supposed her maneuver had a message for him. The least he could do was test its meaning, and the first test was to ask her out to lunch. That cliché was so old he supposed she could not—being bright—have any doubt at all about his intention. Yet, when they stepped out of the Algonquin at two ten, after a lunch where she had laughed at everything he said, she looked at her watch and groaned, "Jeez, we'll be later than is good.

44

Jan Savery laid it on me about not taking too much lunch time when I was slaving for Darcy."

"Yeah," he said. "Only on our way back I want you to meet a writer friend of mine who's got a room across the street at the Royalton." The friend was real—and a real writer. Real enough to have come by Troy's office just before lunch time to leave the room key with him.

Was Margaret surprised to find the room empty on their entrance? Later, she would deny it. "I knew you were up for me. I have a strange sense about those things, though you tried not to let on. And when I saw you unlock the door, I said, 'Oh, oh'. I said, 'Oh, oh, this is it'."

And he remembered how shockingly breathless she had been when he closed the door behind them—as if she did not mean to breathe again, ever, unless he gave her breath. Their first kiss was abbreviated by her panting. "Ooooh. Let me sit down. Sorry. Get me a glass of water, please?"

She sat on the bed. She had kicked off her shoes by the time he returned from the bathroom with water that trembled over the edge of the glass and wet her skirt.

When he thrust into her, she said, "I'm *glad.* I'm so glad!"

Then she went back to Cincinnati on schedule. It was December before Troy saw her again. "We never even had an allnighter in New York," she said when she kissed him at the Cincinnati airport.

They had not. But already, in his letters to her there had begun what was to be the richest and strangest part of the whole affair with her. He had begun to write to her—writing with a heady freedom he had never permitted himself since the bad times of his mental collapse, writing now with no fear of being caught or punished or merely shamed for what he put on paper.

"I've got all your letters on my shrine," she said in the taxi

45

from the airport. "God, you're such a wonderful writer."

"Like Blake? Yeats? Andrew Marvell?"

"All of them. Wrapped in one skin."

"What's your 'shrine'?"

"You'll see. I've been working on it."

Then, when the cab finally stopped in a crumby, lower-class neighborhood that could not even be called inner-city but only a mistaken, neglected sort of sink-trap on the river bluffs, inhabited mostly by the discouraged of several generations, he asked, "Dear young lady, we'll have to up your salary so you can move somewhere at least safe if not pretty."

"It's good and safe. I picked it myself. I don't want to be where anyone but you can come looking for me. I don't make friends with people at the office. Not any more."

Her apartment was one flight up above a bakery. It was large because it was the only inhabited part of the squatty building —three rooms that made up the entire second floor. What was to be her living room was still a welter of Salvation Army furniture, her hi-fi set on the floor, cardboard boxes still bound with ropes, a Navajo rug still rolled up and propped in a corner.

"Next time you come you'll see me as I lived in college," she said, apologizing with sweet anxiety for the present disorder. "I've got some nice things in the boxes. Mother is sending my big print of Titian's *Concert Champêtre.*"

"With the fat nudies on a picnic?"

"They're goddesses. I'll hang it right between these windows. I'll tell you about it, too." She pulled the window blinds as she spoke (and he would never see them open again in two years; for these windows looked out only on the back of a tacky Congregational church).

"And here's our kitchen," she said. "I'll serve you such things! I'm a pretty fancy cook. You'll see." (He would, indeed —and sadly compare her gourmet cooking with Nancy's hit-or-miss, slam-bang improvisations. When the creative mood hit

46

her, Nancy baked bread—good bread—but her real preference was for eating in restaurants. Margaret thought restaurant atmosphere spoiled the "sacrament of eating with someone you love.")

"And . . . !" she sang in triumph. "Here! Here's our shrine!"

He would remember—with a groan of sin—that he had laughed when he saw what she had done with the bedroom, the one room in the apartment that she had carefully finished in time for his arrival.

It appeared at first to have no windows at all, to be merely the stark white interior of a cube. The windows had been boarded over with celotex before she painted the walls and ceiling. She had put a white, shaggy carpet on the floor. And in the middle—the exact, geometric center—of this arctic and austere environment she had placed her queen-sized bed. *Their* queen-sized bed, covered with a white coverlet.

At the head of the bed, one on either side, stood two big wrought-iron candlesticks (made from branding irons, he would discover) each loaded with a lewd red candle three inches in diameter. Behind the candlesticks was an upright screen or bulletin board, also made of celotex nailed on a two-by-four frame, on which fluttered all the pages and pages of letters he had written her since she left him in New York.

When she heard his laugh, she asked in real, girlish pain, "You don't like it?"

"I do . . ." he said (already too late?). "It's . . . surprising."

"It's . . . what?"

"A fit shrine for your strangeness." Knowing he had already spoiled some keen edge of her expectation, trying to joke away his failure. "We'll study your strangeness here."

He went to the bulletin board and glanced editorially over the collection she had made of his unleashed writing—recognizing his own typing, a phrase or two, his longhand inspirations on office memo sheets mailed as he walked to the subway from the office, his signature at the bottom of something he had clipped from *The New Yorker* to share with her. All his —except for a postcard reproduction of Titian's *Sacred and Profane Love.*

"I'm your sacred love," she said from behind him. "I don't care if you have another wife back there."

On the white bed with its white coverlet rumpled on the floor beside them and the red candles growing shorter as the days, weeks, months, then two years passed—they studied her strangeness.

"I have this great woman thing," she said gravely. "I suppose I've always known I had it, even before what I told you about being possessed in Egypt. I don't think it's for child-bearing. I don't even know if there's a womb up there. It's like something else. For making *you* instead of babies three or four. I know it is in there, and it follows you out when you pull out of me. Can you feel it follow out?"

"Yes," he said, and he seemed to be telling the truth.

"You know in the Titian it's the naked one who is the sacred love. The woman in the dress is the profane love. Maybe it was my mother who told me it was the other way around, but I always knew naked was sacred. That painting is where I got my idea for our shrine, really. I meant to always be naked for you in here. Though it was good with the garter belts and the other costumes, wasn't it? And that corset I found that time with the old-fashioned whalebone stays? That was a nice idea. And the masks we wore the second time you were in Cincinnati? They were lots of fun. But from that first night in here when you undressed in the kitchen and I was lying here for you when you came back in, it's always been best when we were naked and I could watch the candlelight on you while you were walking toward me, so you stayed in me all night. That was best. Do you want to fuck me now while I'm talking?"

"Yes," he said.

"I've enchanted you now," she said. "You can't pull it out of me if you want to."

He showed her he could. He pulled it out and showered and dressed because he had to take it back to New York.

From New York he wrote, on yellow foolscap, "I pulled it out like Arthur pulling the sword from the stone."

She wrote back: "Yes, you pulled your prick out, but my strangeness came out with it and followed you all the way. Can't you feel that, you fool?"

Presently both these segments of their correspondence were pinned up on her bulletin board shrine, lit by candle flames that also lit their bodies on the white bed.

She put up her large reproduction of Titian's *Concert Champêtre* on the wall between the blind windows. "Notice," she said, "the two men with lutes aren't paying any attention to what you call the fat nudies who are out in the country with them. Do you know why they are not paying any attention? Because they are mortal and can't see the nude, or naked, bodies there in the forest with them while they make music. They can't see them because the women are goddesses. Only the painter—and now the spectator—can see the immortal ones."

"Terrific," he said. "How did you learn that?"

"I was there," she said. "I helped them with their music. I taught them what they could get out of a plain old lute."

"I believe you were."

"You better believe it."

"I begin to see the depths of your design on me."

"I'm going to fuck you right back into writing. The only

thing I can't forgive your wife for is she doesn't encourage you to write any more. Your short stories are as well-wrought as Hemingway's ever were. The things you tell me about your family, for instance, are just what Joyce said *should be written.*"

"Let's be more modest."

"We don't have to be modest here. That's why I found this place for us. We can do anything. Say anything here."

Very early he had appreciated her cunning in finding an apartment in a building where no one else was present after the bakery downstairs closed between five and six.

Margaret was a screamer. As she approached climax the tendons on her neck would tighten and harden like a ship's rigging. Her eyes rolled back until only the whites showed. And she cried his name in a high, incantatory treble.

"Troh-eee! Troh-ee! Troh-ee! Troh-ee! Troh-ee!"

Back in New York, looking out his office window on the rooftops of buildings spread in magnificent geometry toward the towers of Wall Street with the North Atlantic pale behind them, he would hear the echo of her screams. And imagine . . . well, that the great city was named for him. Troy. This Troy that some fabled beauty would burn to the ground some day.

And, in spite of all the evasions he had perfected to survive by, the funny thing was that in those first months of Margaret he had been a writer. The sort of writer that once in his college days or on long winter evenings at the Marine base in Seoul he had understood he was born to be—witty, passionate, droll, powerful, fearless and lyric.

Or—wait a minute—rather he was *part* of that writer, like a boxer with elegant footwork and a deadly jab but with, alas, only one arm. A writer not limited to the letters and notes that accumulated on the bulletin board above Margaret's bed (their white bed) in Cincinnati but a writer in the way he told stories

50

when they occupied that bed *intercoitum*. The sad shortcoming was that these stories Margaret pulled right out of him never made it to a written page. Hearing himself space and shape and refine the stories he told for her, his editorial mind told him that *not much* more was required for them besides typing them on fresh white paper. But they seemed to print, instead, only on the white sheets under them.

There everything turned into pert, well-shaped fiction. He could tell Margaret candidly about his drunken lunch with Jan and Jan's subsequent appraisals of his "bigamous" situation. "Bind you with hoops of steel, Jan recommends. Jan says, 'I gather our little friend is not only tops in the sack—she's got spirit, depth. A fine animal in a word, in a word.' "

"Doesn't she know we *are* married? Who needs steel?"

"I haven't discussed our, uh, *various ceremonies* with her, darling. They're known only to us and God. But the *idea* of us warms her old blood. She lives vicariously in her own aged, frustrated fantasies of what she supposes we enact in our shrine, the dear."

"So you're married to her, too," said the mistress of fantasies. "Hey, Troh-ee, you could write about our ceremonies, why not?"

"And make an X-rated movie or a How To book, sure. But I don't need to. What we've got going here is total and complete in itself. You keep giving me your hot and hairy Nobel Prize for my work, and what could possibly come after that? Your mistake was you were going to fuck me back into writing. But while I have you I don't need to write and be rejected or misunderstood. So, you see, you outfoxed yourself at your little game."

Someone was surely outfoxing someone in this game of tag and dodge, reaping uncanny and unorthodox benefits if not the Nobel Prize. One of the benefits was that he could be not only breathtakingly candid with her about Nancy, he could be more

generous about his legal spouse than he often was in his purely
private thoughts. For Margaret somehow conceived of Nancy
as the heroine of adventures in Greenwich Village that she
herself had missed. "Nancy was so . . . so *brave,*" she said about
the Midwestern sorority girl who had come to the Great Baby-
lon to dance.

"She was a kind of wondrous bitch in those days," Troy
admitted. His present frictions and annoyances with the bitch
did not interest Margaret in the least. At best she tolerated his
references to them impatiently. The trials and joys of courting
Nancy brought stars of amazement and a kind of delight to the
young fox's eyes. And it made him feel satisfyingly generous to
speak generously of Nancy, though the tales took shape in the
past tense.

"The first time I laid eyes on her she was peeping out from
under the sheets of my friend Kunstler's bed," he told Margaret. "Giving me a mean look for interrupting something."

"Oh!" Now that was the way for the prince to discover his
sleeping beauty!

"Kunstler was a mean sonofabitch. That is to say, he was a
poet and they tend to be ruthless as a refinement of being
egomaniacal. When Nancy came to New York she was full of
romantic crap about art, so she was an easy lay for predators
like Kunstler who could present themselves as the real thing.
I suppose that's what got me in, too, as a matter of fact—that
I passed for the real thing. But at least I was not as mean as
Kunstler. He used to abuse her while she was living with him,
and part of my motive was that I thought I was saving her when
I lured her out of his clutch into mine."

"Oh yes!"

"Kunstler used to tell me he only did it in psychic self-
defense. Even then I had some sympathy with him, because
she was too much for him. He was what is known in these days
as a foul male chauvinist of the purest dye, not only by pound-

ing on her but in what he said. 'All cunts are flip' was the way he put it. 'Midwestern ones are, as well, sly and profound. *Tiefe*, as Nietszche said of the Germans, meaning no compliment. You have escaped the Midwest yourself, Slater. Don't drag it after you by making anything permanent with Nancy.' "

"It's so great you can remember dialogue from that long ago!" Margaret said, shuddering with pleasure so that her breasts quivered.

"He said, 'Strictly speaking, dancers do not have minds. They have neural ganglia and opinions. The opinion Nancy Carson clings to most irrationally is that art is more important than nature, which is what makes her a dancer instead of, say, a gymnast.' And he was right about her opinions. She has cast iron opinions of a New York liberal sort and that's what I can *not* stand about her or ever get around in all these years."

"But you saved her from this male chauvinist pig! That's a happy ending!"

"Not for him. It was a very ambiguous thing, the way he felt about her. After she was living with me he used to hunt me down to talk about her, and being a poet he defined the essences. She was too wholesome for him. He said, 'The women we can get along with are sick, Slater. They don't mind giving it all up while they've still got it. Carson won't. Though she throws a very heavy fuck, she keeps something back, since her strongest opinion is that it's a procreative act. That's the Nebraska mentality. If you marry her, that will make trouble sooner or later. A clit like a rooster's comb! There used to be a Nebraska football player named Bronco Nagurski. What power that name conjures up! Sometimes I would think of Bronco Nagurski when she put the grip on me. Spine-shattering power! But incurable opinions. Even more powerful.' He saw the ambiguity and couldn't handle it. Within a year after she left him he was dead."

"Wow!"

"He threw a mattress down the airshaft behind his apartment and then when he'd made a soft spot six storeys down from his window, he dived into it. Shattered his brain stem."

"She killed him," Margaret said with a little cluck of satisfaction.

"That's the way I'm telling it," Troy agreed. "My stories seem to have more theme than content and detail. Yes. As a poet Kunstler was fascinated by ambiguities. A man that lives by ambiguities dies by ambiguities. Also poets like to dive from high places. Not me. What are you thinking?"

"If you dived six stories onto me you'd land like a feather."

"That may be true, but I'm not brave enough to try. However, I *was* brave enough to go ahead and marry *her* and find out what Kunstler had perceived before me. Oh my. Even before we were married the essential conflict showed up. She kept moving out on me and finding her own apartment when I didn't live up to her goddamn opinions. Like about her dancing. The only thing she could make money at was a belly dancing routine. Well, the fact is, I thought *that* was what was romantic about her and she thought it was 'disgusting.' We quarreled about that and she moved out claiming I wanted a hick with small-town prejudices.

"Which, in an important way, was true. What she'd never come across with for me was the glamor of what she thought was commonplace, her smalltown glamor. She'd begin stories about her childhood that would just curl my hair and break them off before they had a chance to unfold. For instance, she was once accused of setting fire to a neighbor's houseboat on the Missouri River. I really wanted to hear that one. Had she really done it? How? When? Why? The only answer she'd come through with was, 'Oh, after my father and the rest got through questioning me, I didn't know any more if I did or didn't do it. My father wanted it to be that I was unjustly suspected, so that's the way it was left. I don't remember. But

I wish I'd burned it right down to the waterline.' No matter how I maneuvered and pleaded I couldn't get any more out of her about that episode. She won't give."

Then in a swirling meditation, he and Margaret lay in the ambiguous candlelight over their bed, swept far with intimations of a big brown river in the West, a sultry evening with red sky above the willows, a furtive girlchild striking a match and dropping it in a can of picnic litter on the deck of a houseboat . . .

A mute Scheherezade and the King she has provoked into telling her stories . . .

"Nancy is your novel," Scheherezade said. Like many of her oracular statements it was too profound for him to agree with or disagree either.

"I could never make Nancy *or* the novel come across," Troy said. "But at least I'm alive and poor Kunstler isn't."

Perhaps he should have been warned—alarmed? alerted to dangers brewing?—by Margaret's uncanny lack of jealousy about his present cohabitation with Nancy. In fact the absence of jealousy was so comfortable that he refused to analyze it at all. The relaxation of candor let him confide that yes, to be sure, he kept up the level of sex in his legal abode. "There's more than there's been for years. Usually when I go back to New York from here I'm really charged up. That's what you do to me, as you know by now. So then Nancy and I have a high week of going at it every night. Then it tapers off again."

"I'm glad," Margaret said, after a full minute of reflection. She said it with the exact intonation she had given to those words on their first time in the room at the Royalton Hotel.

She was glad, too, that the ring finger he ritually and ceremonially moistened in her bore the golden wedding band that Nancy had put on his finger in Plattesmouth, Nebraska, fifteen years before. In the full stretch of her freedom from

55

jealousy she cared about Nancy as she cared about his daughter Ursula, in transports of imagination finding a sisterly joy in the existences of both. She kept a treasure trove of his anecdotes about young Ursula as a kind of basement to the shrine where she stored all the spill that he would never get into a novel. Pinned on her bulletin board among his letters were snapshots of Ursula from their summers on Cape Cod—Ursula kneeling among blueberry vines below the house, Ursula on a yellow raft being towed behind their boat. "Our Ursula," she called her, but was almost yawningly inattentive to any news of Kevin, as if Troy's masculine alliances made no more sense to her than events reported in the sporting section of a newspaper.

So the bottom line of irony was that she had been for two years a positive and essential bulwark to the marriage that might not have lasted without her—blunting, softening, turning in their tracks his annoyances with Nancy.

She said, "The only thing I could possibly have against her is she has given up encouraging you to write out all the stories in you. I'll get them out in spite of her."

"Ha! Haven't I told you she *does* encourage me? With carrot and stick. Year in and year out I can count on at least a few shrill scenes when she reminds me how she used to work as a waitress to support my dwindling writer's habit. Why am I wasting 'a creative brain' at Stoke & Bywater and their absurdly profitable enterprises. When we go to the Cape in summer she's always arranging parties or invitations to Provincetown to get me in company with summering artists and writers. She's managed to get me introduced to Mailer and Bowman and Tennessee Williams, Kahn, Motherwell, Tworkow, Avery, Capote, Hofmann over the years at big parties. It won't dawn on her they couldn't care less about yet another failed writer. They've seen so many. Then she gets a tragic look in her eyes that they haven't intuited my great gifts. It seems 'unjust' to her that I don't run in their league. Her sense of justice! The whole world gets inverted by her famous 'sense of justice'. Which is phony from the word go and what killed poor Kunstler finally and me if I would let it. But I've always understood it too well. What she's really resentful about is not Chianos and lettuce pickers, but the fact that she was 'just getting started as a dancer' when I snuck a baby into her. The truth is she could have gone on with a modest career in dance —and not just belly dancing either—if she'd been willing to move out of New York. She could be teaching dance in some decent college, for instance, if she'd kept up. She had offers from Illinois and one from Oregon even after Kevin was born. Most of her dancer friends from those days have gone that route. Even in New York there are spots where she might teach dance in the schools. Nope. She burned her leotards when she knew she was pregnant with Kevin."

"To show she had made her choice," Margaret said. "A woman who would burn houseboats naturally goes on burning things. And of course having your babies spoiled her chance to have the career *she* imagined and wanted."

"When you say it, there's some justice in it. But I tell you she uses it as a smokescreen. What's maddening about the woman is she always gives the wrong name to her real resentments. Example: she gets highly indignant about nuclear power plants. Huffs and puffs like a dragon—and I always know it's me she's after, not the power companies. You should see her in her fits of rage against oil companies, bigots, the CIA, OPEC, Ku Klux Klan, Midwestern Congressmen. I ain't them things."

"She rages because she loves you," Margaret said—and her insight had such potency that his prick rose abruptly. They had to postpone the analysis to another time.

"Do me the way you do Nancy," Margaret said huskily. The candle flames beside the bed suddenly danced and spit as if there were little grains of powder in the wicks.

"I have only one talent," he said, laughing at the novelty of her whim.

"You have as many different pricks as you have had women," she said. "Don't you know that yet? How many?"

"I don't know. Maybe ten. Fifteen. Twenty. Thirty. Give me time to count back if you want a reliable answer."

She was not giving him time for anything. She was—by the witchcraft she possessed—taking him out of the ordinary channels of time, of specific occasions, and even of individual personalities. Suddenly she was gripping his prick with a grip as masterful as Bronco Nagurski's grip on a football and pounding up and down on his balls with the staccato rhythms of modern dance. One of Nancy's improvisations that had enchanted him the year he saved her from Kunstler. He had no time to wonder where Margaret had learned it.

"I am Nancy," Margaret said. "Fuck me like a Marine." He felt her legs encircle him and squeeze with spine-shattering power.

The illusion—if that is what it was—may not have been perfect. Indeed, the next day when he was flying back to New York, he saw the shortcomings of it as a piece of theater. He could tell himself then with gloating assurance that Margaret was Margaret and Nancy was Nancy and even the blind tip of his prick could tell them apart when it needed to. Still . . . !

No, he had not at any instant literally believed he was having at Nancy there on the white bed of the Cincinnati shrine. Even in the mindstopping moment of ejaculation when he seemed to be diving from a high place toward a mattress very far below him, he had recognized the delicacy of Margaret's ribcage and the fluency of her smaller breasts oiling his chest. She might be tricky as a fox or witch, but she was certainly Margaret.

Still . . . this time she had not screamed his name. When she had him locked deep and dark and urgently submissive, she

58

put her tongue in his ear, withdrew it to whisper imperatively, "Shoot it, shoot it, shoot it." This time she had a single drenching orgasm, very businesslike and without those teasings to further play he always expected from Margaret. As he withdrew he felt a mysterious annoyance and a suspicion that she had held back the wonderful gift toward which he had flung himself with might and main, stopping him at some dark gate just as he caught a glimpse of the teeming garden beyond.

"How'd you learn that?" he asked with just a tinge of vexation.

"From what you told me about her," Margaret said.

"Hmmmph. I didn't realize I was that good a story teller. Or that explicit."

"Who needs explicit?"

"I guess you're a good listener. I guess you've got ways of hearing what you want to hear."

"Yes," she said with sweet self-satisfaction. "I have ways of learning what I'm supposed to know."

"What did you just learn about me?"

"Hmmmm." She was obviously reluctant to tell him—just as obviously sure of what she knew.

"You can tell me. I'll cross your palm with silver."

"You do more than that for me." Then she made up her mind that he had to be told. "Troh-ee, I know that you *mean* to be generous. You have a sense of justice and you want to be just. But you hold back from her something she needs from you, just as you say she does from you."

"I believe you're crazy."

"No," she said mildly. "You believe I'm a mystic who sees all, knows all. And I have strange powers of communication."

As a matter of fact, that is what he did believe.

5

TROY WAS a rational man, more or less. (Everyone is. More or less.) Yet at the peak of the sweet mystifications Margaret provided for him, he could amuse himself with the speculation that special powers of insight and perception went with her famous "strangeness." (As long as there is no price tag apparent anyone can speculate anything.) The flaw was probably that he supposed he could translate her sacred pronouncements into the language of his profane and legal love.

Flying home to New York from his first full ten days with her (and business deftly tended to at the printing plant) his mind became unhinged with the generosity Margaret had encouraged. He was coming home as a missionary of Liberation which, to his best knowledge, his wife hungered for as much as any woman alive in our time. He wanted to sing the Body Electric. He wanted to stand in the aisle of the 727 and pledge allegiance with the newly purified heart of his earlier days. He felt malice toward none. Charity and justice for all.

He was not irrational enough to believe he could talk to Nancy about Margaret as he had just spoken to Margaret about Nancy. He would have to convey the message of sacred love in the common tongue. Surely he was ready and able to do that.

In the flood of his benevolence, boozed up and choked with what he could not put into words, he had reached for Nancy as soon as they went to bed that night. For the first time either could remember, he was impotent.

Nancy's reaction was characteristic in its spontaneity. She leaped from the bed as if catapulted, yelling, "Let's face it, you shit. You just can't stand me any more."

Naked as his guilt, she raced down the hall from their bedroom to the kitchen. He pulled on pajama bottoms and followed her. He found her miserably slumped on a kitchen chair, breasts dangling. She clutched a gin bottle between her clenching knees. Tears smeared her face.

"All right," she said. "I've seen it coming. Tried to keep it out of my mind. Watched it crawl after me on the street. I'm old and cranky and yell at my friends. At the kids. I see the look in your eyes when you watch me showering."

"You're only thirty-six," he said.

"He tells me I'm thirty-six! Don't I *know* it? Why do you think I threw out all the barbiturates in the bathroom cupboard?"

"How would I know?"

"Or keep the butcher knives in the drawer out of sight? Think it over, Buddy." She tilted up the gin bottle and drank thirstily. "So what did you think you were going to do just now? Give me the big mercy fuck? Face it! Face it, you shit! You used me up and now you can't stand me. *You can't stand me.*"

"Nancy . . ." He could not think of what else to say. *I don't have to take this, too,* he thought.

"He calls me 'Nancy'," she howled. "That takes some gall . . . to stand there *now* and call me 'Nancy.' "

"Nancy, listen, please. Maybe it's time we had a talk." The word divorce formed like a clot of phlegm in his throat. Could you calmly discuss divorce with a naked, raving woman?

She caught up her left breast in her free hand and pointed it between his eyes. The nipple looked like a red bullet, but it also looked like the wound the bullet would make when it hit him.

So this was what they meant by the term *guerrilla theater!* A new style of warfare with ancient precedents.

She let the breast flop from her hand. Her sobs kept her from talking while she rallied her fury. "I'm a rotten, flabby wreck. But who made me this way, you *cur?* Rotten, flabby. Rotten. Flabby. You impotent fag!" With the rhythm of her chanting she began to flap her breast up and down with the flat of her hand.

It wasn't a bad breast at all . . . it was richly mature and swollen with goodies. Noting this, he felt the burn of his resentment and anger turn from a blue to a dull red flame.

"You've got it all backwards," he said. "You misinterpret everything. Every goddamn kindly gesture."

"Kindly? *Kindly?* You were going to *kindly* slip it to Mother Slater but you couldn't get it up? You *shit.* "

"You're the shit. You take everything I am. You drink my blood as long as there's enough left to float a corpuscle. And now this! THIS!"

"Mama? Mama?"

It was Kevin in his woolly pajamas, great-eyed and unbelieving, wobbling in the kitchen door on his way out of interrupted sleep.

Troy rushed at him. He was barely able to keep from slapping the boy. He slowed himself just in time. "It's all right, boy. Everything's fine, Kevin. *Fine!* Now go back to bed."

63

"Fine?" Nancy piped. "Are you his mama, too? He called for mama, didn't he?"

Troy lost the last thread of control and shouted, "Your stupid-ass, *insane* mother is throwing a tantrum. Now get back in your room, goddamn it."

He strong-armed Kevin down the hall. Promised that everything would quiet down before he kissed him and shoved him into his room. Next door he heard Ursula stirring and moaning, so he rushed to get a robe for Nancy before their daughter, too, came out to find her naked on a kitchen chair.

"No! I will *not* put that on," Nancy bellowed when she saw what he had thought of now. "Let them come and see what you've made of me, a woman!" She rose from her chair, waving the gin bottle, pointing at the delicate lace of stretch marks trailing down on either side from her rib cage. "Let them see before it's too late for Ursula how you put the mark of the beast on me! Goddamn faggot pig! You did this and God will judge you. You *did* this to my body. And I wanted to dance. Was that asking too much? Oh God, I wanted to *dance.*"

"I . . . wanted you to dance, darling."

"You lying *cocksucker.* Children, come see what he did to me!"

He had just knocked her to the floor with two heavy slaps when Ursula ran in. Nancy's tears were running like water from a tap by this time and the ends of her hair were sopping. She groped like a mole for her robe as Ursula began to pat the top of her head and croon to her.

"It's all right, Ursula. All right, darling. It isn't your father's fault. I fell down. I'm just coming apart. He's trying to help me." She got the robe on her arms, rose to stumble back to her chair. She took Ursula on her lap, cradling the child's head against her shoulder.

"I am goddamn leaving this zoo," Troy said.

"He is goddamn leaving us," Nancy hissed to Ursula.

Resolutely he went into the bedroom and began to find clothes in the closet. By the time he had pulled on trousers over his pajama bottoms and put on a sweat shirt, running shoes and his woolly jacket, Nancy had come to the kitchen door. Her robe was agape and Ursula was clinging to its fabric. Nancy watched him fumble with the police lock on the front door at the end of the hall. Then yelled, "That's it! Knock me down and one of my teeth loose and then walk out!"

"Now, listen," he said, turning. "Now, listen, we've got to have a talk."

In two years he would never be so close again to telling her that he meant to divorce her and marry Margaret Gill. Then —*then!*—the necessity for saving his life, what was left of it, was totally clear in his thought. The way to say it had been cleared by the brutality of their fracas. At last—for once without hypocrisy—they could face each other as the enemies they had always been. In justice he would declare he loved her. But enemies can not, must not, try endlessly to live together.

With the pretense that the children had now been persuaded back to sleep, with voices lowered to permit that sparing of the innocents, they faced each other over glasses of gin set on the red-lacquered kitchen table.

"It is true," he began in a judicious tone, "that there are *certain things* I can not stand about you. But to say I can't stand you *as such* is another of your wicked distortions. You live by a lot of *wicked* notions about yourself and me. In your opinion you are a perfectionist, an idealist, governed by a massive sense of justice. Mention to you Jews, Blacks, Chicanos, faggots, youth, the elderly—name them all and you'll find Nancy Slater taking up the cudgels to defend them. Very much to her credit.

"But wait! These names of the disadvantaged also turn out to be very convenient code words—to be used when something

65

has been done unfairly to Nancy Slater."

"Oh . . . you *shit!*"

"If Nancy Slater comes home from shopping with clothes that don't look as good on her as they did in the store, why, it's the fault of the Puritan Ethic for not putting out fashions that would show off the good points of her figure."

"You're not leaving. I am. You warped neurotic. They should still have you in Bellevue."

"These distortions have made living with you . . . trying," Troy said. "As for your stretch marks, if you had any *real* sense of justice, you'd be proud of them and goddamn grateful for all they're part of. As a matter of fact, they are beautiful. Your breasts are beautiful. I could continue the enumeration. But . . . ! With all these gifts that could have been accepted, you're a rotten, self-deceiving slob with no real use for a man but to go for the marrow of his bones and dry him out.

"You wanted to be a dancer, did you? You know you had talent. High talent and your belly dance routines produced hard-ons through the entire Great Lakes region. I even hold onto the idea that, wife and mother though you be, in your corkscrew soul you still *are* a dancer. Nancy Slater doesn't have to have a stage to get at the essence of whatever she was supposed to be or God intended. So much for you.

"Don't think for a minute you've made the only sacrifices. Don't imagine one *instant* longer that you've taken me in by nagging me about 'getting back to my writing'. You don't even begin to cover up your guilts by putting it in that language. You put it that way to rub my nose in my failures.

"Only to rub my nose in them. But I have news for you, sister. While that's been your game, I've had my own. The reason I quit trying was I wasn't ever, ever, ever going to give you any more of my best self."

The authority in his voice thrilled him. He saw that Nancy's neck was pointing rigidly at him, like an arm on which her head was a clenched fist. Her eyes were shining in an almost colorless fury, as if all the gin she had drunk had been ignited at once and was shining its light out at him.

"I can't believe my ears," she said softly.

"It's not that you might not have legitimate complaints about me," he said more mildly.

"I can't believe it!"

He went on, milder and milder, "Like Hamlet, I'm only indifferent honest. I measure my shortcomings daily. But . . ."

Then she was on him with fists hammering.

By sheer advantage of surprise she landed one keen blow under his ear while he was kicking out of his chair and another on the side of his neck before he caught her arm and immobilized it over his shoulder.

She got her teeth into the heel of his hand. He supposed he felt blood start. "Stop it, stop it now," he hissed, afraid the children might soon both come running.

She had to stop biting to talk. "You dislocated my arm," she said.

"The hell I did."

"It doesn't prove anything but you're stronger than I am. Don't touch me. Don't ever touch me again, you turd."

But his lips had drawn back in a monstrous grin. He felt something like a burning wire run up his spine and begin to crackle in his ears. He grabbed her and spread her on the kitchen table.

"Don't kill me," she whimpered.

That was not his intent. Like a surgeon laboring furiously to resuscitate a corpse he worked over her responding body on the red table. Pumping Margaret into her, feeling it take.

"Oh, you Marine bastard," she said.

Something very funny had happened.

What was so funny was the way she had conned him—and kept on conning him to bring her everything he kept getting from Margaret. (As, perhaps, he kept taking back to Margaret everything he had ever got from Nancy. Sisters under the skin. You bet. Under whose skin?)

He had never thought any part of this through to its (no doubt) metaphysical bottom line. He had not wished to think about it too much while it was going so well. If the three-way relationship was bigamous, let the law decide that. If it was compensation for childhood trauma, the shrinks must know about it. If it was shore leave and liberty—tell that to the Marines. All he surmised was that something funny was continuing, thriving in the gaps of common sense like alligators in the dense Everglades, thriving between the long super-highways running to the resort hotels. A bit of the Old Wilderness, what? Like Casey Jones, he had wives at each end of his run.

That theatrical person, Nancy, was a quick study. For sure. She began to run through Margaret's repertoire like a seasoned actress with a script open in her hand, still hardly needing it, anticipating lines that would be memorized later.

And still, in her conscious mind, as far as he could ever make out, completely unaware of what he was really up to in Cincinnati.

"Don't kid yourself," Jan Savery said once. "Nancy knows. She may not know the name and the address, but what makes you think you're smart enough to do what no man ever really does, fool a cunt?"

"Then . . ." Troy mused.

"Then she must like it this way?" Jan asked. "Don't fool yourself about that, either, my boy. When the time comes and she gets your balls under the hammer . . . Wham!"

"Don't say that so loud."

"What?"

"That 'wham!'"

But in the times of his impunity he was still lighthearted enough to say to Jan, "Then there *is* a lie at the heart of the charming affair."

"What affair?"

"Women."

"Oh, ho, ho, ho. You bet your bottom dollar, friend."

The rape on the table—as Nancy frequently alluded to it before abandoning all reference, as she charitably forgot all his criticisms of her "sense of justice" and her "perfectionism"—had no effect at all on Nancy's character or general conduct. It neither increased or diminished the friction in their married life.

She and the children had been still asleep when he got his breakfast and skedaddled to the security of the office the next morning. She called him before lunch to say she had been to her doctor. Her right arm was indeed dislocated at the shoulder joint. "So now you've got another bill to pay. I've got to have help with the housework for two weeks, too." She hinted that she was on her way downtown to a clinic for battered wives. Lawyer's bills might follow.

She got a massage instead. When he came home from work that evening, he found her with her arm in a sling, humming quietly to herself as she gimped around the kitchen helping Ursula bake some raisin bread. There was no occasion then— and none came later—to resume the particular line of talk he had begun the night before.

In the following months he noted there was less talk of divorce between them than in any comparable period since their marriage. But—this seemed to be the stumbling point— yes, he had often talked to Margaret about divorcing Nancy. As with other profane and merely legalistic matters, discussion of the subject with Margaret had been easy and flattering to his intelligence because she was so loftily indifferent to prac-

69

ticalities like marriage. In college she had read Milton's *Doctrine and Discipline of Divorce* and prized it as a work of art with elegant prose rhythms. Milton's style gave her a rush.

Troy dreamed he got this much of the truth written in a single night, and, until his hand got cramped and he rounded out his chapter, he assumed what he had written was still unknown to Bronstein and Jan Savery.

Nevertheless, when he quit, Bronstein summed up: "Each of Troy Slater's personalities is sociopathological. But they knew a soft touch when they saw it."

Jan Savery said: "This is not a case for psychiatry. It cries out for lynch law."

II

6

"YESTERDAY YOU said you were reading and today you say you are writing and you're just lying on the floor," Ursula pointed out. Clearly this was not progress.

When he had broken from his busy dream of writing and staggered out to fix himself breakfast, he had found their guppies were dying. Four or five of the tinier ones floated black and dead on the surface of the aquarium. By the time he had finished sausage, eggs, and a richly buttered muffin, there were three more floaters—one a pregnant female large enough to look like a genuine minnow.

In consternation he brought the aquarium from the shadowed corner of the room and set it on the blue carpet by one of the sliding glass doors in the full exposure of the morning sun. It was then he had taken his present position, belly down with his face near the aquarium wall. He hoped to get an accurate count of those still alive, as if that would help.

When Nancy came in from the garden, bringing daisies, he turned his face only to address her bare feet. "They may all go."

She crouched to look. "They might," she agreed. She had more important things to worry about, if he did not. She arranged her daisies in a pair of vases. She put one vase on the kitchen table and the other on the floor by the striped sofa.

"It's my bad judgment," Troy said. "They're probably poisoned from this ugly seaweed the kids and I brought from the Bay."

"Nobody listens to me. So take the seaweed out."

"If the poison is already in the water, it may be too late. I rinsed it off carefully in the sink when we brought it home. I was afraid they couldn't stand salt."

"What are you croaking about? Change the water and *see* if they survive. That's all. It's no big deal."

"I'm afraid of how it will affect Kevin. He may feel bad if . . ."

But Nancy was gone. She could not stand his hairsplitting equivocations, these measurements of responsibility, because she did not know the connection between them and the last ditch resistance he had been forced to in his dreams. He knew the doom on the guppies was a mere prolongation of those dreams.

Carefully as he could, he changed the aquarium water in the kitchen sink. Three or four of the smaller guppies went down the drain.

It was probably eleven in the morning when Nancy stood over him again. This time she was wearing leather sandals stained from yard work and tramping the woods to pick blueberries. She told him she was driving Kevin and Ursula to the post office. Along with the mail she would pick up tuna, wine and Italian bread for their lunch. "While you spend the pretti-

est day we've had all summer reading your crystal ball. I understand you told Ursula you were lying there *writing.*"

"In a sense that is true."

"If you'd do some pencil work, you'd know how much per
hour it costs in the form of taxes, mortgage interest, deprecia-
tion on the house, etcetera, for you just to lie there and not
even enjoy the good weather."

He said meekly, "Six more died in the last hour."

"A propane explosion wiped out two hundred deaf and
dumb vacationers in a camp near Singapore." She squatted to
examine the aquarium. "I don't see any dead ones at all."

"I dip them out when I change the water. I've changed it
twice now. As carefully as I can."

"You put *cold* water on them? From the tap? That's what
will kill the rest."

"I don't have a thermometer, but don't accuse me of not
being careful."

It was Nancy who was famous in the family for being good
with plants and pets. It was she who had helped Kevin breed
the late multitude of guppies from four medium-sized ances-
tors bought in a round glass bowl from the dime store on
Amsterdam Avenue.

But it was Troy who had always contributed *anxiety* about
the well-being of the fish since he had seen them begin to
multiply. It was he and Ursula who kept the body count of the
living and the dead. Just last Thursday they had been sure of
a count of one hundred and twenty-three adults and babies. So
many—after bad losses near Easter and what may have been
some starvation when the kids were preoccupied with school
work in May and their father was traveling after business and
pussy to Cincinnati.

Pussy? Were these sensitive little fish dying for his sexual
sins?

75

"Another bomb went off in a market in Tel Aviv. The damned washing machine is grinding and I smelled rubber burning down under it. If I had known you'd go bonkers over those fish I'd've left them in the apartment in New York for Katie James to feed."

It was afternoon now and the dying had not stopped. It was time to go to the beach, and the wife of the phony writer loomed over him to demand if he was going with his family or not. There was anger in the mere clutch of her toes in the bare carpet beside his cheek.

He rolled over on the blue carpet and put his hands under his head to gaze up. His glance loitered on the always admirable perspective of her bare legs, noting the single, naive curl of pubic hair that escaped the crotch of her scarlet bikini before he dared meet her eyes.

"Maybe I'll ride Kevin's bike over and join you later."

"Ursula says you didn't do anything all day yesterday, either. Are you sick? Have you been fired? Is that what Jan was worked up enough to call about last night?"

"Odd as it may seem to you—all of you—I'm beginning to write something. That's what I was doing all night long and why I'm—or may seem—so remote today. I had a very odd dream that Bronstein was my psychiatrist and I was writing a story for him."

"And that's going to turn into a novel?" Nancy was unappeased but her face was a study. His claims of being a writer were the one defense she could not penetrate—since she had laid so many stones of that barricade herself, wanted it so much to be the truth. "How many left?" she asked, meaning guppies, meaning he had until the last guppie died to come up with something on paper.

Ursula honked the Volvo's horn outside. Kevin came from the basement carrying his inflated raft and a yellow towel. The boy knelt grimly beside the aquarium and stared with a concern

76

that matched his father's. "How many?" asked the Old General At Bay, the Captain of the Alamo demanding a morning report.

"Thirty-three," his father said.

"It had to be that weed I found. Goddamn *sea*weed."

"It's a mystery and we'll never know. None has died for the last twenty minutes, anyway. Maybe the rest will make it through."

"My God," Nancy yelped. "You could write this. It's a soap opera. If it isn't *Moby Dick,* which I doubt. Watching will *not* keep them alive."

Troy patted his son's skinny leg where the few sun-bleached hairs sprouted below a shining knee cap. "Your mother's right as usual, Kevin. Skip along." To Nancy he said, *"Uxorious* means *henpecked."*

"Fuck you," she said. She stormed out of his life, leaving him free to marry Margaret Gill and pursue his writing career under Mediterranean skies.

Well . . . no. She left him to die with the other fish. For that was what was happening in the clear blue day, the clear blue water of the aquarium. The inscrutable poison was at work and would finish them all off. Deaf and dumb vacationers here or in Singapore, Jews shopping in the market, the inventor of the telephone fuck and her uxorious lover, all carrying their stories with them into the great silence. But, at least, he cared. Lying there, with death so close, he mourned for all the stories that could not be told.

If it was a typical little lie to tell his daughter he was writing, the truth was nevertheless that he was composing. He was composing himself to die, since you could not beat the game. He knew his dreams of last night had not been a new start. They were only the debris of disintegration, the floating wreckage that rose to the surface when the ship went down. His faithful watch on the guppies merely gave him a frame for seeing the end of his life. Time must have a stop, oh yes. Thirty-three guppies to go. He remembered that his numeral had been number 34 when he played on the high school basketball team and never reckoned that he was mortal.

But then—into this comfortable dream of extinction, this warm bath of self-pity—Nancy was shouting, "All right! Let's get that thing off the floor! I've brought the Bowmans to have a drink with us. Get it up, Troy!"

He thought at first she must be referring to *him* as the "thing on the floor," and his first dazed effort to obey her was to lurch up on his hands and knees, shuffling his feet for a purchase on the blue carpet to get rid of the body that cluttered her living space.

"The fish! Get that stupid aquarium out of our way before we stumble over it."

He would always remember that the great man walked into his living room from outside his bad dreams. The great writer W.T. Bowman was there to show him what he ought to be, how he ought to live, and how he should handle his women.

Nancy had snagged him at Balston Beach. Brought him home to get her used-up husband back on his feet.

7

DUST-JACKET photos on his novels represented W.T. Bowman as a brawling giant, as ready for a fight as a frolic. Macho man. The John Wayne of literature. Yesterday at the helm of his boat coming into Pamet Harbor with his women up aloft like trophies brought from the deep seas he had looked to Troy no slighter than Ernest Hemingway at the wheel of the *Pilar.* And right now from flat on the floor—his present point of observation—Troy saw a titan looming over him.

Therefore when Troy got to his feet it confused him to find the man he was shaking hands with was not as tall as he. An odd effect—to have the great man close up in his own house and still seem to be seeing him at a distance, diminished from his proper stature by a sort of linear perspective.

"We met at the Rideouts year before last," Troy said, pumping the older man's steely little arm.

"Oh, yes. *Yes!*" Bowman said. "Yes, yes, yes, *yes*. I remember." It was plain he did not remember the meeting and probably not the Rideouts.

To be sure the two women with him and even the willowy boy who came in with Kevin and Ursula were also taller than Bowman, but with Bowman setting the scale—playing tricks with it—that merely made the women seem like gleaming giantesses. Elaine and Jokaanen. The boy was introduced as Vachel, one of the old man's multitudinous children by his six wives. Elaine, of course, was the present wife, who was said to be a sculptor, into earth art. She had a sculptor's hands, a handshake that molded the soft clay Troy held out for her to squeeze.

"Jokaanen is visiting us from Germany," Bowman said. His voice also seemed to come to Troy's ear from a distance, powerful but not overpowering. It was a warm voice, bubbling with chuckles, as if every simple thing he said trailed many amusing implications, implications of droll circumstances to be recounted at leisure. As if Jokaanen might be visiting from the Germany of fairy tales and not the present drab Republic.

Truly Jokaanen looked as if she might have waded ashore in America from a legendary surf with allegorical figures twirling banners and blowing trumpets for background effect. She was just the most impressive piece of womanflesh Troy had ever shaken hands with, though it would come to him later that he had seen her somewhere, someplace, before—not just on the fishing tower of Bowman's boat yesterday afternoon.

Her eyes were blank, so pale a blue as to seem without a pupil. The massive fall of hair on her bronze shoulders was the color of bleached wheat. Troy thought she said, *"Gruss Gott,"* as they shook hands. Then she said, "Hi," and as far as he would remember took no further part in the conversation. Bowman's women let him speak for them when he was around.

Bowman was authority personified and with his authority he put Troy immediately at ease. "Nancy explained you were back here holding a wake for your fish," he said. His rumbling chuckles implied that any man of spirit would have done the same. A patriarch takes care of his flocks and herds. He scanned the tank of dying guppies and nodded affirmatively. "You've got plenty left. They'll come back. They breed marvelously. Marvelously." It was the first optimistic thought Troy had been able to keep on his stomach all day.

From the first, then, Bowman began to lead him, taking survival for granted, making it seem feasible after all. Bowman took nearly everything for granted. Others fell in with him. It was he who decided what his wife and Jokaanen would drink. Martinis, yes, marvelous martinis, since there were no makings for the rum daiquiris they had been drinking on the beach when Nancy fell into conversation with them.

Pleased with her catch, Nancy fussed to make the visit worth their while. "Kevin, you and Ursula might show Vachel your macramé. They do it down at the art center. Or take the TV and hook it up on the deck outside, or . . . I know! Horseshoes. Do you pitch horseshoes, Vachel? You kids can drive in stakes below the deck and have a game. Kevin's pretty good, Vachel. He can beat his father. Everybody got a drink? You should have used the new ice bucket, Troy."

But while she spluttered hospitably, it was really Bowman who gave order to the scene in the room, disposing bodies like a director placing his actors, with a flow of hardly perceptible indications. He brought his wife and their exotic visitor down on either side of him on the striped couch, the two of them reclining like odalisques around their sultan so they would not appear taller than he. Some wordless signal passed from him to his son approving the proposal that horseshoes would be pitched. His projected lines of force placed Nancy in the rocking chair directly facing him, with Troy delicately nudged to the side where a supporting character—or mere spectator— ought to be.

It was theater and, by grace of Bowman's direction, Nancy was to be the leading lady, situated for once where she could speak her piece to the Supreme Authority. With such a listener, her most fervent opinions would be given full value.

"It's not that I have any sympathy with capitalism as such," Nancy said, settling into the rocker with her first martini, evidently splicing a new paragraph into the conversation begun on the beach.

"Certainly not," Bowman said, the distant boom of his voice applauding the distinction she made between capitalism as such and her reasons for taking a course in business administration.

"It's not that I don't see through the system Harvard is perpetuating," Nancy pleaded. Her temples were damp. On the left side a moist curl of hair was plastered against the skin. Her eyes were aglow with that ineffable sense of being on the verge of justifying her thirty-eight years as a second-class citizen, her stretch marks, her patience with the worst writer's block in America. "And I don't kid myself that I am going to beat the system. It's too deeply entrenched."

"Certainly."

"Troy laughs at me when I talk about making millions selling T-shirts by direct mail. He should laugh. He's right."

Bowman shook his patriarchal head. Perhaps the husband was not—entirely—right on that matter, should *not* laugh.

"I only want to get one big juicy bite of it, just once, and run with it, to show the bastards I can," Nancy said. "Troy thinks I'm an illiterate slob, but the poetry I think of is from Piers Plowman: 'Send them summer, Lord, for what they have endured on this earth.' "

"Beautiful," Bowman said. His chuckle slid the compliment

82

past her comment to the passion it came from, but the question in his eyes, twinkling from half-lowered lids, was simply: Why? Troy did not misunderstand what he began to see in Bowman's expression then—a fascination that asked: Why do you still care? Why can't you surrender? Not a hostile question, nor cynical exactly, but seeming to come from the far side of a gulf of cynicism crossed long ago.

"Keep it up," Elaine Bowman cheered. "Get your bite, Nancy. They owe it to us. We'll file our teeth and then they'll learn not to fool with us anymore. We've been down too long."

"I just want to see Troy's face when one of my schemes comes crashing through and I'm the one who pays off our mortgages," Nancy cried, and looked with sidelong disdain at his present face.

"If . . . ," he started to say, but it was useless as whispering into a hurricane.

"There are a lot of mouths hanging open already about what women have done," Elaine said. She addressed Nancy, of course, not the miserable hubby, whose mouth should open only by hanging.

The only one of the visitors who did not join in the cheering was Jokaanen. Now Troy noted that she was wholly concentrated on probing the hair on the back of Bowman's left hand with a fingertip. In total oblivion to what was being said, she slipped her fingers under and around his palm to squeeze it lasciviously.

Bowman said, "Elaine's principles on women are absolutely orthodox. But fortunately for me . . ." He stopped his sentence right there with the plain implication that the real Elaine was a man's woman of the old stripe and let there be no mistake. At this amusing distinction between her principles and wifely services, she turned on him with giggles, rubbing his bearded cheek with her knuckles.

"We're grasshoppers over there. We've given up the battle,"

she explained to the Slaters. She began to rhapsodize on the routine of life over in their house on its dune fronting the Atlantic. It was a picture without details. "Mornings? What do we do with mornings, Jokaanen? Nectarines and coffee. Jokaanen posing for me. Dipping. It's very rarely we go to the public beach. Today was the first day I've worn a bathing suit in . . . goodness, many days. Bowman's so interested in young people. They come on their motorcycles. Sleep down in the yard or out in the dunes. When he's not talking to them or plotting revolution, what do you do, Bowman?"

He chuckled absently. Jokaanen was giving him bodily attention again, making contact like a huge white cat, with a feline subtlety none of the rest quite noticed or quite missed.

"Goodness," Elaine said. "I couldn't begin to tell you what we do with the days. We're lizards in the sun. Of course, Bowman fishes and we have to keep him company on fish days . . . Goodness, now that I stop to think I'm astonished at how we slide along in the peaceable kingdom. The history of most *ménages à trois* is short and stormy, I believe. But then we have Vachel to keep time for us. He's like a clock."

"Automatic," Jokaanen said, tossing Bowman's hand back into his lap.

"Vachel's too good to be true," Nancy said. "Perfect manners, for a boy. The handsomest kid on the beach this afternoon. Perfect . . ."

"Exactly the right words," Bowman put in calmly. "Your eyes and ears do not deceive you, Nancy, but no part of what you hear and see is real."

"How do you mean?"

Bowman said, "I wouldn't tell you that Vachel came to us from Planet X. I'll tell you he came from much farther away than that. Very far."

"He's an angel," Jokaanen Ober said. Her rare comments

84

were as vociferous as her body language, though more enigmatic.

"I speculate that that is literally true," Bowman said with gravity. "But the medical diagnosis has always been that he is autistic."

"Oh no!" Nancy said. The pronouncement rocked her back and reddened her face as if she had been literally slapped.

Prompted by something in the dialogue he could not quite decode, Troy was attempting to fit some key words together. *Too good to be true.* A lot was getting said and signaled that was either too good or too bad or too far or too out of scale to be true as it came to his eye and ear. Martinis or not, no one mentions living in a *ménage à trois* without sending some shock waves. But . . . where was the ripple? Had Nancy missed it? Not seen the body games the German girl was playing? Not bloody likely. But she was taking it so far with unusual composure.

Then, with a queer conviction that Bowman was stage managing every part of this extraordinary dialogue, steering it in and out of reality like a boat tacking always at an angle to the power of the wind, he could still suppose the old man was paying no particular attention to its progress. Surely Bowman was basking in a medium of alcohol and summer and feminine attendance not particularly differentiated by the fact that they had drifted indoors from the beach where they all got together. But yet, indolently, he was after something from Nancy, prodding her, testing her, feeling for what was honest behind her gauche passions. And her unguarded concern about the boy was his signal to move in on her, like a gorged predatory fish responding yet to a trace of blood in the placid water.

"Oh yes, Vachel—named for the poet by his poet mother —is autistic. End of the human line. Dead end," Bowman said.

When he was young, his mother and I had it gone into thoroughly, hoping there might be a cure. Change at least. By now the psychologists know a great deal about autism. There are very good schools for the afflicted. Vachel went for years to one we trusted very much. We thought for a while they were helping."

Nancy refused to accept what she was being told. "He's so . . ."

"Sweet? Alert? That's the paradox we had to accept. When we talk about it, though, language plays its queerest tricks. Jokaanen says *angel*. That's not so far-fetched if you aren't afraid of the term, as we all are. I'm afraid of the total situation, but I must accept. To sum up Vachel's condition—a trick of language I can't avoid—it's very rarely that anything is really *happening* for him in the physical world."

Now, in daylight, realities were losing their borders for Troy, as they had last night in his dream of writing for Bronstein. The language was more hallucinogenic than whatever alcohol was in his bloodstream. "I understand that," he was obliged to put in. Bowman nodded to him as if he supposed he might indeed.

The father of the sweet monster said, "Vachel's down there now slinging horseshoes like a normal kid. But God knows if, in his mind, the horseshoes are ever leaving his hand. They fly through the air and turn and hit the stake . . ."

Now they all heard the glad ring as steel hit steel, verifying their faith in the solid world.

". . . all the time it is Vachel who is in the air, turning and hitting the stake, which is also Vachel. For the autistic there is no distinction, absolutely none, between the subjective and the objective."

It was Nancy who would not have it so. Nonsense threatened her worse than anything. "That doesn't—"

"Doesn't show? It shows," Bowman said. "It shows for those of us who have learned to live with it. Once you admit what

86

you are looking for, you can't see anything else."

Nancy saw something wrong with that proposition. Was not quick enough to be sure of the flaw. Her frown protested the verbal booby trap. "I can't see it at all," she said.

"No. It's admitting it that requires a long, ghastly conversion," Bowman said. "But look at the choice. Not to admit it is to deny the one chance you have of holding on. Either you admit what's hardest to accept or you let go of someone you love. As with the dead, or in a dead marriage. Vachel doesn't have what you call fantasies, my dear. Your kids will sit in front of the TV and have normal fantasies about raping, killing, or blowing up buildings. But Vachel sits there fantasying that he's the TV set."

"Horrible," Nancy said. She rocked out of her chair and took a look outside to make sure the children were all right.

Bowman laughed approvingly. "Your kids are safe with him. Vachel always plays by the rules of the game. As the psychologists say, he *can't* change any rules. That's part of how you can tell the nature of his affliction. The rules—any rule at all—is inflexible as the laws of gravity or whatever makes the TV work. Vachel knows he works the same."

"How does that make him different from me?" Troy asked, but Bowman was paying no attention to him at the moment.

Even as he had been defining his son's tragedy and affliction he had been getting drawn in bit by bit into the game of touch and flirt with the women on either side of him. Elaine made knee contact with him. Jokaanen's hip had slid on the curve of the sofa until it pressed his. And . . . the devil was bumping some sly and secret code message to both, for both. If it wasn't ridiculous, it was indecent. Most of all, it was rude. Nancy was honestly trying to be serious. This languid foreplay threw her seriousness in her face.

"Carter!" she said furiously.

Jokaanen lolled back as if preparing for orgasm.

"If he'd only turned out to be the Populist he promised during his campaign!" Nancy said.

"No," Bowman said. "If he'd tried to be a Populist they'd have shot him before now."

"Who?"

"The sonsofbitches. We've known that since they dropped Playboy John in Dallas."

"Oh!"

"Or they'd have worked him over with the media ploy, as with Sweating Dick."

"He *should* sweat."

"If it entertains you. They took Carter's one little ball off with the Lance maneuver. They said, 'Jimmy, see how we are burning Lance? You want to go with him or be a nice boy?' "

And while he delivered such heresies, he chuckled and purred almost audibly from the attentions of his women.

Nancy still fought to ignore the latter. "If only everyone wasn't so gutless now in the Seventies. Just yesterday our psychiatrist neighbor was giving me a real Cold War line, and I don't want my kids incinerated. You said this afternoon no one was reading your books any more. I don't believe it. You've still got your following, the kids who adored you in the Sixties. If not, it's because everyone's scared of speaking out."

"They have an inalienable right to be scared. I believe it is the ultimate Constitutional guarantee that outlasted the others."

"But what are we going to do?"

Gravely Bowman said, "As for me, I've accepted Jesus Christ as my Master."

Nancy said, "Oh!" but the syllable hardly diminished the pressure of accumulated breath that was reddening her face. A joker with a pin had just popped her balloon.

Her rolling eyes came to rest squarely on Jokaanen Ober. On the voluptuous swell of Jokaanen's breasts and white-sheathed

88

mons. "What do you say about that, Jokaanen?"

"Me too," the girl said vacantly.

"You . . . ?"

"What he said. Accept Jesus Christ as my Lord and Master."

Nancy rocked to her feet. Tottered. Then raised both arms above her head in imprecation and threat.

"Get out," she yelled. "Just get out, all of you." She fled to the bedroom.

In the silence of her departure Troy realized he no longer heard the sounds of the horseshoe game from below the deck. He saw Vachel Bowman with Ursula and Kevin outside the screen door, all aghast as Nancy called across the angle of deck from the bedroom window. "I think it's a pile of shit, if I'm allowed to express my personal conviction. If I may say what *I* think. In my own house. I think it's the biggest pile of shit I ever heard."

"They were so nice and . . . *ordinary* to me at the beach," Nancy wept, hours later, sorting the debris of the fiasco. "It was person to person. I swear I didn't even think of him as W.T. Bowman at first. We just *fell* into conversation. It was so easy. Particularly he was so easy for me to talk to, though I must say that German cunt seemed weird from the word go. He didn't seem like the dull bastards we usually collect. *Friends!* And then to come into my own house and work up to his punch line so slowly, so he could spring his great putdown. To show off for that cunt. It was all a putdown. To show me what a *little twerp* I am. So I am, and fuck everybody."

"Maybe it wasn't intended that way."

"That Jesus Christ stuff? Come on. Whose side are you on?"

"I don't want to side *against* Jesus."

"Shithead! I don't have to take that from you. From you, *either.* There's no one here to laugh at me now, so knock it off."

"Who's laughing? There are still people in the world who believe in Christ."

"Not intellectuals. Not someone with Bowman's record. Elaine happens to be his *sixth* wife."

"True."

"I guess you missed what that sly bitch said about a *ménage à trois.*"

"That was the part I thought was intended as a joke."

"Oh no. Old Macho is knocking them both off. I'm broad-minded," she said, daring anyone to doubt it, "but he can't have it both ways. He wants to boff that Jokaanen cow, okay. But not along with his Jesus act. Oh no! No! No! No!"

Troy might dare defend Bowman's religious conversion. He was not so rash as to praise the shapely German girl. He wagged his head at Bowman's audacity.

Nancy said, "I brought him here thinking if you and he hit it off . . ."

"A good example for me."

"Shit. You're ten times the writer he is. And I'm not sorry I told him off. But in front of the children! Oh, my *God!*"

As a matter of fact, it had been the arrival of the children that permitted a transition out of Nancy's greatest scene. Kevin was impassioned with a wish to hang onto a new friend and a great horseshoe pitcher. It thrilled him to find an older boy with whom, apparently, he could be friends. "I want to get my telescope out after dark and show him the moons of Jupiter." Could Vachel stay for dinner?

"Absolutely we'll feed him," Troy said. "Why don't you set the telescope up on the roof right now? Get the ladder and set it up. Okay?"

"Is mama all right?" Ursula wanted to know.

"You bet she is. She's just gone to the bathroom. Now you kids run outside again while we finish our adult conversation."

But Bowman had got his womenfolks past the door while this diversion was taking place. He lingered to shake Troy's hand. "I'm really sorry," he said. "Tell Nancy . . ." He could not think of anything to tell Nancy.

"Aaaah. She had one too many, I guess."

Bowman looked at him with uninterpretable pity and shook his head. "Sorry you and I didn't get to talk more. Nancy tells me you used to be a Marine. I was too."

"Yes, I know." Who did not know that Bowman's first major novel had been about his experiences behind Japanese lines on Guadalcanal with Carlson's Raiders?

"The kids seem to have hit it off," Troy said. "You're sure we can't feed Vachel and let him look at the stars? I'll drive him home later."

"*Semper fidelis,*" Bowman said, clapping him on the shoulder. "No. It was fine of Nancy to think of horseshoes. You've got a good woman there. Wonderful kids. Fact is, we truly don't leave Vachel alone with other people much. He wouldn't cause trouble, but it wouldn't be fair to him. We think he knows who we are, at least."

It was a shame. It was a shambles. Yet, as Troy finally lay down to sleep beside the angrily snoring Nancy, he saw a pinpoint of light, a glitter in the rubble of the evening, as if the passage of the Bowman *ménage* promised a blessing on the house, a benevolence impossible to name.

The kernel within the kernel of the nut was that Bowman was a living proof that the woman problem could be managed if not solved. No use wondering if he exploited them or didn't, it was the *way* he did it that might provide a usable example. How?

Well now . . . the answer was clear, as from one Marine to another. *Live big.*

Everything about Bowman—except his not quite believable

physical stature—was scaled to be either heroic or grotesque, or a bit of both at the same time, including the story about Vachel's mental illness with no detectable symptoms. If his profession of Christianity was a joke, well . . . it was a hell of a big one.

Semper fidelis, son. You've got nothing to lose. They can kill you like a poor little guppy, but they can't eat you, trooper.

Be true. To . . . what?

Well, how about to . . . uh . . . Jokaanen Ober, Marine? How'd you like to sink your yellow teeth in that and let it drag you to death? She's got ten times the pussy power of both your ladies, soaking wet.

And, as Troy pondered the scale of the German giantess, with a devastating flash, he thought he remembered where he had seen her once, and once only, before. . . .

Flash all the way back to his wedding night with Nancy.

They had spent that night in a suite in a hotel in Omaha, after the wedding in Nancy's hometown of Plattesmouth, Nebraska. The suite had been rented for them by the father of the bride.

"Does he or doesn't he understand we've been shacking up in New York for the last year?" Nancy fretted. "Why this lay-on? To impress who or whom?"

Obviously it had been rented to mollify the Nebraska relatives. It was Walter Carson's compromise between his pride that his daughter was a dancer, making the beginnings of a career in Greenwich Village, marrying a promising young writer, and—on the other side—his self-respect as a lumber dealer in Plattesmouth. Nancy was grumbling because it was a compromise, and in her grumbling the bridegroom was, even then, hearing premonitions of what he was letting himself in for.

In a word, all his doubts about whether they ought to marry were swollen to a head at the very moment she crawled irritably between the hotel sheets and announced she would be asleep in exactly three minutes.

He was moodily confronting the window of the hotel room, shaken with lust entirely appropriate for a bridegroom—but not for her, who gave him ultimatums to hurry up or go without. He had honestly and foolishly expected marriage to give him his first shot at the real Nancy who had never quite come across in New York. He wanted the spunky, headstrong girl-child who, no doubt, should never have left Nebraska. In marrying her he wanted to marry . . . oh, the promise of the past, something already finished but not irretrievable. He had flown west to the wedding with the deadly comic wish to marry the American race, with a hunger for the games of the American night, for the adventure that had never been used up in the small towns. Now, from the hotel window, he faced a wall of glazed brick. It was the back wall of a high-rise apartment hotel, the twin or mirror of the one they were in.

The glazed wall was sterile as their bathroom. Floodlit to discourage crime, it blocked his vision of the night on west over sleeping grasslands to the foothills of the Rockies, the crude granite slabs thrusting up from the crest of pines, the lift of star-lit ranges behind the first chaos of stone. The Carsons out there would all be descended from Kit, and their daughters came to their marriage nights on beds of wild fern.

"Two minutes," Nancy called warningly from the bed. "Is something wrong?"

"Not a thing."

"You're sorry you married me."

"I'll never be sorry of that."

"Then we might as well get my father's money's worth," she said. "Don't blame me if coming out here was a drag and my family is so square. I wanted a J.P. and you remember I said so. It was your whim to come home to Plattesmouth. We'll never do it again."

"Then go to sleep," he remembered saying to her. (Go to sleep for all these years of marriage, girlchild, dancer . . . Is that what he had commanded? Hypnotized her into that night?) He might regret his lack of gallantry then, but the plain fact was that of his own volition he could not force himself into bed with her. Not on command.

He was staring into the room in the building across the courtyard from theirs, a room with a very large window. In the insipid wall the window had looked to him just like the side of a cubical aquarium, and the blue-lighted room it revealed seemed full of a fluid like water. The room was empty. The bed was made. The dresser and the easy chair looked as unused as a display of furniture in a furniture store. Toy furniture . . . but on a scale his eyes did not reliably register. He felt that if he could reach his hand over he might pick up any piece of the furniture between thumb and forefinger. Or he might have stood by a caster of the bed dwarfed as by the wheel of earth-moving equipment.

Then, into this marvelous artifice of a room, a woman came. She was wearing high-heeled gold sandals and nothing else. Her hair was the color of Nebraska wheat and gathered at her nape with a pinching ribbon that set off its fluffy opulence.

Fifty feet tall or five centimeters, like a doll or a mermaid queen, the woman advanced in the fluid of the interior.

He felt the pulsation of her movement through the fluid of his eyeballs.

With the precise step of a drum majorette in her prime, the woman crossed the entire width of the room to the dresser. She put her gold sandals together and crouched like a splendid American housewife combining calisthenics (or even eurhythmic dancing) with the duty of checking her cake in the oven.

94

She opened a drawer. From it she took a huge, blue-gleaming revolver and left the room.

"Nancy," he called with hissing excitement.

"I'm *asleep,*" she said. "You told me to go to sleep."

He was forlorn. It seemed to him that if Nancy had seen what he saw all the compromises around them and between them would have lost their power to annoy.

"Nancy?"

Too late. The vision had retreated.

The best he could do was hop on Nancy and pump her full of boys and girls, whose names would be Kevin and Ursula and who would make up for what was gone. He had never expected to glimpse again that woman in the other room. Now Bowman had brought her back.

Jokaanen Ober, Troy said to himself. *Semper fidelis.*

It was undoubtedly fiction to suppose she was the same woman, but it had the power of truth.

8

T ROY ARRIVED early and anxious at the Provincetown airport to pick up Jan Savery and Genevieve George. The anxiety he deserved was sharpened by his inability to make contact with Margaret again, and he had been brought to the point of hoping Jan would know where she was.

He had several times tried phoning the Cincinnati apartment and not even Bob, the new renter, answered. When he called Margaret's extension at the Stoke & Bywater printing plant in Cincinnati he was told she had quit her job several days ago. Claude Bonito gave out this information. Claude asked, "That you, Slater? The word I get from the other girls in the office is that Gill—Margaret—is going—coming—east to marry you. Congratulations. She's a very able young woman. Very bright. Very *literary*. Anything to that?"

Troy had answered with a laugh so pained Bonito said,

"That's your business, isn't it? Anyway, the bird has flown our coop. You want me to find out if she gave anybody here a forwarding address? But then you must know . . ."

All he knew was *semper fidelis* and *live big*. All this whittling didn't help him grow.

Kevin and Ursula had ridden along to the airport to pick up the "two old ladies from daddy's office" as Nancy insistently labeled them. Nancy was busy at home, as she had been for the last two days, "researching W.T. Bowman." She had got some of his books from the Wellfleet library. Everything carded was on the shelves. The books were evidently not much in demand this year. Her research also included phoning her friends and acquaintances in Provincetown for any gossip floating about the Bowman household. Only Mary Lee Rideout seemed to have heard that the old man had become a Jesus freak. She thought there had been some trouble at a cocktail party where Bowman had proclaimed his conversion to Catholicism. "Mary Lee agrees he's trying to get back in the limelight by being controversial. It may not even have been Catholicism, which would get by in Provincetown without too much stir." Nancy found nothing but agnostic nihilism in Bowman's novels, after he had passed from his Left Wing phase. As for the connection with Jokaanen, even Mary Lee knew nothing about her, though she remembered something similar back in the time of Bowman's wife Marian, who was Vachel's mother. There had been an Irish girl in the picture, apparently tolerated—for a while, *for a while*—by Marian. As a matter of fact, it was very possible that Bowman was still making it with his second and third wives while Marian held the title. All his wives continued their fondness for Bowman.

"There's that woman," Kevin said as they drove into the airport parking lot. Jokaanen Ober was sitting at the wheel of a white Porsche. "Aren't you going to say hello to her, dad?"

"I don't know," Troy said. "Let's go on through the terminal and look at the airplanes." He took the children's hands and hurried them through the little building to the benches in the arrival area. Kevin was up on the fence explaining propellers to Ursula when Jokaanen came through with a carry-on bag.

"Hi," Slater said. His heart skipped a beat as he took in the significance of the bag. "Leaving us?"

"To New York only," she said. "Not yet home." In a linen pants suit she was not quite the creature she had been in her bikini in his living room—or in gold sandals in Omaha—but the authority of her body would show through veils of sackcloth, and as he made room for her to sit on the bench beside him his balls felt honored even to be in such proximity. When she put down her bag something very hard in it bumped against his calf. It might have been the big revolver she took from the drawer in Omaha.

"The plane is late from Boston?" she asked.

"We're a little early. It's usually on time. I brought the kids to pick up some friends from New York."

The prompting made her recognize Kevin and Ursula. "Your boy is enamored of Vachel, yes?"

"He wanted to show him the moons of Jupiter with his telescope. As a matter of fact, they're a thrilling sight."

"I have seen them," she said—as if she meant she had seen them close up. "It was unfortunate. At your house. On the beach we liked your wife. We do not know what happened. Your wife is not used to alcohol?"

"Well . . ." He seemed obliged to defend Nancy as he would defend his flawed nation against alien attack, even by superior extra-terrestrials. "She's not used to people talking about Jesus while consuming alcohol."

Jokaanen smiled and nodded abruptly. "We know." Apparently there had been an enlightened review in the Bowman household of the explosion at the Slaters'. "Bowman is grieved he can not keep his big mouth shut. He said it innocently, but he is too old to be innocent. He would like to make amends. He cares about you that you are a fellow writer and were once a Marine as he was once a Marine. He thinks of inviting you to shoot with him. Yes, your wife told us many things at the beach to make us care. She is very anxious about you. In America you will be anxious about someone instead of love them. Why is it so?"

He could have imagined nothing more banal than this European condescension to American immaturity—and, by the same token, it was exactly what this beauty was supposed to say to him. Her simplemindedness was one charm the more. In the way the Bowmans were working on him, his grossness was being transformed. Instead of mentally undressing her, now it was as if he had mentally lifted off the top of her skull and seen an unwrinkled brain lying there juicy as the white meat of a pear on a plate.

"Do not so," Jokaanen said, exactly like a crone advising a wayward boy. "Love is the way."

The frumpy old airplane hobbling across the Bay from Boston was romanticized by the setting of dunes and wind-whipped beach grass. Waiting for it, watching it dip a silhouetted wing out over the sun-tracked water in the west was like being on an atoll in the Pacific during the war with the Japanese. Douglas MacArthur might step down from it, puffing his corncob pipe, masking his Top Secret plans behind a nobly expressionless face.

Jan and Genevieve got out of it cautiously. It was only when Troy waved and yelled to them that they made up their minds they had been brought to the right place.

"Hey, goody!" Ursula yelled to them. "You're on time. Let's go. We're gonna take the boat out and have a picnic on the sandspit if the tide isn't gone."

"Lovely, lovely," the ladies said. Genevieve went to collect her golf bag from the baggage cart. Jan embraced Troy.

Close to his ear she said, "Margaret's already in New York. Tell you more later."

"What else is to tell?"

"It's got complicated," Jan said. Just as if it had all been as simple as pie before.

By their nature, picnics are inhospitable to complications. Complications get wet from the spray of the boatride and go soggy. Sand blows into them. The smell of burning hamburger fat simplifies everything. With the tide just turning at seven that evening, Troy's family and visitors were spread on a sand-spit in Pamet Harbor like the harmless and guileless figures on a Grecian urn, picturesque and exempt from what was past and what was to come.

Troy had intended to get what information he could from Jan before she got too liquored to be intelligible. Instead of learning what new complications Jan had cranked into his life, or what she had discerned, he was simply busy tending the charcoal burning in the hibachi, the plastic jug of gin and tonic, the spread of paper plates on an oilcloth and the hamburger patties attractive to gnats when their waxed paper wrapping was loosened. He shuffled on bare knees to gather some dry seaweed that would hasten the charcoal. The seaweed caught in a puff of smoke. The crinkle of small flames rose through the grill. He shuffled on his knees to where Jan sat on a spread blanket. "Ready," he said.

"For what?"

"What's the Margaret news this time? You say she is in New York. It's a relief she hasn't run off to Majorca with Bob."

"Who's Bob?"

"Never mind. The complications. Tell me the complications."

"This is a spot of great beauty," Jan said. "She wouldn't run off. Great beauty." It was not the gin and tonic that was cadencing Jan's speech. Second thoughts were nibbling her convictions of right and wrong like the wavelets nibbling at the sand near her feet.

"We love this spot. It's the perfection of the American dream, and don't knock it."

"It may be as good as anything there is."

A day sailor was towing a dinghy past them and out between the breakwater boulders. The family of six on the sailboat looked not only healthier but sexier than the lovers in a Watteau painting setting off for Cythera. Two college boys in a canoe were chasing a pair of girls who kept collapsing their Sunfish. In the shallows, vivid with the turbulence of an offshore breeze, Nancy, the children, and Genevieve George took turns throwing themselves flat so the racing waves would carry them the length of the sandspit before they stood up in thigh-deep water.

"You've got a lovely family. I keep forgetting what an attractive woman Nancy is," Jan said. "I can't get over that she was running a chain saw when we came into your driveway."

"Just a stump I promised to take out a month ago. Nancy's the chain saw type. They make a lot of racket. For her a chain saw is the moral equivalent of a machine gun."

"Pioneer woman."

"She grew up in Nebraska. Sawdust in her blood. Her father ran a lumberyard."

"She's got a strong figure. Like that woman you were sitting with when we landed in Provincetown. I saw you from the airplane window and thought Nancy had come along."

He snorted astonishment. "Odd! Genevieve looks damn good down there in the waves, too. And, my, I guess I haven't told you how trim you look."

"For sixty?"

"You're not and I know it. You forget you're a lush who

confesses the truth over lunch."

"Sixty in December. What's the difference?"

"I like your bikini." He didn't look at her as he said it. It would not be fair. She had no advantage of distance or the aerial perspective that made Nancy a sister of Jokaanen Ober as the night makes all cats gray. She would not suppose his eye could miss the crepey withering of her skin or the freckles like scales on her arms. The freckles came from her efforts at tanning on her roof in New York.

"I must have been nuts to buy it. You know, there I was in Bloomingdale's dressing room and got rebellious. If you ain't got it, deny it. Like Barbara Streisand."

"Well, you had it once. That's what you're proving."

"Careful! Someday people will take you at your word, Troy. Ursula said a while ago it looked super. Your wife had no comment."

"She's jealous."

"Kind."

"Women are never kind to each other. That's why men like me serve a purpose. To appreciate them all. The woman I was with in Provincetown is my latest love."

Jan laughed coarsely, but her heart wasn't in it. The bawdy guffaw was a smokescreen for a chaos of sentiments as unmanageable as his. She patted his knee. "You poor sonofabitch. You never had a chance against us, did you?" Then she gathered her determinations and said severely, "They better damn soon learn how to be kind to each other. Damn it, since I bought this suit, I better immerse the silly thing."

She got up and tried angrily to tug at the polkadot bottom of the bikini—as if it might be stretched to cover the vanity of the illusion that had come over her in Bloomingdale's flattering light. "Margaret's in New York, as I said. She chose not to stay with me."

There was hurt in her voice and Troy guessed—his guess

would turn out to be correct—that this was the only new complication in the advance toward his immolation. It was a guess that opened on a teeming field of guesses, for from it followed the probability that Jan had counted on a sisterly alliance with Margaret when she offered to share her apartment, and Margaret had hurt her feelings by casually ignoring the attempted kindness. Had let Jan know that their ages and ways were much too different to make sharing an apartment, even briefly, tolerable to her.

He had no feeling that this rebuff served Jan right. Unkindness always made him want to be kind. So he whistled appreciatively after her as she walked down to the water. He whistled an anthem of appreciation for the impulse that had made her buy the inappropriate suit, since Jokaanen had instructed him that love is the way. The Bowman people were at least giving him the right mottoes for living big. "Love is the way" was as great as the others.

The picnic worked the better part of its decisive function by glutting them with food and drink and the sound of water moving on undisclosed missions. It made them sleepy. When they came back by boat up the black, winding channel of the Pamet River, all but Troy and Jan were winding toward bed.

None went directly to bed when they were in the house again. The river had taught them you don't go directly to where it is destined you will arrive. Jan and Troy still had complications to examine, but in the lamplight all the adults except Jan fell into a game of "animal, mineral, and vegetable" with Ursula and Kevin. The nature of the game was that one of them would silently select an object visible to the others and then permit twenty questions in the process of guessing what it was.

"We called it 'Twenty Questions' when I was a kid in Ohio," Genevieve remembered.

"Where in Ohio?" Nancy asked, "Cincinnati?"

"Oberlin. Or near Oberlin. I grew up on a farm."

"Mineral," said Ursula, who was answering questions. The only place in Ohio Nancy had visited was Youngstown where, believe it or not, she had once danced when she was a dancer. "Daddy goes to Cincinnati." "Genevieve knows all about that, Kevin." "No, it is not the rock in the aquarium," Ursula said. "I was, however, an Oberlin graduate. Is it that coffee table top, Ursula?" "What Nancy means is that she was a belly dancer. In Youngstown she danced before the crowned heads of the Steel Workers' Union." "It's my *jumping rope*," Ursula said. Kevin immediately declared the rope to be vegetable. "You're silly. It's made out of plastic." "Mama, isn't plastic vegetable?" "Ask Miss George." "Goodness, I thought plastic was just plastic." "Daddy?" Daddy thought it was time they were all in bed.

"That's where I'm headed," Nancy said. "Troy, why don't you drive Genevieve and Jan up to see the night life in Provincetown? It'll be eleven when you get there and should be jumping."

All this while Jan had been prowling around them, looking at the titles of the books on their shelves. She picked up a novel of W.T. Bowman's that Nancy had left lying on the carpet. "Doesn't Bowman live in Provincetown?" she asked. "We'll go look for Bowman in his haunts."

"He's a much over-rated writer," Nancy said.

"I'm too sleepy, dear," Genevieve said.

Troy said, "Animal."

Time for straight talk. Troy began before he had cleared the driveway. What, exactly, had been the nature of the discussion between Jan and Margaret in Cincinnati that had precipitated Margaret's return to New York?

"You're mad at me," Jan said.

"I'm not mad at anyone. I'm in the dark. Things seem to be caving in. Things I supposed I understood."

"Well. In the first place I went to Dan Wiggs and reminded him I'd been promised an editorial assistant as long ago as last fall . . ."

"And Margaret just happened to be ideally qualified?"

"You want to hear what we talked about in Cincinnati? Well, I just said why didn't we have dinner together. She said she'd cook for me, and she took me to this love nest she's been keeping for you."

Love nest . . . ! The tabloid term from antique times came back to serve ideally. Of course, no one could enter that apartment without being smitten with its venereal ambience. He could well imagine Jan's eyes narrowing, her nose twitching. "She showed me the 'shrine'," Jan said now with a suffering cackle that mingled envy, resentment, outrage and unbelief. "Damn bedroom's like an icebox where they hang the carcasses."

"Mmmmmm." But . . . yes, the sacred room would have to seem an abattoir to profane eyes. The odor of spent lust is not universally cherished. "It was her creation."

"But was it a life? Could you call that a life for her?"

"I didn't have a life to offer her. Not the way you mean it."

"Hold your horses, sir. I didn't just walk in and say, 'The dummy's had his fun, now make him pay.' What started it all was her parents had visited her and they'd got a look at that queen-size bed. I guess they whomped her. Landed with both feet on her little back. She explained to them you were going to marry her. Do you deny that?"

"I'm not denying anything. Go on with your story."

"What did I have to contribute? I'll tell you all I had to contribute. Unless you've been lying to me, too, which I doubt, for two years, you care about the little thing and you don't get along so great with Nancy."

"As simple as that."

"If you're mad at me, let's just knock it off. She's not even going to live in my apartment, so I wash my hands. She's gonna stay some place she got from a college friend in the Village until she finds her own. Set you up another love nest there, maybe. But why should she keep laying it out for you when you promise to marry her and then 'don't deny it.' "

"Why indeed if she doesn't want to?"

"She loves you."

"That's the complication, isn't it? I love her."

"So I said . . ." Jan was swinging like a trapeze artist who, at the last moment, decides not to let go the bar and fly into space.

"You said, 'Come back to New York and put the heat on him. Help him over the hurdle.' "

"Wait now. Hold your horses. Not exactly." These had not been her words, but in her repudiation of them there was an admission that maybe that had been the gist of her savvy counsel, as it had been what Margaret was ready to hear. "Troy, it was too much like the young man named Dave in the limerick. Who kept a dead whore in a cave. You gotta admit he was a bit of a shit in spite of the money he saved." So much for sacred loves.

"And you told her that in New York she could start all over again. With some other married stud if Troy Slater wouldn't make good on implied promises and tacit understandings and wishful mishmash."

"I told her to make her move while she still had time if it didn't work out!"

"I suppose you meant well, Jan. Didn't it occur to you at any time that you might ruin something precious and beautiful by putting your big nose into it?"

Jan burst instantly and noisily into tears. Of course, that was just what she must now suppose she had done. Had needed him

—of all things!—to deny it for her. She *didn't* know Margaret. Must have had thoughts of frying pan and fire, but had nevertheless "put herself in the girl's place," the root of all mischief. Had probably never expected Margaret would take advice from her, since so few ever had . . . Therefore, loud tears.

In the face of her collapse, he did the only thing he could think of. Instead of driving on to Provincetown, he turned off the highway toward Highland Light and came to the public parking lot a mile north of the lighthouse. He parked between the cars of lovers and fishermen in a spot where they could see the line of surf like a white flaw across the windshield.

"I don't know why I'm sounding sure of myself," he said. "Tell me what to do, Jan."

Quick as a flash she said, "Marry the girl."

Then in an intense half hour of confession he learned what they had all been up against with Jan. He heard her story.

Once upon a time—right after World War II—a lank, pretty schoolteacher named Jan Savery had chucked her job in Oelwein, Iowa to come to New York. Sure enough, she had been a poet with just enough publications to sucker her along. Sure enough, there was a New York editor who genuinely believed in her talent. Needless to say he was married and had a house with two children in Jamaica, Long Island. No need to scoff at the sincerity of his wish to come over to Greenwich Village where Jan Savery was stashed in a two-room coldwater flat, tending her geraniums and her verse. Twice he had left his wife. Twice the psychic strain had obliged him to consult psychiatrists, who helped him straighten things out and get back with the wife.

"Then he left her for good," Jan said. "We always knew he was going to leave her. I knew that in my soul, and I was right."

Editor X had left his wife and married a sharp young staffer on a fashion magazine. He left Jamaica and moved to an apartment in the East Fifties. "Then he went gay for a while until his psychiatrists got him straightened out so he could fuck his secretaries." The drollery of that circumstance was too great for tears. After all these years Jan could laugh about it. She laughed. Laughter twice as ghastly as her weeping. In the midst of her grim choking she said, "Somebody's got to do it right."

"I see," he said. "You want me and Margaret to make your story come out right for you. You're too smart to believe in that."

"I was too smart for my own good. Take the plunge, Troy. It's your only chance."

"I'll come down to New York soon to see her," he said cautiously.

That was not good enough. "What the hell? What the *hell?*" In a gusting fury Jan grabbed his crotch. "He's smarter than you, Slater. He's the good soldier. Trust him."

It was the deepest truth she had saved from the ruining years. A truth so superior to reason that at the instant she touched him he had a startlingly complete erection.

She had wanted him to *hear,* to agree with the logic of her daydreams in which he had figured vicariously, it seemed. His carnal erection was an irredeemable trespass. A shame on both of them.

"Oh *no,*" she said. She let go in violent repugnance. His erection vanished as quickly. Rather, it seemed to dart back all the way up his spine, like a chipmunk darting up a tree trunk at the approach of Bronstein's cat. He felt the terrified creature trying to get into his skull and hide there.

Like a flash Jan was out of the car and walking back the way they had come. He glanced down to see if he was still intact. He would not have been surprised to see her detached hand still gripping his fly.

By the time he got the car started and turned around to follow her she had covered nearly a hundred yards. As he crept behind her, she was transformed in his headlights. He saw a child walking stiff-armed and rigid with resentment at a punishment she would not admit she deserved. She seemed no older than Ursula—an Ursula cruelly struck and determined not to collapse until she got out of everyone's sight. His foot wanted to jam down on the accelerator and run over her. He might crowd her into the roadside bushes and rape her.

He pulled the car gently alongside her, but she would not turn her face to look at him. "Let's go get a tall drink, old friend."

No answer.

"This is just absurd," he coaxed. Yes, but it was the absurdity of being in the spot where lightning chooses to strike and there was a smell of burning flesh in the salty night air. He drove some distance ahead of her, got out and headed back with arms spread as if he meant to tackle her when she came near enough.

He did not have to do that. Stiff as a soldier on parade she went to the right of the Volvo and got in. By the time he was settling again in the driver's seat she looked composed, with her offending hands folded brittlely in her lap. "I'm so tired," she said—not as explanation but as brute statement of fact.

Halfway home she was prompted by her thoughts to say, "You have a fine, pretty family. If you do anything to hurt them, never speak to me again." Then, when he had shut off the ignition beside the house, before she moved to get out, she said, "I try to do the right thing."

Jan slept the greater part of the next day. "I don't think she's sick," said Genevieve, the emissary from the guest room. "Just wants to be left alone. Did you two drink a lot in Provincetown?"

He took Genevieve to play golf on the course near Highland

Light. "Jan thinks she's going to die," Genevieve said. "And she may. All this drinking."

"She was pretty sober last night."

"For once then. It doesn't get any better. You know how she grabs her bootstraps to come to the office and get through until lunchtime. She still cranks it out! Then goes home and . . . sinks clear out of sight. Weekends are usually the worst. She needs a new interest."

"She's got one."

"This girl who's coming from Cincinnati? Yes, with someone to share her apartment she might perk up. Someone to train in her office. She was cheery on the flight up here, and unwinding. She cares about you. Wants to know that you're writing. Wants to 'get you going'."

"Everyone does. That's what keeps me hogtied."

Genevieve refused him sympathy. "Pshaw, Troy. Just . . . pshaw. You're living a princely life up here. You're living at the peak and if you can't see it now, you will when you look back and miss it."

"A quitter never wins and a winner never quits."

"That's the spirit." She hit a pretty nice drive down the fairway. He followed with a pretty nice drive, thinking like Jan that he was going to die before he either won or quit.

Through the rest of the weekend he got no more out of Jan on the subject of Margaret Gill. Jan was devoting herself to Nancy and to hearing tales of the Harvard School of Business. She encouraged Nancy to show her the operation of the chain saw. In a shower of sawdust the two of them demolished a pine log as if it were the ultimate phallic symbol. They beamed with happiness when it had been reduced to manageable lengths for the fireplace, and they celebrated with Bloody Mary's.

Jan said, "I've heard all kinds of stories about people who got out of the rat race by selling through direct mail. You people could retire up here with a little business of your own and Troy could write *Moby Guppy.*" She had been told the tale of how he mooned all day in front of the aquarium and agreed that it was an evasion of his opportunities. She agreed that W.T. Bowman was a writer whose fad was over and thought perhaps he might be in the pay of the Moonies, as so many were in these times. "Seriously," she said. "The Moonies are buying into publishing in a big way and they would need some writers with track records to make it seem legitimate when they make their bid for world domination."

Hearing these arguable opinions while he sat on the sunny deck with his wife and guests, Troy chuckled at them without argument. He needed a service from Jan.

"Look," he said to her at an opportune moment. "I need an excuse to get to New York and find out from Margaret what her thoughts are. If you can get the Dangleburn manuscript and all that mess up for review this week, I'd have to come in to go over it with Holbrook and Wiggs. We can't keep Dangleburn dangling."

Humpty-Dumpty had been glued back together by sunlight and Bloody Mary's. Jan's gaze was sardonic. "I could do that," she said. "Wiggs thinks you've goofed on Dangleburn long enough."

"And tell Margaret . . ."

"Nothing! Handle that yourself."

"Sure. Just give me her address and phone number."

"There isn't any phone." The address she gave him was on Carmine Street, not far from where Nancy had lived in her dancing days. "Just remember all I ever wanted was to get some things out of the closet, all aboveboard so everyone could take a fresh look."

"Everyone deserves a peep at Troy with the egg on his face."

"Though I still entertain some curiosity. Which way will the cat jump?"

She had put on an affected Voltairean wit. In the daylight he saw that she had a certain resemblance to Voltaire as he is portrayed in old age—the same lethally pointed chin below the quipping mouth, and in her eyes an expression that might be malice if it were not so scornful in its pity.

9

HE WAS debating with Nancy about when he should fly to New York for the Dangleburn conference when Bowman called to invite him for some shooting. "Wednesday morning," Bowman said. It was the day Troy had said he must be in the New York office. "Fine," Troy said.

"How about bringing your son?" Bowman asked.

"He'd like it." But when it came to explaining this to Nancy, he hit a stone wall.

"First you tell me you have to be in New York Wednesday. So I agreed to skip my Harvard class and take Kevin and Ursula to Hyannis, which you promised them long ago. Now you're going out to play cowboy with that man on Wednesday. I'll tell you, Kevin's not going."

"Thursday's as good for New York. Go to Cambridge. We're only going down to shoot tin cans with a .22 behind the

Truro dump. Vachel's going. Why not Kevin?"

"And leave Ursula all alone here?" It would not be the first time they had done that, but Nancy had the smell of a rat in her nose and protested everything he proposed.

Then Kevin got into it, overhearing enough to know his invitation was being vetoed on specious grounds. "I'd be very careful," he promised. "I wouldn't even ask to shoot the gun unless Mr. Bowman asked if I wanted to."

"Remember the talks we had last winter about handgun legislation?" Nancy asked. "In school you debated in favor of it."

"Of course I'm against handguns and Saturday night specials," he said. But of course he was regretting such a political commitment, and was smart enough to see the flaw in his mother's reasoning. Also smart enough to know she would come up with another argument if this one failed her.

"If you'd stand up to her, she'd let me go," he charged his father.

"I don't want to overload her system," Troy said. Not when she was smelling rat. "I'll tell you what I'll do instead. If you'll forget about the shooting, I'll ask Vachel if he wants to go with you on a sightseeing flight from the Provincetown airport. Just you two. You don't have to take Ursula this time."

"No!"

"You told me once that was the main thing you wanted to do this summer. In the old yellow Stinson."

"You're afraid to stand up to mama about anything. That's all." Kevin ran away after that, down into the woods to nurse his shame and his knowledge without a father to help him. He came back, though, in an hour to say, "It's a deal, dad. Do you think Vachel will go with me? He's probably flown so much it's boring. It's all right about the shooting."

"I'll bet Vachel will go. You and he seemed to hit it off."

"He's a neat kid. Is there something wrong with him?"

116

"*No!* Why?"

"That they wouldn't let him stay the night they were here?"

"Things just got screwed up that night."

"In one of mama's books it says Mr. Bowman was a Marine. You were, too, weren't you dad?"

"Oh yeah. Feel my leather neck."

"I remember when I was just a baby you used to tell me about it. Combat."

"It was all lies."

"Didn't you . . . Well, did you kill people?"

"Me? You know me, kid. I was a supply sergeant. Never fired a shot in anger."

"I don't think you were afraid to, were you?"

"Kill people? Yeah, I sure was. I was more afraid of killing people than of being killed. That's the truth."

"I don't understand."

"Well, a human life is precious, isn't it?"

"Yes."

"Your mama is right about handguns. It's like I smoke cigarettes and drink. It's too late for me, but you can be better. Shooting isn't so big a deal for me, either, but I promised Mr. Bowman I'd go."

His adaptations of morality got no direct response from Kevin. But another hour passed and Kevin found him to say, "That was brave."

"What?"

"To rather be killed than kill somebody. I don't know if I could feel that way."

Then it was his father's turn to go down into the woods below the house, to lie face down on the soft peat and pine needles and cry like a baby. Because he was not brave enough to accept all his cowardice had brought him.

The crying helped his nerves, if nothing more could be said of it. At least it restored him to the fatalism he had basked in

117

that day he watched the guppies die. It was a comfort—not much—that, after all, half a dozen of the little fish had survived and by now seemed in health.

On Wednesday the two old ex-Marines slogged into the Valley of Make-Believe Death. Vachel led them. He was wearing dazzling white tennis shorts, shirt, and sneakers. His arms and legs were the color of iron streaks in the sand of the dunes. The hamper and icebox he was carrying seemed much lighter in his hands than the leather pouches of guns and ammunition Bowman had hung on Troy when they parked the car behind the Truro dump and continued on foot.

The fire lane through the pines petered out where they had left the car. Now they were on a footpath curling down among shadowy pine trunks and bars of light so intense as to be hallucinatory. Below them the sandy floor of the valley was moon-colored, whitish.

"Remind you of anything?" Bowman asked.

It did. "We trained on Guam for two months. Yeah, we bivouacked in country like this, more or less. Cane fields right over the top of those hills."

"We have returned," Bowman said with one of his suggestive chuckles. "We always come back."

"You were on Guadalcanal?"

"Wasn't I, though?" His gamy, reptilian eyes sparkled with memories that must be joyful.

"With Carlson's Raiders?"

"Oh. You know about Carlson, do you?"

"Whatever happened to him?"

"That's a great story. It can never be told. I used part of it in one of my novels, you know. In brief he went Communist from his American convictions and got mixed up with Agnes Smedley. Died of a heart attack. I loved that man. There haven't been many like him. I called him Old Hickory, and I believe it amused him, though I was a smart-ass kid then. What a sweet sonofabitch. Smedley was another matter."

"You were out behind the Jap lines with Carlson?"

"That's where we are now, Troy. That's what you learn at my age." He seemed about to deliver some profound and sweeping summary that would translate into religious conviction. Instead he chuckled again, as if Troy could fill in the blanks as he needed to.

The sandpit into which they came was flanked on its northern perimeter by an absolutely barren rise of dunes, shaggy with pines at the top and seeming to curtain a limitless immensity. For nearly half a mile to the south a little valley squirmed. Its floor was littered with uprooted stumps and other debris trucked in from highway construction years ago. A devastation of peace, it was in any case a place of havoc and ruin.

Just at the foot of the bare dunes on the north was a pitiful little scaffold of crating wood. Shreds of paper targets were nailed to it, and on the mutilated paper were black human silhouettes. "Are those the crucified thieves?" Bowman forgave the lame witticism by ignoring it. This was no morning for subtle religious allusion as far as he was concerned.

A litter of punctured cans and cartridge casings thinned away from the target area across the sand. Target shooting here was evidently a popular Truro pastime. Amid the debris Bowman spread the Army blanket and with a certain air of prestidigitation began to lay out on it his arsenal of handguns and ammunition.

"Good Lord," Troy said. "I told my son we were coming out here to shoot a .22." Among the eleven guns there were, Bowman indicated, some .22's, but clearly most had a larger bore. "What I mean is . . . I thought the Massachusetts laws were strict about the possession of handguns." He had been on the verge of asking, How do you get by with it? For there were enough weapons here to defy the Mafia if not the National Guard.

All Bowman said was, "Oh, I've got connections"—leaving more blanks to be filled in. He said, "This baby is a .44 Magnum. Ever shoot one of these?" He chuckled with pride and tossed a cartridge for it to Troy.

"My God, it's an artillery shell." Troy had never seen a revolver cartridge of such size. The big, blue revolver was just as outsized. It was, to be sure, the revolver he had last seen across an airshaft in Omaha on his wedding night. Now he had it in his hand. Its checkered grip throbbed obscenely against the heel of his thumb. Quickly he passed it back to its owner.

"Anything wrong?" Bowman asked. "You know they say about the GI .45 that if you hit a man anywhere in the body it will knock him down. You hit him anywhere with this it will put him in shock. I've seen a man hit with a .50 caliber machine gun round and . . . You feeling all right?"

"Absolutely." Troy had barely qualified with basic weapons in the Marine Corps, but he had always *enjoyed* using up government ammunition.

"You look snakebit. Probably been working too hard. Your wife said you're slaving on a novel besides your editorial work. Takes it out of you. The real pros shoot the .44 Magnum at iron targets up to four hundred yards. It's Vachel's pet, huh?"

Vachel grinned winsomely, shaking his boyish curls. He was spinning the cylinder of a smaller revolver and in a perfectly natural, boyish way seemed rapt in some frontier fantasy about it.

There were automatics of various sizes along with the four revolvers. "Beretta 7 mm. This one's an authentic Nambu. I brought it from Okinawa. Couldn't get ammo for it until about three years ago. I got it from a dealer in Tokyo who caters to veterans with souvenir guns. It was an officer's gun. We burned the poor bastard out with a flame thrower. Now this one is your old friend, the issue .45. I never liked it. This snub-nosed baby is strictly for close work, but we'll try it, too. Vachel, we forgot our sack of empty beer cans. Why don't you gather up some of these lying around? Doesn't matter if they've been punctured a little. They're better than our paper targets."

He means they're more *human* than paper is, Troy thought. He was convinced he had been brought here to be shown what a real Marine was like.

A hullabaloo of gunfire! What crazy fun Kevin was missing! What a drunkenness in the sun as they banged away!

Where are those do-gooding pricks who want to legislate handguns away from Americans? Bang, bang. So much for them!

They began with a .22 target revolver, each firing six long rifle bullets into an assortment of cans set up on the scarecrow scaffold. Then Bowman showed off his Beretta. "Rapid fire. Just hose'm down. Not bad, Troy. Not bad, Vachel." They were firing the automatic from fifteen paces. Vachel seemed taut and nervous, shooting faster than either of the two older men. By luck he knocked a can down with each shot.

"We're pretty deadly at this range," Bowman said. He mopped sweat from his face. Dried his beard and mustache with a handkerchief. "Let's try it from twenty-five."

They paced off the greater distance, dragged the laden Army blanket back behind the position marked for the shooter. Safety precautions carefully observed.

"Vachel!"

The cry was a war cry, alarmed and alarming, tone and syllables honed to a signal that must have been refined from unimaginable practice. What Troy saw—partly saw because his eye was not quick enough to register it all—was a trick that, surely he had only seen before in a John Wayne movie or some other rerun on television. He had to reconstruct what happened because it was so fast.

Bowman had scooped the .44 from the blanket. It spun flashing in the sunlight as he tossed it to the boy. Vachel caught it from the air, already crouching and fanning the hammer with his left hand as he began to fire. The unbelievable roar of six shots, one on top of the other, came in a succession so swift that the ear could not separate them fully. Too fast for Troy to act on his impulse to go face down in the sand.

But what he would remember most was the cherubic smile on Vachel's face as he stood up straight again, so willowy and sweet looking. Like a junkie feeling the rush when a main line shot hits the back of his skull.

"Hit anything?" Bowman asked with loving mockery.

"What do you think?" In just that tone an infant Vachel would have scoffed back at his father when the old man praised him for flipping a Tiddly Wink in a cup.

"I saw three cans fly," Bowman said.

"Four. Want to count them?"

"Four."

Bowman said to Troy, "That boy's the angel of death. It doesn't seem to matter whether the gun has sights or not. He makes me believe some of the yarns about frontier gunslingers. They say they could shoot from the hip and drive the corks in six bottles. Or the French ace Guynemer. Another sweet young thing, as you may have read. Guynemer had a machine gun on his plane, but it was his habit to haul off and bean a Kraut with a single shot from it. Deflection shooting at that. You follow me?"

"I do."

"It's an uncommon gift. A mysterious gift of God."

Before it was time for them to relax in the shade with sandwiches and beer they worked out with all the guns at various ranges. The morning extended as a series of tableaux in which Troy saw his own shadow shortening on the sand underfoot while the sun moved and while he went from posture to posture with guns in his hand.

With the .22 Magnum he was interwoven with the roots of a decaying tree stump a hundred yards from the target on the scaffold. At this distance the front blade of the sight was exactly as wide in his vision as the black silhouette on the target they were using now. Bowman coached him. "You can rest the butt or barrel on a root. Put your wrist on that. You won't hit the target at all if you don't. Don't allow for distance. With a Magnum, if you elevate you'll overshoot."

Whump! Whump! Whump! Whump! Whump! Whump!

"The gun talks to you, doesn't it?" Bowman chuckled. "You've got a tiny bit of Vachel's instinct. We'll make a gunman of you yet."

They went back to a two hundred yard range to shoot the .44. Only Vachel put anything into the target from so far.

" 'Some men there are who cannot hold their water when the bagpipe blows in the nose.' " Bowman quoted. "A good loud handgun has the same effect."

"I felt just a little *squeeze* of moisture," Troy said. "Do you suppose I could have one more try with the .44? I'd like to tell my son I put one shot on target with it."

The gun was loaded again for him and he lay belly down in the sand, supporting his gun hand with a braced left forearm. He had got off two shots across the flat sand and was aware of no sound but the gun's coarse bellow when he felt Bowman's fingers squeezing his shoulder. He understood he was supposed to stop firing.

"Someone's yelling from up in the woods," Bowman said. "I

guess someone is out for a hike and they want to cross here."
Troy heard the repeated halloo.

"It's Jokaanen," Bowman said. He yelled, "Come on, honey.
Safe home."

In a minute she came in sight out of the noon shadows on
the path, wearing white tennis clothes like Vachel's. Watching
her approach on the flat sand, the big, symbolic revolver in his
fist, dizzy Troy watched her loom and shrink. First she was tall
as a tree, then diminished like a bird seen through the wrong
end of a telescope. He had taken too much sun on his balding
head.

He saw her white skirt and jersey rotate like a rotated sheet
of paper with its thin edge turning toward him. She widened
and multiplied like a cut-out row of paper dolls. He worked
some spit into his dry mouth.

He saw her grin whiten as she came the last steps to them.
"It's *true*," she said to Bowman. "I've been to the doctor in
Hyannis. I'm truly pregnant."

Troy saw Bowman lay a broad hand on her head in blessing.
He saw the sun, perfectly white and widening rapidly as it
widened across the whole sky above their sandpit. He felt the
sand turn into a cloud as he fainted.

Fainted had he? Now that was something that required
explanation, the ultimate unmanliness. And he called himself
a Marine! He struggled back to consciousness babbling justifi-
cations. "You said it was the Immaculate Conception!" he
shouted up at the faces wavering over him like faces seen in
the air from underwater.

"Well, not exactly," Bowman said good-temperedly. "I
wouldn't say we could claim that."

"I catch your meaning," Troy yelled back. "I catch them as
they pass." He sank again, but the next time he came up he
was all right. In a manner of speaking.

"I'm not all right. Yesterday I went into the woods and cried. Pressures. Incredible demands."

"Surely," Bowman said. "Quite understandable. Vachel, run and fetch the cooler." They pressed ice to his brow and then he was even more all right.

He sat up and asked Jokaanen, "You went to New York and got pregnant?"

"Ha ha," she said. "Is not how."

He shook himself and said, "The human mind is certainly an odd mechanism. I'm all right now. Please don't tell Nancy. That's what I mean about the mind being so curiously circumscrized as can be found in Finnerty's Wake. *What I am trying to say* . . . That is, don't tell Nancy about *anyone* being pregnant in New York. Though that is a physical impossibility. *What I am trying to say.*"

Glib as he was with handguns, Bowman quoted Hopkins: "O the mind, mind has mountains; cliffs of fall frightful, sheer, no-man-fathomed. Hold them cheap may who ne'er hung there."

Troy was inclined to agree. He said, " '*Tendunt vella noti; fugimus spumantibus undisque cursum gubernatorque vocabat . . .* ' "

"He is gone crazy," Jokaanen said.

Certainly he had. Too much sun, too much gun, had done it. But it was nothing that couldn't be remedied with the supernatural remedies at hand. His extra-terrestrial friends helped him out of the sun and into the shade of silken trees alongside the sandpit. They propped him up with a cold beer in his hand and put an exotic sandwich of Italian bread, ham and cheese in the other. He began to feel as pure as the headed grass around his feet and the gently trembling leaves overhead. Like the leaves he felt responsive to the movement of air. "Born again!" he said and began to chew.

Whatever Bowman's expertise on the subject, he did not rise to the phrase. Now that Troy was taken care of he was free to greet the news Jokaanen had brought. He was doing this with hugs and kisses. Troy listened to their dialogue while various lutes and choral voices embroidered it.

Jokaanen was saying, "It must have been the night of the full moon when we swim in the Bay. I told you it happened. I *told* you."

(Far past the stones grating in waves, out of sight of land, amid salt churning and the glow of plankton answering the moon, delicately and fiercely and clingingly the woman opens for the man swimming over her, belly up as he reared on a wave and came slithering inside her. Salt mingling the white sweet jet of creation as they bobbed and bucked with the rhythm of large waters under them and the moon pulled its tide of life warm through their channels. Ebb stinging the flow, flow stinging the ebb . . . and I swear I am tired of impotent ways of expressing love for men and women, said Walt.)

"The doctor say to me women know the time of conception. But forget. Modern women forget. I told him I knew and did not forget."

"He said that to make you feel good," Bowman told her. "I take no stock in your superstitions."

"I think he'd of said anything to keep poking around a little," Jokaanen said, laughing wickedly as she threw herself back on the thick grass, spluttering beer.

"Now there's a doctor we can trust," Bowman said.

Charmed, Troy did not find it astonishing that Vachel was neither excluded from their talk, nor in any way disturbed. He went along with the mood of easy rapture. "This'll make an even dozen of us for you, daddy."

"Who's counting?"

"Your wives are counting," Jokaanen said. "I think two will throw a fit."

"We must go tell Elaine."

"I phone her from Hyannis. She told me how to find you."

"From others we will keep it secret."

"I won't tell," Troy said and got no response at all. It was as if they knew he wasn't really with them. The situation was like the one in Margaret's painting by Titian. They were alone in their pastoral idyll, happy in their song. They wouldn't see him here with them.

"But if it comes with a mermaid's tail we're obliged by law to throw it back," Bowman said.

"Then I will disappear after it."

"No chance."

"Seriously. You must not threaten like that. What is given you must accept or you will lose me."

"Never!"

"Then you must accept the mermaid when she comes. With flippy little tail."

Chewing on a sandwich now and brushing the crumbs from his beard, Bowman said, "You still look green, young fellow. Feeling queasy? We'll take you home in a bit."

"I'm still a little dazed," Troy said. "By everything."

On the way home they stopped at the post office so Troy could pick up mail. A bundle of it and a letter from Margaret.

"Got your note and so thrilled you'll see me in my new setting Wednesday. Can't wait. So *much* to tell you."

This was Wednesday. This was Wednesday and he had been afraid to face her today. Bowman was supposed to give him some clue but had come across only with blanks still to be filled in. But Jokaanen had said he must accept the mermaid. Maybe that was the message.

When he rejoined Bowman in the parking lot after reading Margaret's letter, Bowman said, "There's no news so good or bad as it seems at first." Troy could not know whether his face registered good news or bad.

10

H E THREW up three times in the night before he went to New York.

"Give it up," Nancy said. "Surely you can postpone it until next week since you already let it slip one day. The company won't go broke if Dangleburn dangles. Maybe you caught something from the guppies after all. It'd be my luck to have you all come down with tropical fish disease."

He insisted that the vomiting purified him. Mottled pink and white where he was not tan, with a little green in the shadows under his ears, he kissed her goodbye at the Province-town airport. "Tell Kevin . . ."

"What?"

"I failed him. I didn't ask Vachel to go flying with him."

"Is that all? I don't think it's a good idea anyway."

No. That was not all. It was in his mind that he might not

return from this trip. For one reason or another. And he wanted Kevin to know he was sorry he had not set a finer example.

"My, you're strange this morning," Nancy remarked. "Are you sure you feel up to it?"

He did not. But it was wonderful what was done for him when he was caught up in the mechanized routine of air transportation. Crossing the Boston terminal, he found his step as brisk as that of all the other morning passengers with brief cases, and on the hop down to New York he could positively feel his skin changing back to its normal colors.

And in the editorial conference room at Stoke & Bywater he was mean, acerbic, alert—entirely his old self. He knew precisely what should be done with Professor Dangleburn and his long-researched manuscript on Navajo horse myths. He had the four years of memos and correspondence with Dangleburn overlaid with market research summaries laid out on the table before Dan Wiggs' secretary passed the coffee. He had copies of his own latest recommendation typed out for Wiggs, Beth Whitelaw, Paul Armbruster, Darcy Holbrook and Jan. Jan was not there. When he asked Beth why, she made a troubled face and was about to go into an explanation when Wiggs said, "Before we go into the Dangleburn thicket Paul wants us to review the distribution figures in the South Central district first. Troy, you've been spared our worries, but it may be a matter of putting on some new young persons or canning Hargrave."

"Send Chester down there for a year," Troy said. "Hargrave has not cut the mustard since '73. As you all know."

"I know you never got on with Hargrave," Wiggs said, "and maybe he's too old school to hack it any more. But let's listen to what Paul has to tell us. Our fiction anthology is way behind Norton's. That's one thing to worry about. Among many."

Armbruster, the master of preponing credits and postponing

obligations, was, unmistakably, in favor of retiring Hargrave by the first of the year. "Troy's right about sending Chester into the South. He's been absolutely invincible in Chicago, and it shows."

"Personality-wise, Chester is more Chicago than Southland," Wiggs worried.

"He's ruthless," Armbruster agreed happily. While he read from a yellow pad to show that Chester's ruthlessness was superior to Hargrave's Princetonian manner in bookselling, Troy scribbled a note to Beth: Tell me what brand of ruthlessness Chester drinks and I will send my other generals a barrel of it.

Wiggs said, "Well, I suppose the thing to do is for me to take Hargrave to lunch and try to be as candid as I can. Shall we give him until spring to try to pull it out?"

"Show him my comparative figures," Armbruster thought. "He's not a fool. My thought would be to give him a slot with the New England group until retirement. What's he? Sixty-three?"

"He's never liked the market research approach. Particularly on literature," Wiggs said. "But New England is a constructive idea. He has friends throughout the Ivy League. Now, Troy, are you ready to fish or cut bait on Dangleburn?"

In forty minutes Dangleburn was dead, as far as Stoke & Bywater, Inc. was concerned. Troy leaned into his work with relish. "I know what Beth always says about anthropology and Navajos. They go together like love and marriage, as the old song puts it. But how many Navajos can the American education system absorb? I count thirteen major Navajo texts extant. Not all thriving, though Prentice Hall has done all right with their backlisting, I suppose, and a couple of others have earned well and may be gaining. *Plus* . . . plus innumerable cross-references to Dangleburn's material in Kapwell's bibliography, if it's a question of serious scholarship. I think Dangleburn is simply raiding Kapwell. I know we've already advanced Dan-gleburn—what? Fifteen thousand dollars? If you'll look at my old memos, you'll see I never recommended more than the initial five. Let's chop him now before the machine writes him another check."

"Well," Wiggs said. He gave his most famous line. "You know textbook publishing is a conservative business, Troy." It meant, in this context that if Navajos had been the Elizabeth Taylor and Princess Meg of popular anthopology so long, there was no reason to think any other tribe would ever re-place them.

"It's a readable text," Beth still insisted. "What I found most attractive was the potential for illustrations. With a really first rate design job we might take the Navajos away from Bobbincott, if that's what is worrying Troy."

"What worries me is that the goddamn manuscript is ninety per cent tabloid filler," he said. "If Jan were here, she could support this. I went over it yet again with her when she was up last weekend."

He came out of the meeting with his hands delicately atrem-ble with victory. Thinking, I am very good at this.

Thinking, Why is *this* what I am good at?

Genevieve said, "It's just terrible, Troy. I'm frightened this time. Jan was all right on the plane coming back from our weekend. Now she'll only talk to me on the phone, and I can't make any sense of what she says."

"Is she home drunk?"

"The only clue, if you can call it that, is she said last night she might fly to Mexico for Laetrile treatments. But, honestly, this is the first I've ever heard that might suggest cancer. She's usually intending to join the A.A. Could you go to her place and see if she'll talk to you?"

He could do that, too, and promised he would, but he meant to see Margaret first. He taxied to the Village, to the Carmine Street address where she was staying. Now, at close to one o'clock, the city was stifling. The shadowed street where he got out smelled of overheated metal and dog excreta.

Her name was penciled in full below that of I. Chasen on one of the mailboxes. He rang the bell and waited for the buzzer with a sudden acceleration of pulse that might have come from happy anticipation. Somehow he did not doubt she was there in spite of the flimsiness of the arrangements and his one day delay to shoot with Bowman. But the guilt of that delay began to crawl on his skin while he waited four, five minutes and there was no answer.

He rang a few more times. She was not, usually, a late sleeper though she was a heavy sleeper and perhaps the heat had made her drop off. Then two young men in jeans came out and he caught the door before it swung shut and locked.

The elevator was tormentingly slow and smelled as though it had risen from a cellar where vegetables and old newspapers were stored. Passing the third floor he heard voices and sniffed marijuana. At the fourth a glitter babe in last night's finery got on as he got off.

There on the door of 4J her name was penciled again. He knocked repeatedly and shouted his own name. "It's Troy." He heard a radio or TV playing and the tribal repetitions of it were certainly coming from this apartment. But perhaps the windows were open and the sound was coming from across the street. It was certainly faint and mingled with the noise of traffic, the grating of a steel door being lifted in the sidewalk. He thought he heard a voice and he thought it sounded male, but since it only spoke a syllable and a slurred half he could find no meaning in it.

"I break your fucking balls. I break your fucking balls." A

woman's voice, but certainly not Margaret's, and it came from another apartment if it did not, in fact, come from the soul of the steamy, odorous building itself.

He went down and sat on the front steps for nearly an hour in case she had stepped out for lunch. At two-thirty he went to Eighth Street where he bought a *Times* and had a hamburger in Wimpy's. He looked in a phone book and found the name of I. Chasen at the right address on Carmine Street When he dialed he heard the healthy buzz of a phone ringing, but that meant nothing much. Sometimes you got that sound even when the number was temporarily out of service.

There were three Hispanic girls hanging out near the front door of Margaret's building when he got back there. One of them demanded to know the time. He carefully noted that it was exactly 3:55 in case a crime had been committed and Margaret's body would be found up there with multiple stab wounds. He rang her bell again and this time noted there was a letter in the mail box. He thought it was something he had mailed to her on Tuesday after he agreed to go shooting with Bowman. Probably it had been delivered this morning. What could he make of that?

At exactly 4:41 he left to walk to Jan Savery's place, since it was only a nine-block walk and would help to kill the time. He needed a drink and surely Jan could spare one.

Yesterday he had fainted. He had been sick in the night. His afternoon's vigil had whipped out of him the last reserves of confidence he had felt as he taxied to the Village in the noontime glare. The heat was, if anything, intensifying, and at Jan's apartment building, though the lobby was air-conditioned, the sun blazed in at him through the glass doors, printing his shadow on the tile walls like a human silhouette scorched on the walls of Hiroshima.

"It's Troy," he shouted into the microphone when he heard

136

some sort of mechanical gurgle.

"Troy Slater is it?" Jan's voice seemed to recall some childhood acquaintance. "Why'n't you come up, Troy Slater?"

But when he got to the fourteenth floor she would not open her door for him. He rang and stood waiting in the long, antiseptic corridor with its green carpet, beige walls and uniform red doors, peering into the glass of her peephole. In its mystifying refractions he saw something small as an insect moving and knew she was only two feet away from him.

"For Christ sake let me in, Jan. I'm thirsty."

"You want to rape me. Oh no. Oh no."

"Just let me in, Jan. Are you all right?"

"I know what you want. No more, sir. If milk is so cheap why buy a cow? That's your thought, is it? Well, it ain't so cheap any more, sir. Ho ho ho. Get down on your knees, sir, and beg for it."

"Are you all right? That's all I'm worried about. Hadn't you better let me in?"

"Women beware women! Women, be wise!"

"Open? Please, Jan."

"You some kind of a dentist? Open wide and I'll fill your cavity. No more! Never shall! Our cavities are our own. Our bodies protected by the Constitution. Away, sir, or I'll set the dog on you."

"Gen said you were flying to Mexico. Are you ill, Jan? Please talk to me."

"The devil is sick, the devil is sorry. Think I tell Gen? There are many false friends. We'll trust them no more, sir. I'm going nowhere. *J'y suis, j'y reste.* If you batter the door down, sir, it will be of no use. The kitchen is closed."

"All right. I'll go. I'll be in our apartment uptown this evening, if you want to call me. You need help."

"You want me to call tell you where your pussy gone."

"Do you know?"

"Ho ho ho. We are on to you. All women united. I have showed her the light. Have told her you are just another husband. Uxorious beast. Married to a beast. Wedded to bourgeois life style. America the beautiful. And your teeny boat and your snotty kids."

"Anything you say."

"I love you, Troy. Expected much of you. Be a writer, Troy. Break out of prison world. Hear?"

"I hear."

"Your fault we lost Margaret. Girl of great spirit. Could've saved you. But saw the light."

"Have you seen her since you got back?"

"Oh yes. You bet. So that's your game. Come here pretend it's me. You want to see her. The lost lady. *La demoiselle elu.* No never, never, never, never, never. She you love is dead and gone. Said I love you. Never said you love me."

"I love you, Jan."

"You lie, sir. Your wiles, your ruses! Think now I'll let you in, sir? Read 'The Lady of Shalott'?"

"I've read it."

"All the truth. Memorized it in eighth grade. Eighth grade in Iowa, so snowy. Cried but should have listened, stayed in Iowa. Now you listen, fucker, cause I'm going to recite it to you and that is *all you get.*"

As she began at what he supposed was the beginning of Tennyson's poem, her voice was sluggish and only intermittently intelligible. But she got better and more eloquent as she moved from verse to verse and told him how the cloistered Lady had seen the reflection of Lancelot passing and violated the conditions of her enchantment by leaving her mirror for the window.

A young couple in summer clothes passed down the corridor behind him, giving him the once over fearfully. It was Jan's rich voice through the door that evidently placated them.

When she was through, Jan was sobbing contentedly. "Broke her fucking mirror. Do me one thing, friend, Troy?"

"Anything."

"Say, 'She had a lovely face, The Lady of Shalott.' "

"She had a lovely face."

"The Lady of Shalott."

"The Lady of Shalott."

"Dumb shithead. Serves you right."

By the time he got home to his own apartment in Washington Heights (exactly 7:14) guilt was trickling out of every pore. It was now obvious to him that he confused Margaret by coming a day late because he had not meant to face his responsibilities to her. The perils of the city counted off in his mind like a platoon of snarling demons: mugging, falling off a subway platform, encounters with the psychotic, electrocution from faulty wiring, heat prostration, white slavery, loss of apartment keys, sniper fire, objects falling from tall buildings . . .

He had done his best after leaving Jan's, but his best was only to go once more to Margaret's mail box and stuff a note in it explaining that he would wait for her call in his own apartment.

He ransacked the medicine cabinets for Valium, codeine, or seconal. Found none. He stood in the shower for twenty minutes.

He paced the rooms with a glass of gin and water in hand running his fingers over the houseplants. The plants seemed to have luxuriated since their departure in June, as if they had taken orgiastic advantage of their liberty. These plants were Nancy's. Some plants love the touch of a woman's hand, some die from it. The plants that thrived here were like her, a bit coarse but sturdy. Margaret had never been able to keep plants alive in the Cincinnati apartment. She blamed it on the lack of light.

The summer flourishing of these plants must mean that

young Katie James from upstairs had been faithfully coming to water them. If he killed himself tonight, it would be a terrible shock for Katie to come in and find his body, even if he managed without blood. Also, Katie would someday tell Ursula how he had looked when she walked in and discovered him. The two girls were terrible gossips.

Certainly he had too many extant obligations to think of killing himself. Jan might call needing help in getting to some hospital where she could dry out. Kevin had asked him to go to Macy's and buy a star chart that couldn't be purchased on the Cape. Bowman needed him for . . . something. While he was with the Bowman gurus, he had felt they were recruiting him and giving him basic training for some desperate, necessary action.

When the phone rang it was . . .

"Of all people! I believe this is Miss Ursula Slater to whom I am speaking," he said.

"You must be drinking, daddy."

"I won't deny it. Is anything wrong?"

"Mama said you'd ask that. She wants to talk to you in a minute. But, daddy . . . !"

"Your team won in volley ball."

"We've got a dragon. An ugly one. I mean, Kevin and Tim Shipley found him in the grass over at Snow's Field and we've put him in a cardboard box."

"Here, Stupid, let me tell him," Troy heard Kevin saying and there was a mild scuffle. Kevin said, "We believe it's a snapping turtle. Genus Torticus Snappicus. And that crappy Ursula wanted to put him in the aquarium with the guppies."

"Will we never learn?"

"That's what I told her, since there's only four left."

"Another one die?"

"Two. But, daddy, you should see this monster. Not so big, he just looks like a monster. When we pushed a stick at him he bit down on it and wouldn't let go. A kid said they don't let go until the sun goes down."

"Like me. Is that what you're calling to tell me? Can I let go now?"

"No. The Rideouts and Joyce Johnson and her friend are here and mama's on the deck barbecuing with them. She said I was to keep calling you. She tried several times this afternoon. Mama! Mama! He's home. I caught him." There was more clicking and bumping as Nancy came from the deck and apparently shooed the children out of earshot.

She sighed theatrically. Then said, "Well, have you got her there?"

"I'm all alone with the geraniums and begonias. Katie's done a great job taking care of them. What are you talking about?"

"That girl who calls herself Rebecca West."

He started to deny acquaintance with Rebecca West, saw no hope in making any sound.

"Ha!" Nancy said. "The way you were acting lately I figured you had something on the line besides Dangleburn, but you screwed it up, huh? The Rebecca West popsy called here *twice*. The first time she said she was calling from your office, but then had brains enough to figure that wouldn't wash, since you were in the office today, I told her."

"I left about noon."

"So she told me the next time she called. She tried them and they told her. If it's Rebecca West, give her a contract quick. It will put you in good with the company."

He made a little noise of appreciation for Nancy's wit, but as diversion it was inadequate. She lowered her voice and said with a somber quiver, "Just remember. Two can play at that game."

"What? What?"

She shouted through his defensive stupidity: "TWO CAN PLAY AT THAT GAME."

She should not have put it that way. If her guests heard it, they would surely understand its implications as readily as he, and if she meant to pay him off, fornication for fornication, he hoped she would not get messy with Harold Rideout tonight, since Mary Lee loved to make trouble.

Speaking in remorse that she knew him so well, Nancy said, "I told her you were supposed to be in the apartment tonight. That she could probably phone you about now. All I ask, chum, is . . . not in my bed, please. I guess we can afford a hotel room. It must be stuffy in the apartment."

"Awfully."

"Is that all you've got to say?"

"I believe so."

"ALL RIGHT. JUST NOT IN MY BED, PLEASE."

The phone had hardly stopped trembling in its cradle before it rang again.

"Hi!" Margaret's syllable was so clear, breathless, and happy it seemed to be made from air inhaled long ago and far away from this hellish city.

"I'm sorry."

"Why? What happened?"

"I bungled everything. I've been looking for you all day. I hung around your place most of the afternoon. Did you find my note in your mailbox?"

"I called Truro. Spoke to Nancy. But it's all right. I told her I was calling on business and she's never heard my voice."

"It doesn't matter."

"You think she caught on?"

"Not to who you are."

"What matters is we'd better talk, quick. I guess my sudden

moves hither and yon must be hard to keep up with. I talked to Jan when she came back from the Cape and she said you were in a dither."

"She's in a dither."

"Poor Jan. I'm hungry. Can you take me to dinner? Tell me a restaurant near Carmine Street and I'll be there before you are."

"Why don't I pick you up at the apartment?"

"I don't think that's such a good idea," she said breezily. "I'm not calling from there."

"That's right. No phone."

"There is a phone. You can call out, but nobody can call in."

"Let's not waste time discussing Ma Bell." He named a restaurant on MacDougal Street.

"I think I've seen it walking around," she said. "Right, let's not waste time. I've got so much to tell you. I've had a big heart to heart with myself and understand *everything*. I'm in Phase Two."

Because they were so exquisitely tuned to each other, because she had so recklessly admitted him to her secret life and her "strangeness," he was very close to understanding all she meant to tell him before he raced from the apartment into the street.

11

Margaret used to theorize that she got much of her strangeness from her father. A black-framed photograph of the General sat below her large Titian reproduction in the Cincinnati apartment. Hairless and cunning, his head gazed out through rimless glasses like those of General Omar Bradley, but General Gill's hero of the Second World War had really been Erwin Rommel, the Desert Fox.

General Gill—then a captain—had been on detached service with Alexander and the British Army when Rommel chased them back across North Africa into Egypt. The experience had been profound as a religious conversion. "Daddy spent years trying to figure out how Rommel did it. When I was little and playing in a sandpile I'd see him eyeing it and later understood he saw the Libyan desert and was trying to figure how to maneuver all his tanks. He said it was a matter of timing and surprise. He tried to tell me all that stuff about gun calibers and throw weight and how you lay out a mine field. All I remember is the timing and surprise part.

"When we were in Germany he went to Rommel's birthplace and where he grew up as well as to all the schools Rommel had attended. He collected Rommel souvenirs and photographs. He got hold of Rommel's astrological chart—all the big Nazis had very elaborate ones done, you know—and I used to think he meant to write a book. It wasn't that. He wanted to understand all life in military terms. Reconnaissance by fire, double envelopments, committing your reserves. I guess I must have learned some of that from him. If I did, I use it loving you."

In college Margaret had rebelled against everything her father stood for. "Honestly, from daddy I'd never understood war was to kill people. He made it sound so creative. I guess I read a poem about trench warfare by Wilfrid Owen and knew that couldn't be right. I want sweet wars, lifegiving wars, like Whitman said, because that's what my woman thing tells me I should go for."

The apple never falls far from the tree, they say. The reversal of codes and values had been so precise as to suggest a military tidiness. Her reclusiveness in Cincinnati, her dutiful endurance of the loneliness that love had commanded for her, the renunciation of temptations to fraternize across sex lines were 180 degree departures from the artificial gregariousness she had known in growing up on military bases in Munich, Colorado and Texas. Her photo in the annual of the American High School in Munich showed a cropheaded ski enthusiast with none of the veiled ambiguity in her eyes that made her seem prettier than she was in the times Troy knew her.

"But even then I knew I was waiting for something," she liked to insist. "I only didn't know it would turn out to be you.

I was preparing my body at least if not my strange mind. I had good health habits and the skiing was good for my legs when I grip you."

Her notions and systems of causality—of what she easily spoke of as "destiny"—were as tightly woven as they were contrary to common sense. "You think my mind is charming, anyway, even if you laugh at some things I know."

She "knew" that after she was totally bound to him it was wrong for her to have any real social life with other males. Hence her circle of homosexual friends, Francis Rittmeister, Keith Chapin, and Bobby Hommedieu. Francis was an angular, diffident book salesman for the company—one of the homeliest men Troy knew. But he dressed impeccably, drove a Firebird, and was a connoisseur of French military uniforms, working on a doctoral dissertation tracing their variety and development from the times of the Empire to Boulanger's time. "And Francis helps develop the military side of your mind," Troy speculated. (What would have been scoffing in other environments was never quite that in the charmed atmosphere to which she brought him in Cincinnati.) "Perhaps," she said. "Costumes and formalities have a lot to do with it. Do you know that when Francis comes home with a boy he's picked up, he dresses him in a Grenadier's uniform with a shako before they go at it? Or he told me that once, at least.

"I learn things—for you—from Francis and the boys. Not that we talk about sex. Almost never! But to see the way they work so patiently closing in on somebody they mean to bring out, or someone who doesn't find them attractive. I learn a lot. You think Francis is dopey looking, don't you? But I've seen him with the most gorgeous dudes, and I know something about how he does it. Timing and surprise!"

Since on most of the occasions he had seen Francis, Francis had looked battered—with bruises or fingernail scratches on face, neck or hands, it astonished Troy to think of him as a master of patient strategy. "I thought he rushed into toilet stalls."

"That's a side of him I know nothing about, if he does. Once, months ago I thought Francis was trying to put the surround on me. I sensed he was and that he might switch when he felt the time was ripe. My woman thing was beginning to respond to him. So I spoke to him, very sorrowfully, and he absolutely denied it. We had a good laugh because he's virgin with women, though he doesn't find us repulsive. Besides, he truly respects what you and I have together. He admires you lots."

"Do you think he might be closing in on me, using you as bait?"

"That's very paranoic to think so," Margaret had said.

Paranoic to ride down through Manhattan on a summer night to wonder if Margaret was putting her military heritage together with what she had learned of homosexual stalking to spring the trap tonight. To wonder if a larger design of malevolent intent was not about to close. The humidity of the weather in the streets, the gradually blooming excitement of people on the sidewalks as the cab passed Fourteenth Street. and pushed around toward MacDougal, and his own fear seemed woven into a web from which there was no escape.

He was prepared for surrender simply because he guessed the battle had been lost a long time back. Congratulations, General Gill. Here is my sword.

The aromas and flickering candlelight above the tables of the restaurant gave back, in a rush, memories of all the times he had arrived from his travels to find her eagerly waiting for him. He knew, though, how haggard he must look to her now as he spotted her in her crisp summer dress, waved to her, and

148

sank into the chair across the table from her.

"I hurried," he said.

"Poor Troy." She patted his hand with excited, soothing fingers. Her full lips trembled with the promise of all she had saved up to say to him. Always during their separations she kept for him the things too good to share with anyone else. "Here, sip from my martini. Did you run all the way?"

"From Sixth. It's one way and the cab driver missed the corner. Well, I didn't run. It's a hot night. Hard to breathe." He finished off the martini she had given him to share. "I've been afraid I wouldn't find you at all. I came down expecting Jan to tell me how to find you—and of course Jan . . ."

"Isn't it wonderful news about her? She's going to quit her job and go to Mexico. And *live*. I saw her day before yesterday. We went shopping and she bought a lot of flashy clothes. She told me all about being up on the Cape with you. Your fun picnic! She's like a different person than I remembered. So young suddenly. Suddenly confident and sure of herself. Like me."

"You are?"

"Wait till you hear! But should we order you another drink? Because there's so much to bring you up to date on all at once."

"Phase Two," he prompted her.

"Yes! Phase Two! I'm in it and I told you on the phone I see everything absolutely clearly now," she began as he waved desperately for more drinks. "You poor man. I can see I must have given you fits with my letters. Which can't have helped sounding like an ultimatum. Even when I was writing I knew I wasn't being fair to you with what I was saying. But daddy had put a worm in my head all right. He kept repeating you were living a lie—*that* old cliché, but it's the only language he knows. It's hard to reason with someone who won't let you use your own language. It was as if he was tearing down our house by repeating simple clichés over and over.

149

"That's the main thing—that I could literally see our place, the shrine and all, coming apart as if one of those big machines with a ball on a chain was breaking the walls. I didn't give daddy an inch in arguments. He left saying he was heartbroken and did he pay twenty-seven thousand dollars for my education just so I could prostitute myself for a married man and hadn't I heard of Woman's Liberation? Phooey.

"I did what I swore—to you, to me—I'd never do. I let him destroy the shrine. I mean it was only a stupid white bedroom by the time he got through with it. It wasn't . . . alive with us any more. So . . ."

(She was pronouncing her *so*'s and *then*'s like crashes of little silver cymbals.)

"*Then* I said, All right. I'll play it his way. I'll move in on Troy. I'll use every trick in the book to put him in the spot where he'll leave Nancy and marry me."

"Phase Two." He nodded dreamily, not exactly protesting, since he had foreseen all this so thoroughly.

"Oh *no!*" Merrily she grabbed his sleeve and shook him, as if he were the sleepwalker who had to be wakened.

"Oh no, though that's what was guiding my strategy when I sold out and came to New York. I knew it wouldn't work. I was in despair, that's all, and I didn't want it to work. I counted on you to see through me and tell me you wouldn't do it. But I was going to go all the way to the end."

"You don't want to marry me?"

"Oh no. That would degrade everything we were and everything we had."

Paté for him and a cold soup for her had been served before the wild gleam of candlelight in her eyes signaled that she was ready to hand over the real truth. By then he was as prepared for it as the taste of meat and alcohol could make him.

"I didn't plan to stop long in New York. My thought was

to come to Provincetown soon and confront you on your own ground. I was going to Provincetown and bunk with Francis. He's up there with a new lover from Texas and said he'd give me a bed."

In a world where meek Francis Rittmeister abandoned everything for love, Troy cut a poor figure, admittedly. Yet Margaret had meant no reproach. What she was leading up to was the heroic intimacy in which the two of them were immune to conventional measures. He had never seen her more ecstatic than now, as she spooned her cold soup and tasted something brewed in the world beyond.

"All my strategic thinking was foolishness. When I got here to New York and talked to Jan about you—about you and me —I saw they would only make trouble. I couldn't just barge in on you and bring more walls down. Then, I thought, why don't I just stay in New York this fall? Irene, whose apartment I'm in, may not be coming back. She may go to grad school, and I guess I could have her apartment if I wanted. Then we could see each other every day. More often at least. And it would save you all the bother of divorcing Nancy.

"*So.* This isn't Phase Two, either. I'm *coming* to that. One other thing I saved from all the trash daddy dumped on me. He said, 'The grass is always greener on the other side of the fence'. See how profound he is? He said lots of men want to marry someone else until they actually leave their wives. Then afterward they wonder why they did it."

"The general is no fool."

"He's not. But if I can't be the greener grass for you, then there's no excuse for me in your life. That's what got it started and that's the way we had it so long. Am I right?"

"Very green," he said, with an ache of nostalgic love. As if the two of them were very old now and recalling something that flickered beyond a gulf of many years.

"Nor is mother a fool," she said. "I told her that, sure, I

would like to marry you and have a baby for you and carry him in a back pack when I went shopping in the market in Verona."

Verona and Padua and the Tuscan spring . . . Of course they had talked about that. It seemed maybe they had done it once. A holy family slipping out of the Porto Romana in Florence in the golden dusk, the road to the hill country dusty underfoot.

"Let's do it," he said.

She didn't even hear him. "So mother's advice was 'make him jealous'. You! It would degrade you. I don't *want* to make you jealous because that would be untrue to everything we've had together. We've had our times of ecstasy. Kierkegaard says the eternal mustn't be confused with what merely lasts a long time. What we've had is *eternal* and nothing can spoil it even if we turn away from it to something else.

"*So* that's why you mustn't fail us and be at all jealous of Phase Two."

For a ghastly minute the veal he was chewing seemed like a muscle of his own mouth that his teeth had clamped on by mistake.

"*So!*" She said. His fortune teller, turning the card of destiny. "All these ingredients were in my mind, but they hadn't jelled. I'm not a decision maker, as daddy says. It drives him wild, always has. 'Command decision! Command decision', he says. Even when I was little and we'd be in a restaurant I'd drive him wild because I'd keep reading the menu long after everyone else had ordered. Even coming here to New York wasn't decisive. I blew here on the wind.

"Then, *bam!* Here's the way Phase Two really began. Monday I was walking on Carmine Street, paying no attention. Somebody had tied their big dog to an iron stair railing. A big yellow and black dog with crazy eyes and a red collar with metal studs on it. As a matter of fact I think I've seen the same dog three or four times here and there in the Village since I started walking around and thinking. It's the sort of dog you believe you recognize, but maybe are only sure it's a German Shepherd.

"Just when I came even with it, it lunged. Not at me. At something like a cat or another dog on the far side of the street —which, by the way, was all in shadow, so I couldn't see anything over there even if I had been paying attention.

"It lunged—and you know how clumsy I can be—I tripped over the leash it was tied with. I went down hard. Full length. But what brings everything together and made it all happen the way it happened afterward is: I saw stars.

"I saw *the* stars. Real stars. You know what I mean. Whether just because I was jolted by falling doesn't matter. Among the stars, like they had come from the shadows across the street, there were these two black dudes standing over me.

"They looked at me a minute and never reached down a hand to help me up. One of them said, 'Come with us'. And, Troy, I *had to*. I just knew I had to.

"Oh, and they were some dudes, I'll tell you! One of them was tall and one was short and that's the way it worked out for us mostly. Oh, and one of them was left-handed and one was right-handed . . . . "

Somewhere, ages and ages hence, when Troy was still trying to get her story straight so he could endure it himself or perhaps write it into the history of the end of the age, he would be saying: I didn't hit her then. I never hit her.

She said, "You . . . hit . . . me . . . . "

But even if he had, this fatal brutality did not follow instantly from her revelation. She must not have been watching him at all, focused instead on something among the stars that still orbited in the remote world of her reality. She talked on in the same confiding ecstasy—so sure he would understand

153

her conversion precisely as he did. In a way (he would always tell himself) the enchantment that had twined them during the Cincinnati years had never made her so confident of his sympathy.

"*So.* You know what I've always suspected about my occult female power. It's true! It's been proved! But what Phase Two is is that now I know what I can do I'm going to live by myself without putting any more burden on you or putting you under any more tension. You'll get your share of me and others will get their share. You can go on with your family, and that will be easier on all of us."

It was then he put his hand out. Reaching for her with what was a fist first, then a spread of fingers trying to grab her as she fell from the highest cliff of his mind. Would have fallen from a window ledge of Manhattan's highest tower if he had not had a little sanity to serve them both.

He had a grip on the cloth just below the yoke of her blue-flowered dress. He held on until he felt the tug of her plunge controlled. Then, as her eyes opened on him, it was like meeting the eyes of a drowned corpse, seeming to scan him without recognition.

"Is that why I couldn't come to Irene's apartment for you? That they're still there, the dudes?"

She shook her head. "They're away tonight."

She seemed to bow as he released his grip. With her hands modestly folded in her lap, she tilted stiffly over her plate. Tears began to run down her nose and fall from its exact tip into her hardly touched food. Tears of a swiftly shattered innocence, streaming through the firmament.

He lifted a glass to hold wine to her mouth. Tears ran into the glass, drip, drip, drip. With despairing gentleness he put a hand on her shoulder to straighten her up. She would not budge.

Presently the waiter came and with Troy's permission took

their plates away. Margaret was still rigid as stone.

"You surprised me, that's all," Troy said. "Now that I'm over the surprise . . . I'm going to understand all this. All perfectly natural. We sail right over things like this. All unimportant. You know what we always said about Nancy. 'It's only skin'. Skin doesn't matter. We'd always laugh that part off because we had so much more."

The tears kept coming off her nose onto the table cloth.

"Margaret. Can you hear me, Margaret? I'm listening."

Now she shook her head, shook her long hair back over her shoulders and gave him a game smile. "So's everyone else. We can't talk any more here. Everyone's watching now."

"As a matter of fact, they're not."

Eerily she nodded and put her finger to her lips. Lowered drowsy lids as if to cover the nakedness into which he had waked her with his blow.

12

ISN'T IT clear yet? Doesn't the whole fabulous, ribald, unlikely story of Troy Slater's long affair with young Margaret Gill now, at last, fall into a comprehensible—if not quite run-of-the-mill—pattern?

See . . . the middle-aged would-be writer, grinding along between contradictory definitions of himself, lucks into an affair with a late-blossoming mutant of the Flower Children. He finds her zany manners and lifestyle not only convenient to his crypto-bigamous wishes and his actual business situation —he is enchanted by the whimsicality with which she colors the simple convenience of getting his rocks off in a homelike environment at both ends of his commuting run. Enchanted, yes. Her hair was long, her eye was wild, a fairy's child. She bends sidelong in the saddle (watch your dirty mouth, John Keats) and sings him a fairy song.

Enchanted, the would-be exception to the laws of nature and matrimony abandons for two whole years his ground-gripping hold on the wisdom of the sages. "Crazy girl," he tells himself, licking his lips. "Sacred love," she says. He rides the shuttle back and forth between parallel universes, pretending it is only a commuting flight between New York and Cincinnati, congratulating himself on the stability it has brought to his creaky psyche.

Crazy girl, crazy fellow. Crazy fucking in Cincinnati. A few little touches of *angst,* but *angst* is the spice of spicy stories written in a serious literary manner.

That's the situation, pat. Now for the denouement. Whack this out on the typewriter with crunching simplicity:

The crazy girl turns out to be . . . *crazy.*

The word slips from one meaning to the next like a sentence turning into a life sentence, a desert into a just desert. His bold adventure with the daughter of the Nile was his holiday from sanity, hair of the dog from his Bellevue binge before he took the pledge. His dribble of lunacy fed hers and together they put on a high wire act without a net. Now she tells him there is no wire, either.

After such a slick twist in the story, what's left for the next chapter?

Nail your balls to the diving board and take the plunge, Slater.

Semper fidelis.

He kept her in Nancy's bed that night, giving her shelter with the same impulse that would have brought Ursula in to sleep between him and Nancy when she was feverish and had bad dreams.

He bathed her before he put her to bed. The bathing came from a more confused impulse, as if he were washing away not only her recent mortifications but any smell of abuse he might

158

have left on her in the last two years. But his abuse had been abstract. He found on her legs and back assorted bruises and pinch marks. These he couldn't wash away. "They were a little rough," she said with a refined detachment.

He kissed her forehead as she lay down in bed, smelling so fresh with Nancy's bath oil. She fell asleep almost at once.

At first he felt like father or physician sitting beside her in the bedroom lit only by lights from the street outside. He thought the impact of what had happened had not reached through to her yet, as someone who has lost a limb in a street accident doesn't quite admit its absence in the first shock. He guessed they might be total strangers when she woke to a realization of the event.

He sat there wanting to blame someone or something, to fix anger at a single specific target, but his anger was as diffuse and edgeless as the hot darkness crouching on the city. He could not hold in mind the names of the men who had picked her up from her tumble over the dog leash. He thought of them only as citizens—those who wait in the city for its daily windfalls of ruined beauty and spoiled hopes. In an Arcadian setting nothing bad could have happened to Margaret. At worst she would have been ravished by satyrs, raped by a swan. There was no Arcadia except in those wishful fantasies that had brought her now to this.

He had munched on the lotus, shared her invented world recklessly and he was not cured yet of its seductive lunacy. Now still—in spite of anger, fear, and a tinge of disgust—he could feel a stir of envy that she had gone where he was not allowed to follow. It was envy cut from the same cloth as his envy of old Bowman and his legendary Jokaanen. Based on nothing except some treacherous need in himself that he was still afraid to name.

Later, when he lay down beside her (wearing his shorts as testimony that he had no carnal claim) he dozed fitfully and

159

woke, thinking he heard her shuddering love cry—"Troh-ee!
Troh-ee!" But it was the siren of a police van or ambulance
deriding him.

The sun was well up when he woke before she did and went
around the corner to the deli to get something for their breakfast. As he set orange juice, milk, eggs and English muffins on
the counter beside the register, it seemed that old Ramirez, the
proprietor, was reading these items like a bulletin of family
illness. ("Your leetle girl got butterflies in her tummy? Feex her
nice poach egg on toes she feel better.") What Ramirez actually said was, "You lucky be up in the ocean breezes all summer, Mr. Slater. Weather report for more thees damn humidity. You go back today? Go back today."

The sun in the street threw reliable, hot shadows from cor-
nices, lamp posts and a passing bus. The sun knew east from
west. Had its head screwed on right. Was not deceived by
fantasies of satyrs, mermaids, Bowmans, serpents of the Nile
and Phase Two. The voice of the sober, pathfinding sun was
unmistakably like the voice of Nancy: You mean this babe of
yours orgied with some spades under the impression that they
were forest divinities? Come on, Troy. Come *on!*

The New York sun had no patience with metaphors. It
prescribed a long rest cure for Margaret Gill in a comfortable
asylum. It was only right that Troy Slater should help foot the
bills for that.

Margaret had risen when he let himself in with his sack of
groceries. Naked as a Samoan in the morning heat, she was
idling in the living room, admiring Nancy's potted plants.

"Mine always die because I'm an unfertile woman," she said,
matter-of-factly. She had a way of making such comments
sound entirely rational. It was merely that everything—the
houseplants, the economy of the Manhattan underworld, the

United Nations, the seasons, the tides, the cosmos—referred to her sexuality and its mysteries. She ran her thumb pensively up the crease of a lavender and green leaf. "I know Nancy better by her plants."

Plants! Katie James! In the jangled instant of remembering that Katie came in daily to water the plants and give them their chemical stimulants, he heard her key already in the door at the end of the hall. He got Margaret into the bathroom, turned on the shower full blast, begged her to stay locked in until he got rid of Katie.

"Whooo! You scared me, Mr. Slater," Katie called from the entrance. The whites of her eyes flickered in the dimness. She clutched the doorknob, ready to scamper back to the elevator in case it wasn't Mr. Slater. Might be a burglar or child molester instead of the father of her best friend. "Did Ursula come down with you?" Had the sound of the running shower already signaled this bright child he was not alone in the apartment?

"The shower is leaking badly. At this very minute Ursula is kicking a soccer ball at Snow's Field," he said. "Since I'm here, I can water the plants today if you've got something else to do."

"It's no bother and I know how." Katie made her way authoritatively to the kitchen. As she ran water from the tap into the scarlet sprinkling can she said cheerily, "I should have realized you were in town. Yesterday I didn't come in the morning since I had a karate lesson. So in the afternoon when I was in, someone called for you."

"Oh? Any messages?"

"Wouldn't leave any. She sounded kind of . . . well, not disturbed, but funny."

"Funny?"

"Well, it was a *nice* voice. Kind of breathless. Like someone who's been kidnapped."

Breathless? Kidnapped?

"Like she really needed to get ahold of you. So I gave her your number in Truro. Was that all right?"

"Certainly. It's no secret. It's in the Truro phone book anyway."

"Afterward I worried about giving the number. Because of the way she sounded."

Illicit. That was the word to describe how Margaret would have sounded on the phone to any bright child, though Katie might not have the term in her working vocabulary. It was another tally of Margaret's helplessness to protect herself in a world of workaday suspicions.

All at once, without having watered a single plant, Katie returned the sprinkling can to the sink. In a constricted voice she said, "It's Okay, Mr. Slater. You can water the plants today, since you're here." Holding her arms stiffly at her sides, glancing neither to left or to right, she left the apartment.

If she didn't know everything, she had figured out what signified. As he watched her leave, Troy understood that while she might not share her discovery with his wife, someday, somewhere, she would review it with his daughter.

In that unveiled chamber of the future he heard Ursula reply in a mature voice: "Yes, that must have been the bitch that daddy left us for. Right after that they went to Europe, you know. We loved him but he had to fulfill his tragic destiny."

"The die is cast," he said, setting a white bowl with a perfectly poached egg on the kitchen table in front of Margaret. "The leap of faith is made. By what small promptings come the commands of destiny. *Semper fidelis.*" Margaret had taken advantage of Katie's intrusion to wash her hair. Now her head was wrapped in a great turban of toweling, and she had found a light robe of Nancy's to put on. Thus she would look as his wife when routines were established.

"The die is cast," he said, more grimly than he wanted to

sound. "I love you and want to marry you and keep you always, amen."

Accept the mermaid when she comes. They all have flippy tails.

She was moved by the recklessness of his declaration. No doubt of that. It had no sound of ambiguity. If he had never, in so many flat words, proposed marriage before, he was doing it now, and that was to his honor. She wrinkled her nose, as if to keep back tears. But at last she shook her head. No.

"Why not? Let's make your daddy and mother happy." He set his own breakfast on the table and sat down facing her. "I will not use my ticket back to Truro and the bourgeois life. This time . . . no cab to the airport while your little white hand is waving goodbye." His voice kept its momentum, dragging him like the tail of a kite rising. "I hear the waters of the Rubicon rushing behind me. The thing is *done.* Let the details fall where they may."

It made her smile her best smile to see him so brave. She spooned a bite of toast, egg, and milk into her smile. Rubbed it off with a paper napkin. "It's too late," she said.

That's what he had told himself in the night. In the full threat of daylight he denied it now.

"Even when I left Cincinnati—how many days ago?—I thought that was what I wanted most." But her mind had changed and with Margaret there was no distinction between mind and sexual strategy. She had *thought* her way into Phase Two, maybe with the help of the stars she saw when she tumbled in the street but nothing else. With a certain majesty she let him know that her black fuckers were not the agents of the change in her but mere servants of her mutation. The absurd thing about this was how absurd it was. But "What's true is true."

"That's my line," he said doggedly. "What if it's true that *I'm* in a new phase? Things have happened to me this summer,

163

too. I fainted when we were shooting in the sandpit . . ."

From there he began to tell her about Bowman and Jokaanen, thinking that Margaret was the one person in his life
who would understand how Bowman had loomed into his mind
as father-figure, guide, example, promise-maker or whatever
the hell Bowman had been. Margaret never saw people in their
social identities, always as myth figures, and surely that was the
right way to make sense of Bowman.

But the story of Bowman that would have charmed her back
in Cincinnati in the light of the candles fell curiously flat here
in the sweltering daylight of the apartment among Nancy's
virile potted plants.

Probably the way he was telling it was warped by this environment. In his own voice he heard notes that mocked and
belittled Bowman, cutting him down to size, making him seem
the phony and poser Nancy had perceived. The figure he was
creating was not Bowman the Master of the Guns and of
Women, Prophet of the New Life. It was Bowman the
Bearded Runt chuckling fatuously in the Slaters' living room
as he explained how easy it was to let Jesus guide your boat over
the shoals of life.

"It threw Nancy into a terrible snit," he heard himself
saying with hangdog defensiveness, "and I don't say Nancy was
entirely wrong about him. After all, I don't really know him
well enough to be sure of anything. But you and I know how
important it is to be *tuned* to hear what's behind the smokescreen, behind appearances. And I swear that when he said you
had to be 'born again' I heard him calling me, like the calling
of Matthew in the Bible. He said, 'Don't be afraid. There is
nothing to fear but fear. Come over, come over, Red Rover,
Red Rover. We will fight them on the landing grounds and on
the beaches'. Something like that. And in the sandpit when we
were shooting, it was clear as daylight to me that he wanted
me to join the army."

"What army?"

Well now, that was the question he had expected Margaret to help him with. He didn't know. Had no answer to persuade him over the line. He was willing to go—into lunacy, destruction, heaven, hell—those glamorous places—but no one would give him the decisive tug.

He sighed sweatily and said, "All right, I can't make you hear what I thought I heard. The call."

They were not in the old harmony. Their private language had been damaged. But not entirely ruined. *Something* he tried to tell her about Bowman got through the damaged lines and switchboards. He knew that from the sparkle of excitement which, slowly and then faster, swam up into her eyes.

"Bowman, whoever he might be, is just someone else I used to get the message to you," she said. "It wasn't him calling you to be born again. It was me. Through him." As if people were no more to her than wires and diaphragms to project her voice. Crazy presumptuousness. Crazy girl. Yet he wanted to believe, now that it was so difficult, now that the price seemed to be exactly his own sanity, laid deliberately on the line.

She said, "I've got messages through to you this summer you don't even know yet. You remember the night you called me from Truro?"

"After I got your letter, sure."

"To be born again was what I was telling you by having Bob fuck me on the phone."

Before she went on to explain this he knew she didn't really have to. He knew that—deeply, down where sanity and craziness coil around each other in the pattern of the double helix —he had known it all along. But now she seemed to have a little silver hammer with which she was pounding knowledge like a nail straight into his ear.

She said, "Bob had just fucked me before you called because I was already going into Phase Two. When he heard us talking he came back and did it again. I thought you might know from what I said."

His bone sockets were burning with something as sticky as napalm. Now in the silence of the hot room he heard her voice exactly as it had come to him in the phone booth while the wind blew off the Pamet Marsh. "I love you-oooo-oooooo. . . ." While . . . !

"That hurts you," she said, astonished like an infant at its first discovery that it can inflict pain.

"It hurts to be born again," he said gamely. "I'm still with you because we're going on from all the best we've had in two years. We can say things to each other we could never say to another human being alive. Yes, sure it hurts me about Bob and your black men and whoever else you'll tell me about next."

"No one since boys in college."

"But the hurt comes from seeing why you had to do it. That it cost you so much to get me in motion. Now I want to share and take care at the same time."

"Oh, you want to *take care!* That's what can't be done with me. Do anything else you want. That's what Phase Two is all about. If I married you, you'd start taking care of me and I couldn't excite you like you were excited on the phone that night. Did you come when I did? All that would be ruined."

"*That!* I guess it would be ruined. Why shouldn't it be? We can live . . ."

"A good safe life. That's not what you want from me. Right now you're just scared of what will happen to me next in New York."

She was outrunning him and he was too tired to deny it. "I sat up last night figuring how to get you to a psychiatrist."

"Have me locked away! That's what daddy threatened me with. If I married you, I'm scared you would do it someday. Marry me just so you'd have the power to do it."

166

He was afraid of her then. More afraid that she might be right. And truly he did not want her locked up, so he made another promise. "I didn't know what I'd find when I came down here to New York. I guess I came to get a sign from heaven. Heaven says 'Go'. So we're going together. They won't lock you up until they've got me."

She shook her head in doubt. "You'd try to mean that and live up to it. Like you try with Nancy and don't make it. Being born again is different." (Her authority was that of one who has been through it.) "After it happens you simply know you're a servant and aren't scared of it anymore. Now I'm going to be a perfect servant."

"Of your strangeness," he said with the bitterness of finding his bid refused.

"Of my woman thing. You thought that was only a metaphor or something. I have to live with it, and obey."

"I thought we were all right in that department."

"Last night when you were bathing me in the tub, nothing happened, right? It just was dead. The woman thing didn't speak to you."

"It wasn't the time, for heaven's sake."

"No. You couldn't reach it, or it would have been the time, all right."

"And your black boys reached it?"

With terrifying, undeniable honesty that made his skin crawl, she said, "Clarence always could. Ishmael, no."

He got up from the table, went to the window and leaned out with both hands on the sill—perhaps to see if the sun was still shining or if it had fallen into the gutter. It shone. It drove arrows of light into his eyes like slivers of broken glass. He sat down again.

"I'm not going to ask you to tell me how you think they did it," he said, "because you might just sit there and tell me. And I might understand. And I guess I don't want to."

167

"You'd be jealous of me, not them," she pronounced. "They didn't have so much to do with it. I was up for it, that's all."

"And then I might kill you. Not just for this. For everything you've done to my life for two lost years. All my fault. I listened to your manias, your 'strangeness,' your 'woman thing', Cleopatra from the Nile."

"Troy . . ."

"Be reasonable? Be careful what you say now, Margaret. The drawer is full of knives."

He had never seen her afraid of him before. There had never been an occasion for it, though, not even last night when he had hit her in the restaurant. Now it seemed to come on her fast, to run like a poison seeping from capillaries to veins and then swept with a rush to the heart.

"I'm getting out of here." She started to rise.

"Sit!" The tone of command held her. General Gill's daughter, he thought, his chest heaving with the brutality of his rage. "Don't you know how sick you are? Do you think I can turn you loose to go back to those animals? Damn fool. They'd have you on the street in a week, because you are too sick to notice the difference. What is your Clarence, a pimp?"

"I don't think—"

"All right. No reason to suppose that just because he is black."

"I think . . . his brother is."

"It keeps coming. You talked about being a whore? Is that what you really mean by Phase Two?"

"No!"

"But you talked about it?"

"It wasn't talk like you and I talk. It was . . . another kind of poetry."

"Poetry!"

"Things were said. It was like a make-believe or a dream. I don't even know if he has a brother, really. I never saw him.

Maybe he's in Las Vegas. Puerto Rico. Why are you tormenting me?"

"Because I see now that something has to be done about you. I promised not to lock you up, and I never will. But someone has to stand by."

"I don't want it. It won't work any more. You're afraid of me as much as you're afraid for me and it's all a mess. There's part of you that's always been afraid of me and what I might do. I brought you love, but I'm too dirty a girl for you to love. That's the truth and you know it now. I made you see it."

"Truth!" The truth slithered over them and around them like a boa constrictor feeling for the grip that would strangle them both. It could find no death grip and the hot hours went down the hill into wasteful argument. They were no good at arguing with each other. They had no practice at it. Worse, she seemed to have the jump on him for she had less to lose and probably more to gain. She had a sweeping overview of life and love. He was sweating down among the particulars. He was tangled with the need for consistency. She took the freedom to say whatever might mix him up.

With one breath she could say, "Don't you think I ever cried in Cincinnati when I knew you would be going home to Nancy?" With the next she said, "I know you think I'm sick. Don't imagine I haven't learned a lot by being sick, things that you could write about if you had the nerve."

She said, "If we got married, it would only be paying me for services rendered. But I wasn't serving you. I only serve men indirectly. It was really always Venus. You never took me seriously when I told you this before and now you're sorry. I guess I never told you everything about my special female powers. You know, like karate experts can break boards with their little fingers. There are techniques for concentrating powers. It stands to reason I couldn't have found out these things by myself."

"So I taught you some things. That's not important."

"I don't mean *you* taught me a thing. So if it wasn't you it stands to reason *something* had this service in mind for me and was preparing me. Or testing me. Getting me ready to serve better."

He was being worn thin by these flickers of outrageous and irrational assurance. On the other hand, when she thought of her destined service, the idea made her skin glow. He was powerfully and shamefully tempted to give up and let her serve him as she chose, but each wave of lust came as a reminder that he had been the lover of her illness. She yawned prettily and her eyelids fluttered closed. She had to have more sleep. He let her go into the bedroom alone and sat there studying their dirty dishes.

In mid-afternoon the apartment was an oven thickening his blood like the juices in a pie. He thought he could sense the slow gorging of the potted plants, and Margaret's sleep was part of their vegetable orgy. He would have slept himself if he had not been afraid they would change him into one of them in his sleep.

Around four o'clock Nancy called. He cringed at the recognition of her voice. In his weakened condition she might worm out of him an admission he was trying to persuade Margaret to marry him.

"Why weren't you in the office today?"

"Touch of the virus," he said. "I meant to call and leave a message with the kids for you not to meet the eight-thirty plane. I haven't the strength to get home tonight."

He was braced for the onslaught of her suspicions when he made this announcement, but none came. For Nancy, she was extraordinarily calm. "I knew you were coming down with something. You wouldn't listen to me. Is it hot there?"

"A descent into hell. In this weather."

"Poor Troy. There's a northeast breeze here. You know where we've been? I took Vachel and Kevin flying. They went in the old yellow Stinson, then we all dipped at Race Point. Superb! You poor bastard, you're missing it all."

"Yeah."

"Have you called Dr. Smollett?"

"I don't need a doctor."

"In the medicine cabinet, in a brown vial marked 'For cough' there should be half a dozen of those dysentery tablets we got in Mexico."

"I don't have dysentery. What the hell are they doing in a bottle with the wrong label? They must be ten years old."

"Nine," she said. "We were there when Ursula was two, remember?"

"Look, I'll make it home tomorrow if I can."

"Not unless you're feeling better. We're getting along fine. Just don't suffocate. And if you don't feel like trekking down to Macy's, for heaven's sake, don't worry about Kevin's star chart."

"I'll get it," he growled with such iron-clad determination that she said, "Mercy!" Then she chuckled with an ambiguity that his ear recognized as the authentic Bowman chuckle.

He felt something bristly and soft rubbing his elbow while he was still assuring Nancy that he would be on the plane for Provincetown as soon as his health permitted. It was Margaret's pubic hair. He hung up the phone with a jolt, as if otherwise Nancy might hear the crackle of his nerves disintegrating. Margaret came from behind the chair and sat naked on his trembling knees. "What was that about?"

"A star chart," he said. "I have to go to Macy's to buy a star chart for Kevin."

"Right now?"

"What time does Macy's close?"

Instead of giving him a mundane answer she presented a

nipple to his lips. He took it gratefully.

"I'll guide you among the stars," she said. *"There*'s a planet that everybody knows. It moves in a big, wide orbit. Here's another one that goes with it, just a little down toward the horizon. Can you trace the orbit?"

"Mmmmmm."

"It's held in orbit by gravity. Can you feel the pull of gravity?"

"Mmmmmm."

"All right. Here's another one known as the dark planet, and no one ever sees it. Its year is fifteen of our years long, and its Christmas is only the same as ours once in nine centuries. And then there are three more planets, one so big that it pulls all the others off course when it passes, and the other two are faster than anything else in the solar system, all invisible. Come with me."

He followed her into the bedroom, knowing the precise sensation of a captive satellite swung through light and dark without will of its own.

This was Margaret triumphant, not only all transformed into a priestess of arcane mysteries but full of kittenish high spirits from her nap. He had no doubt at all, as he followed her, that she had claimed him and was going to make him pay for all his middle-aged caution and vacillations.

The kitten at play nudged him flat on the bed, covered his face and chest with a sheet odorous of her sleep and opened his fly.

"Tell me the rest," she said.

"What?" he asked from under the sheet.

"How you fainted in the sandpit. What you knew before you came out of it. About Jokaanen Ober."

"She's . . . different from us."

"Yes! Different from whom?"

"Us people."

"Beautiful?"

"Beautiful."

"Big?"

"Very big. Very big."

"But you wouldn't be afraid of her? To go all the way into her?"

He didn't answer that one except with a little gasp that was surely from a fear unspecified. Maybe the fear of losing himself absolutely and forever unless he could reclaim his own will.

"Would you be afraid if she mounted you like this?" He felt Margaret's knees pressing the mattress on either side of him with a weight that seemed like the pressure of granite, polished smooth and warmer than blood.

"I am Jokaanen. Do you know me?" Slowly, careful not to crush him until he had made his assent, she encircled him and slid down. "Do you know me yet? Now? Now? Now? Now? Now?" The bright shaft eclipsed centimeter by centimeter by the omnipotent weight of darkness. Halfway to extinction. More than halfway. Nearly there . . .

He snatched away the sheet that she had covered his face with. He saw that her eyes were open to the wall above his head but blind. He saw the frailty of her body that belied the force she had made him feel. Very gently he said, "We mustn't play these games. They're not good for . . . us."

She seemed to wake then with a foolish, half-shamed smile. "Was it just pretending? Wasn't it fun? Was it fun?"

"Let's just love each other as ourselves."

Fair enough. *Not* enough for what she required of him. He felt her expelling him, refusing him. Then shaken by a spasm of pity for them both he found he had nothing to love her with.

"Let me just hold you tenderly. We're both worn to a frazzle," he said.

173

That was not quite all that happened that night. They listened to records—ah, *Die Zauberflöte* and Mahler's Fourth Symphony—had a quiet supper in the kitchen, drank a bottle of wine, went to bed and made a domestic type of love like any married couple fond of each other's bodies and in need of the relaxation healthy sex can bring.

But morning came and they woke into the wilting banality of yet another summer day in the city. They were rested but not at ease with each other. They tiptoed through the apartment either in fear of Katie James or of the rightful owners returning.

Margaret went with him to buy the star chart at Macy's. On the subway they sat knee to knee, sweating and jostling with the iron movement of the train, but they had nothing significant to say to each other.

Back in the apartment he raised the question of where they should go for dinner. "By then we'll have our thoughts in order. We can settle things then," he said.

She said, "Not tonight. I'm leaving."

"Where?"

"Back down to the Village. To my place."

"All right. We'll go there. I want to see it."

"No."

He wanted to chuckle. A chunk of steel wool blocked his throat. Finally he said, "To find Clarence and Ishmael?"

Her answer was not so much brazen as just recklessly, overwhelmingly candid. The shock of it was merely that she did not admit or recognize his feelings now. He was not in her universe. "I want it," she said.

The room echoed like the interior of a bass drum with the percussion of her intention. Everything shattered. Nothing changed.

He heard his voice braying, "Look! Walk out that door and I swear I will get hold of your father and tell him you are shacked up with nigger pimps. Go ahead if you don't believe me. You know he'll come looking for you and we'll put you where you belong."

The threat made her recognize him. Not as she had ever known him before. A different kind of male brute in the zoo of her reality. When all had been lyric between them, the matter of his age had never mattered. But he could threaten her from another generation. From the grim authority of age.

"Would you do that?"

"Don't force me. I love you."

"What do you want then?" She was all wilted. "For me to go back to Cincinnati? It would never happen to us again the way it did. My father wouldn't like that much better than black friends."

The lead basketball was in his hands. "All we need is time to settle ourselves," he said, saying it once more for lack of anything else to offer. "Here's the solution. You told me Francis Rittmeister was in Provincetown. Come up and stay with him on the Cape until I can settle with Nancy. Fresh breezes up there. You'll only be ten miles from me."

"You won't just leave me alone up there?"

Yielding to him—suddenly plaintive and bewildered—she was more a stranger than he had imagined possible. And it came to him that he trusted her submission no more than he would have trusted a stranger's promise. But it was all she would give him now.

"Provincetown?" she asked wonderingly. "Yes! That will be better than going back to the Village. What an idea!" She burst into uninterpretable laughter.

IV

13

A ND NOW his little mermaid Margaret had brought her strangeness all the way from the icebox apartment in Cincinnati to Provincetown on Cape Cod, and to a lodging known as the Deep Six, where even the rambling roses along the driveway were gay.

Perhaps a hundred times in their years of domicile on the Cape, Troy had driven past The Deep Six, always admiring its jaunty look. Fundamentally it was a rambling nineteenth century house on the waterfront. To the basic structure had been added a warren of cubicles, outside stairways, gazebos and whimsical towers dotted with stained glass. Its eccentric protrusions and the large deck behind, which floated on pontoons at high tide, had been intensely decorated with found objects of wrought iron, bunting, hurricane lamps and mementoes of seafaring. In high season the Deep Six might house as many as forty rent-payers, though with the comings and goings of night visitors probably even the management had no accurate census of occupants at any given time.

Sometimes holding his children's hands Troy had walked past its rose-rimmed driveway opening on Commercial Street, and the pace of walking permitted more time than driving for appreciation. "Look at all the flags!" Ursula had cried in delight at the yachting pennants aflutter over the sunbronzed young men on the floating deck. "Don't call them that," Kevin hissed. "They're gay." "What are they gay about?" asked Ursula.

Troy thought he remembered that down the drive, wafted on the offshore breeze, had come an odor of semen and perfume, mingled with smells of roses and the fishy Bay.

It was the best haven he could now imagine for her strangeness. At least it would cool off Phase Two. At least he had rescued her from the frying pan of New York and whatever flames might run through the Deep Six, they would surely not lick at her.

Rescued? Well . . . Rescued. The term would have to do, just as the arrangment would have to do until he could invent something better. Maybe an inexpensive, safe mobile home that he could drag behind the smoking Volvo . . . ? Oh, hell.

He had not seen her since they got a room in the Deep Six, where Francis Rittmeister had been acclimating himself since July. He had only seen her onto the plane at LaGuardia, before he pulled himself together and made the same trip two hours later on Sunday night. He was mindful of her dread of being left alone on ice up there. At least he had managed to chat with her on the phone.

"The weirdest night of my life," she reported after the first twenty-four hours. After New York he took that as exaggeration.

The second time he talked to her she was trying not to be

180

demanding, but plainly she was not happy. "My so-called room is only big enough for the bed and a gas plate and a toilet that folds out and a telephone that sits on the bed. The part of the toilet that doesn't fold out is under some slanting stairs and men run up it all night long. There's a porthole instead of a window, and I hear spooky things from somewhere down below."

"That's good."

"What's good?"

"That you're finding it is something to laugh about."

"When I close the porthole there's absolutely no air to breathe. Francis has a big, airy room on the second floor, but I stay out of his way, naturally, because his friend took off with a bookkeeper and he's making new acquaintances. It's his hunting ground, after all. Mornings I go out on the floating deck to read because none of them are up from the night before. I hope it doesn't make them all too nervous to find me around."

He said, "Look, I've got it all worked out so I can see you tomorrow and have a look inside the Deep Six. We have to drive Ursula to Provincetown for her riding lesson in the morning. Maybe I can slip over for a while when she's riding. Stay on deck where I can find you."

"You mean Nancy's coming along?"

"Not to your place. Only to Provincetown."

"You told me she went over to Harvard to school on Wednesdays."

"She's quit. So she tells me."

"Why?"

"That she hasn't told me. I avoid intensive conversation with her since I got back."

It might have been closer to the truth to say Nancy had spared him any interrogation about his fling in New York and the calls from "Rebecca West." Mostly she just smiled at him

181

knowingly, like an elder sister who has seen the lipstick traces on her brother's shorts. But he knew very well how busy her mind was as she hashed over the problem he presented for her. When he suggested she needn't ride along to Provincetown just to deliver Ursula to the riding stable—it was a lovely day, a beach day, why couldn't she and Kevin take a lunch to the beach, he'd drop them off there—she briskly announced that, of course, she would see Ursula ride.

"I quit Harvard so I could devote myself to the children, watch them in this setting. So I'll remember. This may be our last summer up here."

"Why our last summer here?"

"Oh, the crisis in the economy. Farmers and truckers. Everything causes cancer. The whole powder keg may blow. Some asshole Senator has found Russians in Cuba. Imagine that!"

A distinct touch of autumn was in the air as he and Nancy sat on a shady bench above the riding ring at the Hiram Godiva stable. Troy was puffing a cigar, tasting in its smoke the tragic languors of Latin America. He was trying to recall the old days before Castro spoiled the fun.

Fifty feet down the slope Ursula was bumping around the dirt track beside the stable on Judy, the buckskin mare. Senile as Judy might be, she nevertheless looked to the anxious eye too big for the child in the saddle, and Troy mentioned it.

Nancy knew better. "She's ever so much improved this year. That's what's so gratifying about both children. You missed Kevin's flight with Vachel Bowman. Kevin was not at all kiddish about it, before or after. He was living up to Vachel, because he thinks older boys are keen. Ursula gains every year and then loses it when we go back to New York. I think I'll find a stable for her this winter. Jersey has a lot of rings where she could ride."

"We'll do that."

"You're great with promises." She eyed him with melancholy fondness.

"Because they're so cheap. Especially in the large economy size. They're what is wanted from me, so they're what I give. Man is the animal with the ability to make promises, the philosopher said. If I had blood to give instead of promises, I would be a turnip."

"Going to New York always improves your wit. Did you truly get Dangleburn settled?"

"All but writing him the Dear John letter. I must do that this evening. Or this afternoon. I'll drop you and the kids at the beach and drive right home and get it on paper."

"You need the automobile to write a letter?" He could not think of an explanation for why this might be so, but he didn't have to. She said, "Of course you can have the car. We have to think of your needs, too, since you're our meal ticket, hubby."

"My needs!" he marveled, blowing cigar smoke at the spots of pure light winking through the shade tree over them. No philosopher had named his needs with precision enough for him to accept, nor would be likely to take the trouble, in view of the billions of human beings on the globe they had to think about. Which other of those billions had a mad young alternate wife stashed half a mile away in a male whorehouse expecting his imminent appearance while he depended on his wife's indulgence for transportation to get there?

"It would be unfair not to give them their place in the whole picture. You're on the threshold of a new phase of life . . ."

"Phases!" He felt Nancy, like Margaret, was about to tell him she had entered a new phase. "I don't have phases. I'm a male of the species, a cat of the stripe."

"As Bowman puts it, you're in trouble with your soul."

"Bowman puts it? In what book?"

"Oh," she said with kindness appropriate to her smugness.

"You're not in any book of his yet. And won't be because he's given up writing. This was in conversation."

He still had not quite got it. He could not remember Bowman saying anything of the sort on the occasion of his disastrous visit to their house. "He said this about me before he ever saw me? I don't say he's wrong. But the occasion for diagnosing me is not apparent. It's true I fainted when we went shooting, but that is not a weakness of soul, it is probably . . ."

"Yes, he told me. You never mentioned it."

". . . an early warning of heart attack. He told you? Oh, he came to keep an eye on Vachel when the kids went flying?"

"The night before. And don't say I didn't warn you that two could play at your game."

His eyes must have looked scrambled like eggs before they have begun to congeal in the frying pan. He could believe his ears, but his ears simply refused to believe what they heard.

"You're joking," he said.

"Of course. Though he did come to see me. And he did come to discuss the troubles of your soul, ha! Apparently you must have babbled more than you thought when you fainted down there in the sandpit with him."

"What? What did he say I said?"

"Just look deep in your conscience and you'll know."

"Bull shit," he said. "So this cheap imitation of Christ said I had troubles? That's totally unwarranted. That goes beyond the bounds."

"You can call him that," she said with the chuckle she had appropriated from the old dog. "But remember, I was the one who warned you that was a fraud and a pose. It certainly is. That's all right. He's an astonishing man anyway."

"It can be said of anyone. That he is sick in his soul. What else did he tell you about me? He came over just to tell you about me?"

"I wouldn't say so. And I wouldn't say no. I admit I said

184

something very ugly about you on the phone. It just popped out of my mouth because of how I was feeling just then, as you can well enough understand—you boffing this West piece in probably my bed. And he didn't reply while we were on the phone. We just arranged the flying for the boys. I'd forgot what kind of asshole I might have called you and was getting over my mad. I'd gone out on the deck with my drink to think us over, you and me and this collapsing marriage. And then I heard something thrashing around in the brush. Like the troll in Billy Goat Gruff. 'Nancy, Nancy,' he called. Which happens to be my name. I thought he hadn't come by car at all, but just out of the woods. That he was whatever it is that springs on you out of the dark, you know. Which made no sense and turned out not to be the case. He'd actually parked down at the end of the lane and didn't know there was no path around to the deck, like I always told you we needed. He glimpsed me through the glass doors and came around that way."

"Why'd he park at the end of the lane?"

"He's played this game before. You know how it's done in Truro when the hubby is away."

She was making every bit of this up, Troy thought. It didn't fit. Innuendo and teasing were not Nancy's preferred revenge. She liked dripping chunks of meat, sliced off with a broad axe.

Nevertheless he said, "You dreamed all this."

"It seems that way now," she said with the generosity of one who has been elevated above threats. "Actually he'd come as a peacemaker because he knew from both sides that we couldn't stand each other. His message was that love was the way to see us through."

"You're quoting, of course."

"I couldn't think of anything that highflown myself. It takes one of you geniuses, or jeany-eye, as the case may be."

"Go on. He came on a mission of mercy."

"You might say so. Though he started talking about Jesus

185

again. That's all right. It's just his style of expression. As for his being a *real* Christian . . . pooh! I showed him up on that. Now he can't con me." Her scornful, throaty laugh was exactly that of Sadie Thompson in Somerset Maugham's immortal cliché, *Rain,* and Troy heard old Sadie scoff, *"Men!"*

While his mind raced toward extinction, she went on, "Believe what you choose, and I'm sorry I can't get his real message across to you in terms you'd be receptive to. He's no Christian but he's lived through a lot, and we did have the most honest talk about marriage I can remember before—"

"Before what?"

"I talked him into taking me out to see his boat. The tide was in. We took a little cruise and went skinny dipping. He does care about you. You got through to him somehow. Maybe by your fainting. Or being married to an uxorious like me. Or because you're both Marines under the skin. Because you're struggling to break through and be a writer. He said you are like Faust. 'Him we can save'."

"I don't want salvation!" If the old con man Bowman offered it to him on a silver platter, he would kick it down into the middle of the riding ring where his daughter went pointlessly, innocently, round and round.

"You don't fool us. You were hooked by his Jesus talk. It is just his way of talking, but it gets through to some people. I think I know you well enough to know why you bit. You're not at home in life. With me or with anyone."

"This is too much! I can see it was a very high level talk."

"Yes, it was. The . . . *other* was, in a real sense, merely incidental."

"Driving home the message!"

"A kind of old people's joke between us, to show we could still play. And it helped me understand better that you need to play and not believe the world is all on your shoulders. I've been fed to the gills with you. Always. I thought you'd get over it. Now I have more distance. I can honor your suffering."

"I am not suffering."

She laughed. Charitably. "Bowman's opinion is that you are one of those who can't let go and let God."

"Let Him what?"

"Have his way."

"Your language boggles the mind. This can't be you talking."

One of the multitudinous voices chirping in his mind just then advised: this is your chance to tell her about Margaret—where she is and how she got there. Smack her with it, right in the chops and see how much *she* can let go and let God.

He might have done just that if God had not, at that instant, intervened.

Child and horse were both bored by the shambling trot around the track. Ursula dug her bare heels into Judy's flanks, but the mare certainly did not mean to canter. She had done her morning's duty and wanted to go back to drowse in her stall. She began to buck.

One of the hard-eyed girls who supervised the lessons shouted from the shade of the stable wall, "Give her the stick, Ursula. Show her who's boss. *Jerk the reins!*"

Instead Ursula dropped the reins and grabbed the pommel with both hands. The whitening of her face flared like a light flashed in Troy's eyes as he flung his cigar and ran for the rail fence around the track. Judy was prancing and swinging her head nastily as the reins whipped dirt between her legs and to either side.

He should have vaulted the fence and snatched Ursula right out of the saddle with any clumsiness required. It was an impulse of decorum—maybe things weren't as bad as they looked, what did he know about horses?—that made him follow the fence around to where the instructor stood in her faded jodhpurs. She was now yelling more furious commands at both the horse and the tossing girl.

"Get her off that horse!" Troy put a lot of percussion in his voice.

The eyes in the girl's sunburned face blazed on him with absolute loathing. "She's still got twelve minutes in her lesson."

"Get her off or I will!"

"Goddamn you, Judy! Fucking bitch! Ursula! Lean up and grab the reins or she'll stumble. Oh, Christ! You've got to let her know you're boss." The tough girl was looking and shouting right past Troy's shoulder as if he were not there.

He stepped into the ring—saw that the girl whose business it was to control this was now moving in faster than he. He shuffled back to lean against the stable. His mouth was dry and open for a command his mind would not supply. Nancy had run down now and was digging her fingers in his arm, counting on him.

"I told her to get Ursula off," he said.

The instructor sprinted to catch the lashing reins. Spry as a cat, she did so with a show of deftness and mastery that was partly reassuring to the parents. She brought Judy to a halt by planting both feet wide and plowing with her heels.

"Bring them here," Troy said. The air did not seem to carry his words.

The instructor knew her business. She looked half horse herself, though handsome in action. She explained tersely to Ursula where she had failed. "Keep a tight rein. Jerk her head. Cut her mouth. The bit's made to hurt her. Don't *ever* grab for the pommel or you're in trouble, see?"

Maybe Ursula nodded. She did not let go of the pommel.

Obeying a cruel jerk on the bit, Judy followed the lithe girl to the edge of the ring. The girl rummaged in a clump of beach grass and came up with a stick three feet long and heavy as a ball bat.

Holding the reins in her left hand, she clubbed Judy with all her might across the nose.

Judy might be old, but when she was hit like this she reared powerfully enough to lift the snarling, spitting instructor onto her tiptoes in the dirt. Then the girl set her heels once more against the drag of the backstepping horse.

"Why don't you make her stop?" Nancy cried.

"She knows what she's doing."

And in the appearance of the moment this was so. Judy had halted and closed her eyes in submission, though her barrel was heaving and the sweated skin twitched behind Ursula's skinny leg.

"Lesson's *over,*" Troy said. But as he started to walk across the ring he was still getting no acknowledgement from the girl in cut-off levis and dirty white blouse. In the tone of an exasperated gym teacher she was telling Ursula once more how to dominate a horse. "Here," she said, passing the reins once again into Ursula's vague left hand.

"It's all right, daddy," Ursula said. "I boo-booed."

"Here!" The girl put the big stick in Ursula's right hand. It was a nice trick of teaching. It got Ursula's hands off the pommel of the saddle as no coaxing could have done. "Hit her between the ears if she acts up again. *Got* to show her you're boss. Don't be afraid of hitting too hard. 'kay, you got about eight minutes left."

She turned away then, her eyes skimming Troy's face with a pure and mocking malevolence. She blew a puff of pink bubble gum. Walked past him on her way to the shade.

Instantly the abused and now demented Judy began to run, and Troy ran after her, straight across the ring, south to north.

Without changing her gait, the mare crashed head-on into the heavy rails of the fence. The galloping Troy threw up his arms to catch his daughter as she was flung from the saddle

. . . but of course she was flying in the other direction, straight away from him.

She flew like an angel riding a cloud. Right over the timbers that knocked the demented mare back on her haunches in recoil from the collision, toppling her on her side with legs still churning in a parody of running.

Like an angel or a flying squirrel with limbs symmetrically distended, Ursula soared an instant and landed in a clump of beach grass and silky sand. To her father it looked as if she landed on her head. Surely it was her forehead that traced a furrow in the sand and sprayed it up like the bow wave of a boat before her momentum was lost.

Yet before he wiggled through the fence to gather her up, she was sitting upright. It was the unmistakable embarrassment on her face that struck to his heart more than the sand-burn that reddened her forehead. She had done wrong, wasted her lesson money, boo-booed, proved herself a coward and incompetent.

"Oh, daddy," she sobbed as he gathered her up (thinking as he brought her to shoulder level that if her neck was actually broken he might be doing the wrong thing), "daddy, I blew it." Then, "Is Judy all right?"

"Give her to me!" Nancy had caught up to them now. Gooseberry green. Of the three, she was probably in the worst shape. Her breathing was an arhythmic caw from her throat, but the arms that claimed the child from Troy's relaxing grip overwhelmed him with their authority. "Honey, can you move everything? Wiggle your fingers and toes." Sensibly she put the little girl on the grass and knelt beside her, checking her over and over.

Mother and daughter kept smiling confidence into each other's faces, as if the sky might crack otherwise.

Yes! All fingers and toesies wiggled! No, it didn't hurt when she took a deep breath. So surely her bird-frail ribs were not fractured.

Were they? Better be sure, one says. Better trust a licensed stranger. "I'll call an ambulance," Troy said. Nancy said, "Wait," and he waited.

The sand-burn on Ursula's forehead was oozing lymph and turning scarlet. The paler burns on her arms and knees truly did not look serious to either parent. "How's the tum?" Nancy asked with a return of breath control. "Feeling a little sicky?" Concussion accompanied by nausea? She peered in the child's eyes to see if the pupils were contracting. She knew so many things, this capricious woman. "Carry her up to the car, Troy. I think she's going to be *just fine*. But we'll run her to the Medical Center to be checked out."

Ursula held on tight to his neck as he marched with her. The sweat and tears from her face greased his shoulder. As he put her in Nancy's lap in the front seat of the Volvo, she said, "Daddy, wait. I want to go see if Judy's hurt."

He had not even wondered until now why the goddamned animals who ran the place had ignored Ursula's spill. He turned to notice the ring and stable for the first time since the accident. The ring was empty now under a perfect noontime stillness. A pretty place, quainted up for tourists. "The Hiram Godiva Stables," said the black and white sign on the red wall.

"They've led her in. That means she's in good shape."

"No, go see," Ursula insisted and Nancy nodded that he must.

Stiff-legged with anger he went to the stable door. He blinked to adjust himself to the abrupt darkness of the interior. Far in its depths he saw a dazzling wiggle—a sliver of pure sunlight coming through the planks to twitch on the flank of a horse. The place smelled quaint. Marijuana and horse manure.

To his left in the tack room he saw the girl who had nearly

murdered his child. He heard her rusty steel voice in the expanse of a world rapidly regaining its full dimensions.

She was saying, "You remember Memorial Day I said to him. 'Pinky, you remember Memorial Day what you did?' " She was leaning on her shoulder blades against the wall, teasing her mouth with a Coke bottle. A roach was smoking between the dangling fingers of her left hand.

The boy she spoke to was almost prone in a tipped-back director's chair. He was plumper than Troy, wearing only mulberry swim trunks. He balanced a Coke bottle on a hairy navel. His black eyes swiveled to Troy as Troy came in on them. Swiveled right back to the girl's savage face.

" 'What you did Memorial Day was make a fucking ass of yourself, Pinky, as far as I am concerned'. What else could I tell him, Willy, because he made a fucking ass of himself?" Now she angled her head a few degrees toward Troy and said smoothly, "Yes sir?"

"Listen, freak." He leveled a forefinger at her as he heard the director's chair come down on all four of its feet. The girl's eyes flicked a derisive signal: cool it, I'll cool this creep. "I intend to see that this place is padlocked until it can be run with some respect for the safety of the customers."

"Oh, yes, sir."

"And I intend to see that you are *out* of here before your boss is in business again. You're not the boss, are you, Fat Boy?"

The boy studied him, decided not to grin.

"Hiram Godiva! That's a cocksucker name for a cocksucker crew. I'm on my way to the police station to report what just happened."

He was blind with rage, all right. But on the screen of his blindness he saw the fat boy set down his Coke bottle and grope for some kind of steel-ended tool on the tack room floor.

That leveled his voice and he said, "Don't touch it! I'm a black-belt karate. Touch it and I'll smash your windpipe and take both ears." The boy's arms hung slack on either side of his chair.

"The *police* station?" The girl blinked very slowly, as if she truly could not believe her ears. She took a long swig from her bottle and wiped her mouth with the back of her hand. "Did you just threaten Willy? That's a criminal offense, you know. I heard him threaten you, Willy. Break his windpipe? Oh, sir, I'd like to see that done. Willy, call the police."

"And yours," Troy said. "Want to reach for the phone, Willy?" The voice hardly seemed to be his own. But he liked it a lot. Trusted it.

Without really shifting her shoulder blades from the wall that supported her, the girl slowly lifted her chin until the arch of her adam's apple curved out, tempting his blow.

The temptation was real enough. It united the two of them in a searing intimacy, and he would remember that she was not merely daring him to make his threat good. Strangely it was a minute in which she recognized his potency, as if she might say: hey, you could be for real. I'm not ignoring you now.

"What's Hiram Godiva's real name? And phone number?" he asked pleasantly.

"Fuck you. Asshole."

He put his hand out slowly, like a man drawing a bead on a snake. With the gentlest of caresses he traced the line of her jawbone with his forefinger. For an important minute he smothered her will, and they both knew it. Then her derision sprayed his back as he wheeled out of the room, into the blinding sun.

For an eyeblink he knew he had done something decent for once. Not so much right or good as . . . *decent.* Whatever it was he had better try to hold onto it. He knew that a morning which might have been wasted was not.

"Judy was fine. Eating her oats," he told Ursula. "Just banged up a little, like you."

Ursula was lucky, said the woman doctor at the Medical Center. "It's very important to be lucky," she said as she gave the child a lollipop and dismissed her. "Be sure you stay that way."

Not a bone broken. No positive sign of concussion. Only a white bandage on her forehead like a badge, and bright patches of Merchurochrome for her arms and knees. These banal reminders of her dreadful flight were not enough for Ursula. She threw away the lollipop as soon as she got into the parking lot. "The doctor talked to me like a baby." By which she meant she had seen death and flown right over its head.

No parental heartiness about her "luck" could reach her on the drive home. Troy made some headway by telling her how much she had looked like a flying squirrel as she crossed the fence. But still she was a disconsolate and petulant all the afternoon. She tried to nap but quickly woke with a touch of fever and a growly stomach. "The doctor said I could have aspirin and you didn't give me any."

"What hurts?"

"Nothing hurts."

"You don't want aspirin when the tum is queasy," Nancy coaxed.

"I *do.*"

She wanted to share with them some great new wisdom, Troy thought. Her language was inadequate, so she resented language along with the parents who could not help her speak. She would punish them for the shortcomings in communication.

Stormily she jerked the phone cord when Troy tried to reach

the owner of the stable. "Don't do it! Then I could never go back and ride Judy."

"You're not going back."

"I am. I *am.*"

He saw in her perversity the precise flare of lightning Margaret had shown him when she spoke of Clarence and Ishmael. "We'll find you a better place," he said. "I guess it's important to get back in the saddle when you've been thrown. That's my girl."

"I'm going *there,*" she said wildly—and he inferred that for all his compromising Margaret had left New York wanting to see the black men again. His women fled him in dimensions he dare not enter.

Ursula accepted a dish of ice cream instead of aspirin but promptly threw it up in the middle of the blue rug. She ran crying to her room while her parents exchanged questions over the mess. "There's your sign of concussion," Troy said anxiously.

"I think it's just emotional," Nancy said, and, of course, she was right. There was a chord of sympathy between mother and daughter that he would have to respect though it was beyond the range of his understanding.

Then Kevin came romping in from a day's fishing with the Bowmans. He was carrying a bluefish half his own length. "Mr. Bowman caught it. We were out in the Atlantic Ocean. I had one on the line but it threw my hook."

"I might have been killed," Ursula said, belittling the fish and all such sport. Kevin's high excitement dwindled in competition with her increasingly grim interpretation of her mishap.

To make up, as best he could, to both of them, after dinner Troy took them all for a boat ride down the Pamet River and into the surf of the Bay. The sundown was red and purple, a vast flag unfurled by giants marching through their trivial universe.

And, yes, through all the distractions of that day, Troy conceded his failure to look in on Margaret. He had put first things first and done what he had to. What he had to do bore no adequate correspondence to what he should have done. He realized he might, at least, have phoned to tell her not to wait for him in her stifling cubicle at the Deep Six while beaches and sun called everyone else out. His conscience was agile and sore.

Toward two A.M. conscience woke him with a nightmare of smashing some mermaid's windpipe while both he and she were being trampled by poor tired Judy.

Quietly he sneaked through his sleeping house and dialed Margaret's number at the Deep Six. For once he did not prepare a deception or cover story in case Nancy heard. Margaret was asleep and it seemed to take forever for her to understand who was calling her now. "Troh-ee?" she asked at last. Nothing more.

"Tomorrow for sure," he murmured.

"You better haul me out of here," she said dreamily. In the background he heard a chorus of whinnying, as of forty impatient stallions.

Nancy had slept right through his furtive call. He went to sleep telling himself that—like everything which had happened to him or he had learned today—was what he deserved. If Ursula had been hurt seriously in her fall, he would *not* have deserved it.

14

THE DOOR to Margaret's cubicle at The Deep Six had been harmonized with the rest of the place. It was narrow and badly fitted. It must have been retrieved, along with the splintery door jamb, from the demolition of a sub-marginal farmhouse. But it was decorated with a superbly painted mask, vaguely Gay Aztec. Like everything else at The Deep Six, the mask advertised the organizing principle: Art over decrepitude. Taste spread like mayonnaise, creamy on a dry crust.

He knocked—and immediately a gay voice said behind him, "Is it Mademoiselle Gill you cherchez?"

"It is. I do."

"I suggest you try the room just at the head of the stairs and to the left. Mr. Rittmeister's quarters. I have the notion that Miss Gill is a friend of Mr. Rittmeister's.

"She is. Thank you." How did the fellow know she was not

in her room? The afternoon was well advanced. Surely her tiny room was a sweatbox now. But had he seen her leave it? A woman on these premises must be as noticeable as a pheasant in a hen yard.

He climbed the creaking, beautifully waxed stairway up a dim stairwell into a radiance of light from windows overlooking the Bay. He looked out at the sightseeing schooner under full sail rounding the Point.

He felt diffident about knocking. Would all the doors on this landing pop open at the sound of his knuckles? Would he be interrupting something that tact should overlook?

Francis Rittmeister responded almost at once. He was immaculately dressed for the afternoon in white shorts and jacket, with a madras shirt of muted lavenders. He looked uglier than Troy remembered him, but full of cheer.

"Troy, come in! Margaret's left, but I have a message for you, and I want you to meet Mr. Parkinson."

In his youth Mr. Parkinson must have been a Dandy—fit spoil for Somerset Maugham, André Gide, or maybe a centaur drunk on unmixed wine. His rounded face and full lower lip were, except for coloration and wrinkled dryness of skin, those of Bronzini's Bacchus, and his chocolate eyes must always have been faintly disdainful of the men who wanted his body. In his —what? sixties, seventies?—this body still had the look of constant care, in diet, creams, massage and such exercise as would not exaggerate his muscles in their sleek curvature. His perfect nose held a pair of rimless half glasses and his red hair was curled like a sea god's. At the instant of seeing him Troy was reminded of an aged geisha he had met once in a geisha house in Kobe, a being refined beyond crudely natural distinctions of male and female. His handshake was Papal.

"Margaret's gone," Francis explained at once. "To the beach with a carload of the fellows. You are to join her there —that is, in the event that you are free this afternoon. But do have a spot of gin and bitters with us before we go, won't you?"

Troy shook his head, but Mr. Parkinson suggested he sit down and he sat. Mr. Parkinson's sibylline air hinted there were some things he ought to reflect on before he dashed headlong in pursuit of Margaret. "She's certainly caught on here. In the very brief spell she has been among us. Wouldn't you say, Francis?"

"I would. I never saw anything like it."

"A truly exceptional young woman," Parkinson said. *"Vraiment enchantante.* At first I took her to be your ordinary American college girl, in spite of Francis's exception to that. I'm sure you would agree she is anything but ordinary, Mr. Slater. You know what I mean."

"I know her pretty well," Troy said.

Mr. Parkinson's laughter was the real thing; it came from the profundity of his experiences on top and on the bottom. "You know her well," he said, as if this were the rarest of jokes. "Yes, you look with the eyes of love, no doubt, but we never have the full measure of those we love best. I'm quoting. As I often do, don't I, Francis?"

"You're remarkable, Pierce."

"I found the little thing reading on the deck," Pierce Parkinson said. "I supposed she was one of our neighbors—not one of us—who was taking advantage of the morning calm to use our facilities. And they are charming, in their roustabout American way. I spoke—one early riser to another. I was soon enlightened. She was indeed a guest *de la maison* she told me. She was, she said, a lady in waiting, who had not been quite sure when she came here why she had come. She quoted me a line of William Blake's about the overflowing fountain and I responded in kind. From that our friendship grew, for everything about her had quite piqued my curiosity. Francis has subsequently filled me in on biographical detail. We were chatting about that just before you knocked, to tell the very truth."

Troy waved his glass in a gesture of deprecation. *Biography* meant that Margaret and Francis had been gossiping about him. What was there that could be said that wouldn't make him appear ridiculous? He must assume that the old queer saw him in comic profile. He did not so much mind that as consider it a waste of time, and he was in a hurry.

"Quicksilver, my boy," Pierce Parkinson told him with another chuckle. "A young person like that is quicksilver in the hand. A passerby in our lives. And there are passersby. Fleeting as dreams but exquisite. Exquisite in their passage. A dream of youth as we grow older, what? But then, you know all that. I've only known her two days. You've known her, what?"

"Two years."

"Yes. So she told me. I became quite a father surrogate to her in so short a time, didn't I, Francis?"

"You have a lot of experience to draw on, Pierce," Francis said.

"Not all of it wasted," Parkinson said, with a vanity so creamy that he had to close his eyes and wallow in the memories that sustained it. "I've been father to so many of the young that I've accustomed myself to their moving along. Birds of passage. My rule is never to lift a hand, never to bat an eyelid when the season comes for them to fly to other climes."

And that, Troy translated, is the message Margaret is passing on to me through him. She told the old cocksucker that she was trying to untie from me. "Excuse me," he said. "I'm really pressed for time. Francis, thanks for the gin."

Getting on his way was not quite that easy. When he asked where he could find her, Francis made a prologue—or another forewarning not to be disappointed when he caught up.

Francis said, "Margaret's really caught on here. You've no idea what this place is like, Troy."

Parkinson chuckled and said it was a boy scout camp, actually.

"You're so right, Pierce. Troy, you've seen gay places before but this one takes the cake. The rowdy element in particular, and we have our share of rowdies. I never saw anything like it. The way they've adopted her, as if they had to prove something."

Parkinson closed his eyes above a creamy smile. "Princess Meg with her regiment!" he said.

"Last evening I was afraid she might be lonely, since I had neglected her a bit," Francis said. "I found her on the deck— as you did, Pierce—but absolutely surrounded by young men. They had *swarmed* to her. Oh, I should think as many as a dozen or fifteen had either pulled their deck chairs around her or were sitting on hers. And it is my impression she went off early to the A-House with several of them. I've hardly had a word with her since. Except she *was* concerned that you might come today. So when they were after her to go to the beach with them, she instructed me you could find her, any time before six, on the beach at Truro."

"Your notorious beach," Parkinson said.

"The *nude* beach, yes, Troy. That seems to be where a number of our fellows like to go in the afternoons, though I must say, I can't see the attractions. I'm in no way a prude, and I am not in disagreement—not exactly—with the youth cult tommyrot about frankness and candor of exposure. But my own taste is for a measure of decorum. It's all innocent as can be, I'm sure. *De gustibus*, I suppose."

"You can never knock *de gustibus*," Troy said, fleeing at last.

Today he had the time and determination to find her and keep his promise not to leave her abandoned, withering in his neglect a moment longer. The family was off to Chatham with the Dillards. Some matter of watching a balloon ascension, he had dimly registered. He would go to the nude beach, but he meant to stop by his house on the way and pick up his swimming trunks. *De gustibus.* A matter of taste, and his taste was not to parade down the nude beach on a mission requiring decorum with his middle-aged prick shriveling under the gaze of connoisseurs.

There was a strange car in his drive, and as he pulled in beside it, a balding, deeply-tanned gentleman stepped out as though he were there to make an arrest. A man with perfect teeth, all of them displayed.

"I'm Professor Dangleburn. Roger. A pleasure to meet you, sir." His handshake was a grip of steel. He was here to rectify a great mistake. Somehow he had already got word that Stoke & Bywater meant to reject his manuscript, and however he got that unacceptable decision—more of God's superficially capricious tampering with the potentials of modern communication —it was tangled in his mind with the myth that Troy had been, among the various editors of Stoke & Bywater, the one who had showed most genuine sympathy for and understanding of what he was "trying to do with his material." Therefore he had flown across the continent and rented a car in Boston to come and plot with Troy a means to reverse the decision.

"I knew you were out of the office for the summer. I've been checking in occasionally by phone to prod the negotiations. I told myself and my wife Marie that someone was trying to pull something behind Slater's back. I know some of the intrigue that goes on in publishing houses."

"It goes on everywhere," Troy said.

"Aha! Aha! And in the academic profession, as you no doubt know well. We could both tell such stories! In any event, I took the liberty of waiting since your son was here when I arrived a while ago. He said you should have been back an hour ago."

"Should have? Kevin said . . . ?" Oh, my God. Now he remembered the breakfast conversation with perfect clarity. He had promised to drive Kevin to a birthday party on Depot Road. Yes, all were going with Dillards to Chatham, but mother and daughter were being dropped off in Orleans to go sailing on the Spiegels' catamaran. He was to deliver Kevin to the party.

"Kevin!" he shouted at the open windows of the house. "Hurry. I'm here."

"Ah," Professor Dangleburn said. "He was afraid you'd had car trouble. Something about a muffler. He left at three."

"Walking?" He had promised to get Kevin to the party at no later than two thirty. Yes, he had said he might go to the garage in Provincetown to see about the muffler.

Professor Dangleburn could only testify that the boy when last seen, turning to the right at the end of the lane, had been afoot. Whether a motorized vehicle had, beyond that point, accelerated his progress toward his destination, a scrupulous scientist would not venture to say.

It was now 3:27 by Troy's sweated wristwatch. "Sorry," he said. "I'll have to try to find him."

Professor Dangleburn leaned in the window of the Volvo as Troy turned on the ignition, saying, "With your permission, I'll just wait here. I'm in no hurry. I have all the time in the world."

He drove as far as Depot Road without spotting Kevin. He could not remember the name of the kid who was having a birthday, so he could not stop to ask if Kevin might have arrived. He began to circle, trying every blacktop road in the network around Truro Center, uphill and down.

While Margaret . . . ah, not two miles away as the carrion crow would fly it, teams of lesbians prowled back and forth in the surf assessing her labia with discriminating eyes. The vision was like something electronically projected on the Volvo's windshield, and he was late again for the rescue, and . . .

. . . in the midst of this trouble he saw a sweated, red-faced boy trudging doggedly uphill ahead of him. He saw the kid turn

203

and lift a hopeless thumb when he heard the car. Kevin. In his left hand he carried a brightly wrapped flat package.

"Kevin, I'm sorry. I got stuck in traffic in Provincetown. You weren't home when I left, but I had every intention . . ."

Fortunately Kevin would not meet his eyes as he slid into the front seat beside him and gave the little, catching sigh that had always signaled his refusal to break into tears.

"You left with the Dillards right after breakfast, and I wasn't sure I was to pick you up there or at home. Hey! I'm glad you had time to get home and pick up the present anyway."

"Dillards brought me that far."

"Why didn't you ask them to take you to the party since I wasn't there?"

No answer—because the answer was so obvious. The broken promise had spread its damage in all directions, like the famous spreading circle around a stone dropped in water. *Because I wanted the Dillards to think my dad kept his promises . . .*

"I get it," Troy said. "Sure. Well. You taking a record to . . . ?"

"Jennifer. Jennifer Toland. Better turn next left. They live down on Fisher Beach."

"Oh. Jennifer. I guess I don't know her."

"It's not a record. It's the star chart you brought from New York."

"Sure. That was thoughtful of you. Damned thoughtful. Much more imaginative than a . . . *record.*"

"Look, dad."

"Yeah?"

"It's kind of my fault we got messed up."

"It's *not.*"

"Well, it is too. I could of not gone with the Dillards and been there to remind you. Could've started over here earlier. It's not that much of a walk."

"Sun's awful hot to walk. All right, it's nobody's fault."

"So let's not talk about it any more."

"Okay," Troy said. He held his tongue as long as he could. Then said, "Only, I like it a lot that you would think of giving a star guide to Jennifer. You must have planned it a while back."

He had never realized how ugly human genitals could be. And there he was among hundreds of them dispersed at the nude beach along the blue and white shoreline, where the dunes stopped the Atlantic swells.

Dangleburn would have trapped him if he returned once more to the house to pick up his trunks. So, at four o'clock in the afternoon, he was the only fully clothed specimen of the race within sight on a mile of beach.

Fully clothed—he the fully-clothed *voyeur* or maybe cop or maybe parent in search of a wayward child, what else could they think?—he patrolled from north to south between the hissing water and the naked horde.

He was there to find someone, and to find requires looking. But each time he turned his head to look for Margaret, he found himself peering between pairs of feet, straight into a vulvar crease or at a prick empurpled and swollen by the direct rays of the sun. The faces of all except those who raised their heads to watch him pass with hostility or suspicion were effectively hidden from his view by pelvic bulges, breasts, straw hats, or arms draped to keep the sun from their eyes.

It would have been tactically wise to shed his clothes at some point in his walk. What kept him from it was fear, the strangest of fears. As if, in stripping, he would be more naked than any of them—a streamer from his heart dangling ridiculously between his legs like the prick of a baboon grafted onto the body of an editor with a respectable house.

Once when he was very much younger he had been hitchhiking in Utah on a desert road. Needing to urinate, he had gone some yards off the shoulder of the highway to hide himself among some totally barren shelves of desert rock. It was only after he had relieved himself and turned to retrace his path to the road that he saw coiled and sun-drugged rattlesnakes on *each* of the rock ledges over which he had made his way and over which he would now have to get back to the cheap suitcase he had left by the road. Evidently some miraculous camouflage of light and shade on the desert stones had kept him from noticing them until he was completely trapped and cut off.

He remembered it was not the fear that one of the snakes might rouse to strike him as he crept back that had given him so profound and lasting a shock. He was shocked at their ugliness.

Now it took sheer will to turn his head and review the genitals among which Margaret lay sublimely hidden. The pricks curved up over the contour of leg muscle and tendon like a species of huge, purplish maggots. Hair-fringed labia sagged like the wounds left by these larvae crawled from the sea. He shut his eyes.

"Hey, Blackbelt!" From beyond one of the neater wounds rose the derisive face of the girl he had threatened yesterday at Hiram Godiva's.

She nudged the sun-bronzed cadaver beside her, darted her head down to hiss something in his ear. He sat up lazily to grin at Troy. Around her, alerted by some signal Troy missed altogether, other athletic louts began leisurely to stir. Some of them put locked hands behind their heads and, as if in a gymnastic exercise, pulled themselves up into a curved arc of readiness. Their show of teeth looked instinctive, primordial, with no real flavor of amusement and certainly none of irony.

Troy stopped walking without any decision to do so. *It's my legs,* he thought. *They've stopped here to see what will happen.*

The girl called, "Wanna break some windpipes today, Black-belt?"

He believed his answer was polite. "Whatever you say, sugar."

Again her head darted to the ear of the boy beside her. Whatever she told him made him laugh out loud, a fart of laughter still untinged with mirth. Then she called, "C'mon up here with us, Blackbelt. Don' just stan' there with your eyes buggin'. Dinja ever see one before? C'mon. Come join mean my friends. Wanna tell you something funny, Blackbelt."

He shook his head politely.

"I mean *come here!*"

Now his legs were beginning to understand what his deeper nervous centers understood. They were trembling crazily. He had to lock his knee joints to keep the trembling of his legs from betraying him.

"Well now, Blackbelt, I remember how you put it to me. It was I couldn't sleep all night thinking maybe you meant it. Gonna bust my windpipe. You didn't mean that, didja?"

Why is this happening here? he wondered. It was a combat that had been postponed all his life. As if until this singular moment he had been whirled in a pattern of evasion—an inauthentic Marine who had never heard the Chinese bugles blowing through the snow around the Kaesong Reservoir, never fired a shot in anger, a listener to the stories of others, the Bowmans of the world who had been behind the Jap lines with Carlson and his Raiders. How weird that what had been delayed had caught up with him on a beach supposedly public, within sight and shouting distance of dozens of people who would surely intervene. Would they intervene in time to save what had to be saved? And that was a funny question, but there it was.

"Wyncha take off your pants, Blackbelt? Wyja come here

wearing all that like you didn't mean to be friendly? It might hurt some people's feelings, y'know."

His clothing might bother everyone on this beach. The little viper knew that, knew her advantage.

"Nice to meet you again," he said, intending to walk along. His legs refused.

"God*damn* it! If you'll just drop your pants so I know what I'm getting I'll go over the dune with you and we can settle this. One on one." She stretched her arms above her head in a breast-lifting gesture intended as a brutal signal of entice-ment. "Or mean my friends will take you over. That's what you came looking for, isn't it?"

He shook his head. He heard the soft pad of several bare feet passing behind him in the sand, between him and the pleasant swish of wavelets in the shallows. He refused the chance of turning to see who might be there to support him in this savage farce.

The footsteps passed. The girl coaxed, "We just wanna see if your whang's as black as your belt. Don't we fellows?"

"Gotta know," the boy closest to her said. "Got to."

The boys—there were seven of them, not six, as he had thought for a while—began to rock up onto their knees with the economical, lazy-looking efficiency of seasoned troops eas-ing into an action.

"Gotta see if there's anything there at all," said one who had been silent up to now.

The biggest of them began to jerk at his cock, with concen-tration and care, a combatant teasing his familiar weapon. As the member hardened partially, he raised his voice to say, "Gonna stick it right in his mouth."

His mind, which all summer had woven a complication of circles and tied itself up in them was all at once amazingly simple. Happily simple. He knew why his legs would not run though this was the time to run. His legs belonged to the father of a boy who was taking a star chart to a wonderful girl named Jennifer. It was what men did for women, no matter how many crude genitals might be swooping around at any given time.

The lout with the hard-on had scrambled to his feet, still fisting himself arrogantly. The other six were rising, looking toward the reclining girl for her command to attack.

Troy did not see her give it by a nod or a word. He only saw the rising boys galvanize in a roughly circular formation around him and begin a sportive advance toward him. He bared his teeth.

"Greg, he gonna bite you off!" one of them said to his demonstrating friend, giggling exorbitantly.

This was play for them, and somehow as Troy was swept into the comradeship of their violence he remembered someone telling him you must trust God and *play*. In the spirit of the Marines, the most playful branch of the services, he was going to take out an eye, rip off an ear, he thought happily. He put out his hands with spread fingers, playing at being the big American eagle. The boys were not quite close enough yet to jump him with a single leap, but he thought he had picked the one who would come straight at him, with blue eyes open and targeted.

Play!

With a great mouthful of sea air he made the cry of Lord Greystoke, Tarzan of the Apes, and charged through them.

For every man there is a perfect war cry and a time to use it. It may be all he has to spend when the time is right. Each man will hear its perfection himself if no one else hears. It may sound, to derisive listeners, only an imitation of Tarzan, or sound like a stadium full of dullards cheering a football game. But it may also sound like the boys in Butternut Gray breaking out of the wooded draws to run across a pasture whizzing with grapeshot. Sound like a happy Kamikaze pilot alone in his cockpit watching the side of a battleship thicken and then go up like a gray windowblind rolled by a spring. Banzai. Ten thousand years, Emperor!

It sounds like your own name shrieked in the night by a transported girl. "TROH-EE! TROH-EE!"

His own rebel yell.

He turned and saw one of the boys sitting down in the sand, holding a bloody face. He felt the knock of his own heart. Like a war club beating a wooden drum. Not much. The high tide of his life.

His deliverance was clean. Not for long.

His exultant yell was answered, after a moment of clean suspense, by a high, catamitic shriek. "Are you *mad?* Are you *quite mad?*" A bulky man with the face of a dean of men and even a gold pince-nez to temper his nakedness sprang with astonishing speed—considering his age and size—to confront Troy. The dense gray fuzz of his chest was heaving with outrage.

"If you've hurt that boy you will be in very serious trouble, I can promise you. There are witnesses."

"Shut up, cocksucker."

If the man heard him he was too wound up to acknowledge it. "What a shame to cause an uproar here, sir! You appear not to have the excuse of youth for your mischief. Let me tell you, it is entirely inappropriate and will be resented. Enough that you should come here to *ogle*—as, clearly, you have done—and that you can not control your emotions. But try to understand that there are those who come in the spirit of reverence, to be free of oppressive customs . . ."

Even this sermon pleased Troy. He walked on feeling purged and forgiven for failures past, and some of those perhaps still to come.

He recognized Margaret by the excruciatingly feminine curve of her buttocks amid a sprawl of pampered male limbs and torsos. She lay face down in the center of her gay court, the sleeping beauty, under a chartreuse and white beach umbrella so big it had the air of a sultan's tent. He came deferentially into its shade, nodding to the young men who glanced up with unspoken questions. He was tempted to wake Margaret with a kiss on her bare shoulder, but settled for kneeling and tickling her ear with the tip of his fingers.

"Troh—ee!" Her wakening eyes were glad as ever to see him. Sleep had softened her face so it bloomed like an infant's. But a thought troubled her, and the shadow of it dimmed the petal gleam of her innocence.

She was naked!

For once in all the time he had known her she moved to hide her loins from his eyes—flipping a marigold towel corner across her lap as she sat up and swinging her long hair down as if it would veil her nipples.

"I'm glad you found us." Us!

"Sorry about yesterday. Ursula had a small incident at her riding lesson. Shaken up but not hurt."

"Well . . . !" Ursula was someone she had heard about, once upon a time, somewhere. Not flesh and blood and cranky fears to be worried over. "I want you to meet all my friends. Bart, hey Bart, this is my good friend Mr. Slater. Get him a vodka and tonic from the cooler, please. Timothy, Patrick, Jonathan, Norman, Eric, Edwin, Stephen, Hardy, Mason, Roderick."

Golden-haired Bart with his coral love beads . . . all of them acknowledged the introduction with well-bred patter. But, damn it, they were all naked too, now that he had arrived with his conventional clothes and his air of heterosexual proprietorship over Margaret. When Bart delivered the drink Margaret had commanded, his free hand seemed to flutter uncertainly in a screening motion across his dapper prick.

"And you live really nearby?" she asked. "Where is this beach, actually? I fell right asleep when we got here and I'd had a campari."

"You were sleepy today?"

"I'm not used to the sun yet. I've lived under a rock so long."

"Two years. And now you've come out of the closet into the closet. Phase Three? Are you serving the goddess obediently?"

"Can't you tell?" She made a humble, maybe defiant, gesture to number the adorable bodies murmuring around them.

"Frankly, I can't. It's too subtle for me. But no doubt explicable with a diagram."

"It's . . . explicable. Do you need diagrams?"

"I think probably I do. Being this near the end of the string. Having other obligations."

"Well . . . " She gave a small, throaty laugh. Definitely hurt, definitely shamed by the pressure she felt from him.

"Well?"

"I didn't think you, of all people, would need a diagram. Not after all that happened in New York."

"It's that simple?"

"It can't be, can it? Given my strangeness and all."

But then he found she had—still—the trick of making all the world go away when she chose to ignore it. One minute they were duelists, both grappling for a single knife to cut the other away. Then she said, "Look!" and pointed seaward. Just on the horizon line a white ship shone in the dark rainbow colors of water and misty sky.

It may have been a very ordinary ship, some freighter swinging the long way around the Cape on its way up the coast to Boston. But at this distance and in such light it sailed among enticements toward the gates of the Mediterranean, the Italian coast with its green mountains, the swampy delta of the Nile itself.

"Troh-ee!" she said. For the last time he was ever to hear

that peculiar signal from her mouth.

They loved each other beyond bound, scope, or measure. No doubt of that.

But not in this world, where such odd things happen. Profane good things and sacred shames.

"Hey," she said. "Emperor Troy is wearing his new clothes today."

"Don't you believe it. I'm naked as a jaybird."

As if to protest the vanishing of the white ship, the wakening, he reached to pull away the yellow towel with which she had covered her nakedness.

All the young men around them saw his move. Evidently they had not been as engrossed with each other as they seemed.

After a short, hostile lull of suspense, Bart said, "I think that's not done, Mr. Slater." His voice so smart and preppy!

"Well, I did it."

They smothered his boorishness with collective silence.

"Hey," Margaret said, "you've got blood on your shirt, Troy."

How precious that blood was she would never know. Now he had no impulse to tell her. "Wine stains," he said. "And you shouldn't believe it is a real shirt. The Emperor is bare assed naked. Stripped. Down to his bare shinny bones, you better believe it, Margaret. I can't strip any farther. Go any farther than I've gone."

"No. I'm sure it's blood. What happened?"

"A ruckus down the beach. Some sex fiend was interfering with the sun worshippers."

"You shouldn't have got mixed up in it."

"If a dragon is in your way, what can you do? I came to take you out of this menagerie. Remember, once we said we were going to walk right out of Sodom?"

"This is more like . . . Gomorrah," she said pertly.

"Come home with me now. I want you to meet Nancy in

person. And Kevin and Ursula. I want to see what you all think of each other, face to face. You can come as you are. They're all naked, too."

She looked at her painted toenails. Wiggled them. "I love this beach. So free," she said, choosing sides against him. Refusing to come into the only world he truly had to offer anyone.

He got on his knees, preparing to rise. "Come on. Now's the time. Let the chips fall where they may."

"You don't need me any more," she said.

"Then," he said, "forgive me."

"For what?" she asked. Her eyes reflected the color of the sea. Empty, wide, tranquil in the failing afternoon.

15

NO TEARS. No gnashing of teeth. Only the banal whoosh of nature rushing in to fill the vacuum of his loss. In the realm of causality, his farewell to Margaret inspired him to be very kind to Dangleburn that evening.

"You mean you've asked him to stay for dinner?" Nancy asked disgustedly.

"He's come all this way. He waited like a lamb in the driveway for probably hours this afternoon while I took Kevin to his party and did errands. I can't bear to disappoint him."

"Disappoint? You've already put the shiv to him, right under the ribs. That's what you went to New York for, wasn't it? And now . . . ."

The Dangleburn he had demolished was only a name, an abstraction. The Dangleburn now sitting on his deck entertaining the children with lore about whales was a living soul, and hence evoked the same impulse that had made Troy watch over the dying guppies.

Jennifer Minot had come home from her birthday party with Kevin—the star-finding chart had worked like a charm, and with Kevin and Ursula she was learning from the professor that whales are a kind of oversized human being, liberated from the degrading appendages of arms and legs to pursue their superior existence. The children hardly noticed when Troy rejoined them in the charmed circle at Dangleburn's knee. Troy brought with him a double martini, in case the loss of Margaret should suddenly spring out of the ambush of his submissiveness. Dangleburn would drink only what he called a "wine cooler." White wine heavily laced with club soda. Feeling himself somewhere between the human and the whale on the evolutionary scale, Troy listened humbly.

Once (the story-teller explained) the enormous mammals had lived on land, like Kevin and Ursula and Jennifer with their parents here on sea-girdled Cape Cod. Over the ages it dawned on them that there was a choice to be made between the land and the sea—and that arms and legs—or call them just legs, if you must—were what were always influencing the choice in favor of doing constructive, ambitious work on the land, while the trunk and the head wanted to be cradled by the waves. Now, which is the more important part of the body? Obviously arms and legs only serve the royal part, and if they make it do what it would rather not, then goodbye to the arms and legs and other disloyal encumbrances. Shedding legs, the wise old whales took to the hospitable ocean to float their lives away in ponderous self-gratification. Up the evolutionary ladder they went, into the peaceable kingdom.

Listening, Troy marveled that Dangleburn had come, at just the right moment, with a fable to explain Margaret's choice. *She* had opted with the whales, rising to the peaceable kingdom of the Deep Six where the old impediments of marriage, concubinage, social encumbrances, or even the difference between male and female could not trouble her again. With the dregs of his martini, Troy saluted her. Swim on, dear Margaret, beyond the gay horizon.

Whales, Roger Dangleburn told them, migrated without boundaries, for, in truth, there is only one ocean, though the vanity of humans pretends there are several. To eat, they merely opened their great mouths as they swam. They frolicked and basked, he said—and though he was almost nattily dressed in what Californians wore for the more formal occasions of summer, his lurching excitement with his subject could be interpreted as frolicking and basking in the whale manner.

As for love (yes, Dangleburn spoke of love, for all children are interested in that aspect of life, as they well should be) the whales mated with perfect ease and without anxiety and jealousy as they went from arctic to tropic seas at a Californian pace. They cherished their young without needing to teach them rules or restraint. And if they died somewhere, sometime on their happy migrations it was hardly noticeable. They swam on in the great web of life, as protein and then as atoms. Death was a fable the whales had abandoned when they gave up their legs and took to the sea. Their existence was a cycle without heartbreak of seasons beginning or ending, Dangleburn said, his teeth and eyeglasses flashing with such anticipation of the future that Troy could hardly bear to see them all rush away from him after this Pied Piper. But he knew—it was a strange but perfectly firm thought—he could not go when the others plunged joyfully to ruin or ultimate liberty. Someone had to stay behind and report how it had been with whales and all such before the transformation. There had to be . . . there *had* to be . . . writers. And he was one, if he never wrote another story, as he had been one before he ever wrote and published something in the time when getting it on paper and selling it seemed definitively important. He was a writer because he was a guardian of things that merely happen and do not change when the whales depart and pretend that what used to be is not so.

On the beach with Margaret among her newest friends he had declared himself the Naked Emperor, though everyone had taken him to be fully and shamefully clothed. A man knows when he is naked, and when Troy was naked he knew what he was and what it was his duty to guard. He was the abandoned keeper of the past and what had happened, no longer needing Margaret because he had her. ("Troh-ee, the future is all nonsense. We're always in Cincinnati, with the candles burning around our shrine." Cheers, he said, nodding in both affirmation and farewell.)

"We'd better save them, daddy," Ursula said with anguish. She meant whales, or maybe girls like her.

"I couldn't even save the guppies."

She was glaring at him, so he said, "Tell me how and I'll do my bit."

"Not just make cat food or dog food of them," she said.

"All flesh is grass." He wanted to keep her forever in this moment. He wanted her to swim with the others. He wanted her to fly from saddles and bash her head against a rock, but he would keep her in his heart's core when she did.

"It isn't either!" she said. "Daddy! Professor Dangleburn sees them all the time in California, and we never see them here, though Kevin claims he saw one at Balston once."

"Mama was reading *Moby Dick* before she had me," Kevin said, and suddenly blanched at the secret he had almost spilled. His mother's white whale, swimming in unfathomable oceans. Breaching to see the stars.

Jennifer said, "I've only seen the big one in the museum in New York."

"Take these kids back to California with you," Troy pleaded.

"I'm inviting you all," Dangleburn said largely. "Mr. Slater,

I was telling Ursula a while ago about the school of bluefins we once followed in our sailboat down along the Mexican coast. And about one in particular that my wife and I named Topsy. It may be superstition, but I believe Topsy watched and learned more about us than we learned about Topsy." (Oh, call her Margaret, Dangleburn, and stop this unnecessary pretense of parable.) "I suppose she is still out there, Topsy, telling the tale and having a good laugh at our paltry human ways. Another time, as I was telling them, I was in Australia doing research on a fascinating group of bush men when I had the opportunity to sail south with a scientific crew, and I thought of writing my own *Moby Dick*. I may do that yet before I'm through."

"So may we all," Troy said.

"Yes, yes. I know you're a writer, too. I've researched you, Mr. Slater, and know about your excellent book of short stories."

"I'm at work on a novel now," Troy said with the sudden, confident arrogance of the professional claiming his vocation. "Like Melville in the customs house for all those years. He was never more a writer than when he wasn't writing. That is so."

"The seed beneath the snow," Dangleburn said. "I know that feeling so well. And frankly, if I hadn't invested so many years in my Navajo book I'd be tempted to discard it."

"That might be the wise course," Troy said. "Listening to you—I'm speaking as an editor—I wonder if there might not be more sales potential in a book about your whale Topsy. You could jazz it up a little with an episode in which she makes it with a couple of spade octopusi to work in the brotherhood theme, and then you'd have a very marketable property."

Naturally Dangleburn did not follow the private allusions, but he said, "I gather you're trying to tell me gently that too much hostility has built up against my Navajo project by now for me to have any hope."

"No, I wouldn't go so far as to say that, though you put your finger on it when you said this afternoon not everything is open and aboveboard."

To maintain the integrity that Troy lacked, Nancy served Dangleburn a very poor dinner. There had been a big piece of leftover meatloaf she meant to parcel out in sandwiches for lunch throughout the week. She sliced it and confected a tomato sauce to spread over it because in her scheme of things Dangleburn was an atrocious writer and a one-note California bore who put saving the whales ahead of getting a SALT pact.

"I always think in priorities," she said repeatedly while they ate without wine. "I have nothing at all against whales. As long as they are adult and consent freely they can dispose of their bodies as they please. But seriously, the first priority is to line up about nine or ten key Senators and shoot them."

"Priorities, of course," Dangleburn said, wolfing his portion of meatloaf with uncounterfeited relish. "I understand the priorities, Mrs. Slater."

"You'd understand mine better if you had children," she admonished.

He admitted that he and Mrs. Dangleburn had opted for vasectomy.

"What's that?" asked Jennifer.

"Like having your tonsils out," Troy said, balanced between past and future by this duel between Nancy and the spayed wretch. He congratulated himself that his children knew about vasectomies and would be cooled in their ardor for going to California by Dangleburn's confession.

"I understand your priorities, Mrs. Slater," Dangleburn said, looking around hungrily to see if there was another slice of meatloaf. Then he began to belittle the intelligence and personality of whales since, after all, he had come here wanting help in getting his book published and the good will of hen-pecked Slater was an ingredient of his game plan.

Somehow—perhaps because his belly had been filled with second-grade meatloaf—Roger Dangleburn construed his mission as a success. He did not say in so many words that Troy had promised him anything. He simply acted as if now he could count on Troy's advocacy for his interests at Stoke & Bywater.

"You have made me a very happy man tonight," he said as he stepped into his rented car and drove back toward Boston. Troy was glad if he had, thinking that much was salvaged from a day of titanic losses.

He *knew* his loss had been immense; he simply could not feel it. Thoughts turning toward melancholy were only thoughts. They had no ballast of pain. What had happened to him might have happened to someone else, a fictional character whom he could regard with as much astonished amusement as sympathy —and now his overview permitted a rudimentary moral judgment on the order of my character shouldn't have done that. While Margaret had been his love and his albatross he had never been able to get any moral frame at all around the circumstances.

In this new detachment he was going to remember how he *could* have held on to her—not with any promises or stratagems available in recent hectic days, but with the right stroke of courage long ago before there seemed a call for courage.

Once when he had lain beside her with candlelight flickering over their spent and well-used bodies he had said, "We have it all. How do we hold on?"

As usual then, she had been exquisitely tuned to his thought with its unspoken foreboding. She took two deep, shivering breaths and said, "The only way is to give me a baby. I'm healthy and strong. I'm built for it. Then I couldn't blow away

221

in the breeze." He could well remember the shock of his excitement at her proposal. He had felt the word stir and rise in his flesh; his prick rose again to cast its own separate shadow in the radiance of candleglow.

"All *right*," she said gallantly. She scampered to her bathroom where he heard water running and saw the flash of a towel like a cockatoo's feathers as she dried herself. When she came back to him she was carrying her case of pills in the palm of her left hand. "Here, you throw them away," she said. He took them into his palm for scrutiny. They had an unwholesome color, and he imagined he could see tiny grains of poison sparkling in the compound like mica in a rock.

Well, he had foregone the chance to throw them away. He gave them back to her, and their poison had eaten away the time they trusted each other purely, the time when the world balanced with opportunities that might have tipped it toward an adventure with more dignity and more danger. "Babies bind," she had said, his young oracle. They had chosen what they supposed was freedom.

Well, he was bound by his legitimate children, and that would have to suffice. When Dangleburn was gone, Troy must see about returning Jennifer to her house at Fisher Beach. "You come along, Kevin," he said. "Aren't you going to ride along with us, too?"

"Aw . . . ," Kevin was embarrassed for obvious reasons. In this moment of delicacy he must wobble between considering Jennifer his friend and his girl friend. His father urged the greater danger.

"You've got to come. It wouldn't be right for you not to see her safe home."

"I suppose."

"And I'll need company on the long ride back."

"No you don't. But I'll come."

Yes I do, Troy thought. Henceforth I'll need all the company I can get.

Driving back, just the two of them after Jennifer was delivered, they thought they saw something funny in the sky, up along the road toward Provincetown.

"Flying saucers." But they were both too sophisticated to believe in flying saucers. Yet, uncanny, huge, and portentous disks of light were moving in the sky. Moving around in odd, slow patterns.

"Helicopters," Kevin said. "Daddy, wouldn't it be helicopters?"

"Why? Where from? It looks like three of them. I don't know, Kevin. They might be helicopters."

When they drove through the tiny cluster of buildings at Truro Center they lost track of the moving lights. But then they saw them again when they climbed the ridge north of the Pamet River.

"Maybe it's a maneuver and they're up from Otis Air Force Base," Troy said.

They went into the house to find Nancy and Ursula both out on the deck watching the helicopters and their searchlights. The craft were making nongeometric swoops across the narrow neck of the Cape and back, up and down the beaches on the ocean side and over the unforested hills to the west. Sometimes they went low enough to disappear completely behind the dunes and ridges.

"They're looking for someone, all right," Ursula said. "Maybe a child is lost. Would that be it, mama?"

"Perhaps. I don't know."

Kevin said, "I think spies have come ashore from submarines."

"Unlikely," Troy said. With one of its impractical flourishes, his mind fashioned the thought that the whole organized world, with its mighty machines, was out looking for the lost Margaret and would never find her.

He put his hand on Nancy's shoulder and it was like touching a charged wire. That touch, he would remember later, told him more than the wastebasket of information that was about to spill on him. Told him, somehow, that public and private worlds had fused in a single ominous signal, beamed right between his antlers, as if he had been then and there elected as a prophet to bear the word to the peoples of the earth.

"You kids watch it. You keep watching," Nancy said as levelly as she could. But now the hysteria was boiling over. "Troy, come in the bathroom with me?"

"Bath . . . ?" He went with her, holding her slow so she would not spread her alarm to the children.

The bathroom still had a steamy warmth from showers earlier in the evening. In the fluorescent light the whiteness under Nancy's brows was exaggerated, like the white bone of her skull showing through.

"It's Jokaanen Ober," she said, nodding hard as if she couldn't believe it either unless her head hammered the truth of it through. "Winfred Carlson called a little while ago, because they were on the road when the police were setting up roadblocks. I was afraid Ursula might . . . Well, I squawked when I heard. Someone pulled Jokaanen out of her car and gunned her down. Which was bad enough. But now they've turned out the Air Force for something. Troy, who was she? Why is this happening?"

Because nobody gets away with anything. He had supposed that people who lived on Bowman's scale might.

Oh no.

V

16

"I CONSIDER IT a death in the family," Nancy said in the days that followed. It seemed at the same time banal and uncanny that there *were* days that followed the preposterous, graceless shock of the tidings that came to them the way tidings come in these preposterous years. The next morning the newscasters had it packaged in a story that fitted the time slot:

> "European terrorism apparently has spilled over into America. Last night on a road on Cape Cod a young woman known as Jokaanen Ober was assassinated, gangland style, by unknown assailants. Authorities in Hyannis refused to comment on the rumor that the dead woman was really Gosta Haberman, wanted by Bonn authorities in connection with the bombing two years ago of a NATO installation near Stuttgart. The victim was driving alone when her car was forced off the highway. She was

dragged from the car and killed with five shots from a pistol. Her assailants fled on foot to evade police roadblocks, and an intensive manhunt went on through the night between Provincetown and Orleans. So far there has been no report on any arrests. The victim had been staying in the Cape Cod home of novelist W.T. Bowman."

Nancy also said, "It's like they had shot another of the Kennedy's." Because the death of Jokaanen was distinctly not part of their family concerns. No business of theirs. Their involvement with Bowman and his people had been laced with intense glimmers, distinctly not familiar. The main thing Troy registered was that, as a death, it had no fixed range or distance at all. It was in him like the failure of his own brain or heart; it was remote as the death of an antique queen. A pure Platonic principle, and it brought with it, like a taint in colorless air, a special kind of fear, which he would think of as perfect fear. The mother and father of all other fears.

And it was something he shared bountifully with Nancy from the night they had seen the helicopters in the sky and she got the word by telephone rumor. The eruption of their feelings that night drove them out of their house. In the late hours they were sitting in the middle of their sandy lane like refugees under the slow drift of the stars. As if they knew the house condemned by a global scourge that had now come very near to them.

Nancy was trying to make a confession. At four A.M. she was saying, "I want you to know mainly that what I told you about me and Bowman was a lie."

"He didn't come here when I was in New York?"

"He was . . . here. We did . . . go on his boat. Those are facts, but . . . It's the way I told it that is really a lie. The way I tell everything turns it into lies and that's what's spoiled my life."

There was abject need in her voice. A brute hunger to

confront the truth, even if it was like a chipmunk going up against Bronstein's omnipotent cat.

She said, "What I told you was only more of the lies I live by. I think somewhere, down inside, my life is simple. But what I let on to people is either to please them or to hurt them. I usually stick to facts, but not very often the facts that count. I leave out what counts. That's the worst thing most of us do, Bowman says. I didn't explain what a mess I must have sounded on the phone the night I lured him over. He must have thought I was cracking up. For the rest—shit, I wheedled him into it, and you know it.

"Once you told me my sense of justice was a phony, and it is. I didn't argue when you told me, because I don't argue when I know you're right. I've always been afraid you were going to leave me—and pick your moment when I had no moves left to make. But I always believed in justice, except how can you when something like this happens to that lovely girl?"

Her voice shifted gears and she skated past the abstract horror of Jokaanen with an affectation of toughness, honoring it by giving it a wide berth. "How I got to Bowman . . . there you were, putting the wood to this broad in my own bed in New York, and after I had the kids in bed, the sheer presumptuousness of it came over me. To tell the truth it made me horny, too. It came over me, bam, I could fuck a walrus, and in case you've wondered I've done that on similar occasions before. Walri among our dear friends and acquaintances, and don't say it wasn't tit for tat. Two tits and something more, buddy. Which are bygones unless you'd rather hear that story and we'll balance our ledgers."

"They don't really matter. Go on."

"That's true. They don't. But this does if I can tell it right. It doesn't matter either why Bowman came over, and I still think he did it out of kindness, to patch over a family quarrel if he could. He got used for that, too. I spilled it all—all I knew about your woman in Cincinnati. Which didn't surprise him as much as it seems to surprise you I always knew about her."

"Oh," he said. "Her." It was only the top of his mind that would have been surprised by this revelation. The awful news of the night had blown the top of his mind right away.

"I still don't know her name. It was a point of pride never to snoop, but . . . was it her you were with in New York?"

"Yes."

"I was sure it *was* before Bowman came charging out of the brush. I told him what I knew about her, that she really had the grip on you. He asked, Did I *care* that you had another broad in the stable? I said, How do you suppose it makes me feel? Inadequate, naturally. He said I didn't *need* to. Ha! How about that? Well, I *must* have needed to or I *wouldn't* have. He asked if I loved you. How can you tell if you *love* a person after so long? If some Gallup pollster asked me I might say yes just to get him out of the house. But with a man talking Jesus, I thought I had to be candid, so I said I didn't know. He said I had to know. He said, 'If you don't love what you have, big or little, whatever it is, there's no sense to the game'. He said I was merely keeping the cork in your bottle otherwise and being a dog in your manger. I told him as long as you weren't being square with me, why should I put out sauce for the gander. I'm keeping the cork in the bottle and I don't know about love.

"He says, 'Act'. He says we know things by doing them. What we do is the sign to ourselves of how we feel. Feelings are very stupid and don't know what they are until we do something that shows them, then they fall into line like good little soldiers and march with whatever we do and whoever we do it with. Which makes some sense, even if you've acted on some crazy impulse, I think.

"He said if I gave you up for this other woman—who might get the cork out of your bottle, one never knows—that would be the sign to myself I loved you. Like the woman with the baby and Solomon. That idea tempted me. It really did. I had the impulse to give you up then and there and it began to make me hot. *That* was the surprise. How hot it made me to think of not being married to you.

"But it seems like a no-win proposition when you realize love's all a woman has for social security—to get it by giving it up. Phooey. You know I'm not the kind of broad to accept an argument like that. He kept saying I had to 'have faith' and it was at that point I began to get cute—which I'm regretting now—and I asked if that was how he kept his women lined up in a meenadge ah Troy. He laughed, but he said that was when you particularly had to have faith.

"That made me *determined* to show him up. That was when I began to put the moves on him. I guess putting the moves on someone you're determined to knock over makes you hot, too, if you see they are starting to work."

Troy heard something move in the underbrush beside the lane. At first his ears detected no rhythm of progress in the crunch of dry oak leaves or the even fainter swish of displaced branches. He supposed it must be one of the neighborhood dogs, but his nervous system told him if it was not a dog it was whoever or whatever had murdered Jokaanen. It might be whatever it was that chewed up all human efforts to love or to endure the consequences of love.

"What we were saying didn't sound as solemn then as I'm making it sound, because now I'm scared," Nancy said. "But it was sort of solemn, even then, since fundamentally we *do* have souls, as he says, even if they are terribly, terribly decayed.

"Decayed. So we went out on his boat beyond the harbor and anchored and swam. The cold water made me hotter. He could tell that. So we went at it on a boat cushion on the deck, and Troy, here's the awful thing—I was on that cushion and I opened my eyes and saw the starry sky and came like . . . Talk about a cork coming out of a bottle! I nearly blew him over-board."

"It was the Revenge Orgasm."

"But not against you. It really wasn't revenge against you."

"Against life. The big one you'd been saving."

"I didn't know it had a name until now," she said, humbly deferring to his wider experience. "The Revenge O," she said in awe. He hadn't known, either, that it had a name until he spoke it, but now they were like two naturalists who, by independent research, have identified a rare form of life. There was no doubt that it was a distinct species.

"It sort of changed my life," she said, "though that may not show. Changing is so hard."

"Yes," he said. He heard the thing in the underbrush again. It seemed to have moved several yards from where he had heard it before. He supposed it was the angel of death, come to zap them both for eating of the Tree of Knowledge. He supposed that Nancy had seen the same stars that Margaret had seen when she was tripped in the street in New York, and after such revelations there was no way back to the life lived before.

"So," Nancy said, "what I'm trying to get around to is that Bowman was right, and I'm going to love you, so you're free to go to your woman in Cincinnati. I'm going to give you a divorce without any arguments and no strings attached. I thought I was ready to tell you that when we were up at the riding ring with Ursula. Then she got thrown and you were so good about it I thought, No, maybe we can stick it out."

"She's not in Cincinnati anymore," Troy said. "You don't need to be generous about it. There's nothing to be generous about anymore."

Grandly she missed the sense of what he was trying to tell her. She knew herself now, and that was what mattered. "I'll admit I blew it again. There we were watching Ursula ride and it was the right time to say it. I didn't and we slopped back into the way we always are with each other, the way it's always been between us and that was no good."

"Some of it was good," he said stubbornly.

She pitied him his stubbornness. "Oh, *no.* Tonight I don't know what you're feeling about Jokaanen, but I know what I am. Envy—"

"Don't say it!" It might be easier to envy the dead than the living, but he choked on the obscenity of admitting it.

"I *have* to say it." She might or might not have believed what Bowman told her about the ironies of love, but at least she had used the old man as a means of coming to her ultimate knowledge. "It's there to be said, so why shouldn't I say it? I envy Jokaanen because she was a woman being herself. I envy her because she at least took it with her before you men could spoil it."

The beast of the night, the thing in the brush, charged. Troy felt the wind of its passing. He seemed to smell the sweat of its belly hair as it galloped over them. And it went over without really noticing they were sitting there.

It was death, raging after the fine flesh of lovers taken at their prime, claiming for splendor the girl who died young and fair and hardly known to them.

They were ignored and left alive. *Deserted*—that was the worst of it now, the very worst. They were left holding the bag of times to come.

17

THE ASSASSINATION of Jokaanen Ober was the sensation of the summer. Locally in Truro, and in all areas of the globe reached by the far-flung media, there was a splash of amazement at the publicly reported facts and speculation on what was not reported—on "the real truth behind what we're told."

Whatever "the real truth" might be, the event rocketed the girl into legend, where she belonged. Troy had known she belonged in legend from the first time he saw her, wherever that was. There was no use saying she was a mortal like everyone else. No doubt, no *doubt*, she had her sweats and frivolities and digested her food, breathed the common air and painted her own toenails. But her mortal part had never impacted on his awareness as much as her legendary shape had got into his potent dreams. It was simply being true to experience to admit this to himself.

Trapped on a public American road was she? Right behind a Chevrolet with a vacationing family from Quebec and one car ahead of an aspiring entertainer from Tennessee who had temporary employment as a chamberperson in the Howard Johnson Motel in Provincetown. These were facts. Of a sort. Such things as her martyrdom do happen, and they have to happen someplace. Artists of one tradition compose a setting of a magnificence and dignity that will dramatize and re-echo the pathos of the chief agonists in the scene. In another tradition—that of Peter Breughel the Elder, say—the artist will populate his picture with homely and ironically irrelevant figures and detail, counting on the sheer contradiction between the trivial and the mythic to worm the point of his vision through to the quick heart of the spectator.

As Troy Slater was writing the story of Jokaanen it would probably come out in the mixed modes of Breughel and Piero della Francesca, success of the mixture unlikely.

Writing Jokaanen's story? Writing?
Yes.
Why?
Not because he had information or insight unavailable to the pundits, executioners, heads of state, fellow-conspirators, or hacks who might also try to shape the story to a point—but because he had to.
Why did he have to?
Because he was frustrated and offended to the bottom of his soul by journalistic versions of the well-publicized event. For him, around the figure of the eradicated girl—like a handful of dust organized by an ideal paradigm—the grand mystery continued. There was a pattern in chaos. He did not know

what it was, but he had glimpsed it. Therefore . . . he was writing.

"I'd give a dollar to know where Bowman has gone to," Jerry Bronstein said. "That would explain a lot. I'm not prepared to believe he is in custody, though one thing is sure, there's nobody to be seen over at their house except people driving around to have a look at it. We drove past the driveway yesterday afternoon and didn't go in, of course, but saw at least half a dozen cars and some motor scooters on the property." Bronstein was holding his cat under his arm. He had come over to retrieve it since the Slaters had been known to chuck stones at it when it stalked chipmunks on their lot.

"Why should he be in custody?" Troy asked.

"Aha! I know he was a friend of yours."

"We knew him only casually."

"A fellow writer. He has a history of association with Left Wingers, and all that may not be as innocent as we sometimes assume. A man like that with worldwide contacts might have been in it *up to the hilt.*"

"How does that fit with anything?"

"Yes. Well, the informed theory is that this German girl was not disposed of by criminals or terrorists, but by some government. Perhaps by our own government, or in conjunction with an anti-terror squad of the DBR." Bronstein caucused almost daily with other psychiatrists on Balston Beach. When he referred to "informed theories" or to "informed persons" he was passing on something gossiped by them. They inclined to complex stories of conspiracy within conspiracy, of secret governments within governments, and they might have known whereof they spoke. "All those helicopters in the air. Consider the timing, my dear Slater. Knowing the inefficiency of the police and the military, is it likely—does it seem credible to you

—that they could have been so johnny-on-the-spot . . . unless it was all prearranged? They were not pursuing the killers. They were providing a distraction so the SWAT team could escape."

"Mmmmmm."

"What?"

"I'll think that over. That's assuming that Miss Ober was a terrorist herself."

Bronstein laughed and nudged Troy. "You think that old man had other reasons for keeping her? You're a dreamer, my friend. I think we can assume that a certain amount of deception was requisite. Dr. Paley, who practises in Teaneck, knows as a fact that Bowman had a considerable arsenal and that he and the girl had been training with them in the woods right here in Truro. Now, I don't know of my own knowledge that anything was being planned, but I have been studying Bowman's personality, including how he displays himself on the beach, frequently in company of more than one attractive woman. Macho affectations. Dr. Ross, who practises in Queens, considers this a sign of latent homophilia, but say, rather, that it is a revelation of anxieties about failing virility. Given the fact that he is a writer—and we know how writers are, don't we?—my own disposition is to see him as a mythomaniac, constantly impelled to construct a personality for himself. Dr. Steffens, who wrote *The Armed Mind,* feels that such a personality never goes all the way in the enactment of his fictions, but agrees that he tends to associate himself with violent elements. So Bowman may have gone farther than he intended this time. Someday we may get the whole story."

"From whom?"

"There are people who know. Like Chappaquiddick. Do you think, my friend, there isn't someone who knows the real story on that and is waiting for the time to spring it?"

"Things are not what they seem," Troy said.

He hurried to the basement, back to his writing—which was

not what it seemed, either, since it explained none of the questions Bronstein had raised about Jokaanen.

He was writing about Jokaanen—or so he told himself—because there were so many blanks in what he knew about her. And that's what writing is for—filling in the blanks in a life shot full of blanks.

Some time back he had realized if he wanted to know anything worth knowing about Bowman (let alone Jokaanen) he would have to fill in a hell of a lot of blanks indicated by the old fellow's enigmatic chuckles.

But what do you fill the blanks *with?* That is the question always smirking back from any writer's mirror.

Fill them . . . er, umph, wellllllll . . . with *the imagination!* Hurray! Even Dangleburn knew the imagination was "the seed beneath the snow." Schoolchildren knew it. They were encouraged to be "creative"—and that was no help because when you had to put the imagination to work to save your life in the labors of love there were no formulas or directions given.

Still . . . the imagination went on working in its own capricious way. Whenever bumbling, stumbling Troy Slater came to an absolute dead end, why . . . they *imagined* an alternative and swung free on it like Tarzan swinging out of danger on a grapevine. The imagination was not merely the source of belief in miraculous rebirths; it was the primary miracle, all by itself.

He had to imagine he could write his way out of his summer losses, filling one barrel by drawing on the emptiness of the other one. His loss of Margaret would never be made up. It would come upon him, rather, as a long story of grief and comedy. And he was ready for that, had been made ready. At least he was free of anxiety about her, anxiety spoiling love. Whether she was loony or lost, floating right as a cork at her own level or fooling him with more of her whimsical games it no longer mattered. She was not his to save. She was not his to cherish in the flesh. She was right. There was nothing to be forgiven, and so both were free.

But even with his loss of Margaret he had lacked the ultimate push of pain and fear he needed to put muscle in his typewriter until Jokaanen's death shoved him over the edge, terrified him to the bone by its violation and senselessness.

He had better make sense of it.

He might not know the facts about her, but he knew—as Nancy, for instance, did not—that Jokaanen had died pregnant. The embryonic mermaid with flippy little tail was the token that consummated his fear. If it, too, should die, then there was nothing left except the world as it is described on television news. The kingdom of blab, whirling through space on an orbit once assigned to an earth of marvels and wonders, faith and hope.

So the mermaid had to finish its gestation in the slimy counterfeit of a womb behind the frontal bones of his skull or be nothing, forever and ever. It terrified him to imagine how slimy and fish-smelling it was, that lightless rose of flesh he called his brain—to remember how an unthinkable brutality had invaded it and left the mermaid swimming in it as his guppies had swum once in the poisoned aquarium. (Yes, the guppies had their part in the composing picture, too. Many superficially trivial details of the summer fused to become an imaginary thing greater than the sum of its parts.) But the chief dynamic in writing is fear. He was scared shitless, as any good Marine would put it.

And . . . *perfect fear casteth out fear.* That was something Bowman might have said to him if Bowman were truly as wise as he had once imagined him to be.

"What's going on down there?" Nancy asked, somewhat in awe, anxious. "I hear your typewriter going night and day. Catching up on your summer work for the office? Reports?"

240

"I'm writing."

"A novel? It must be long enough for that by now at the pace you're going."

He could not say it was a novel. A novel has a certain length. What he was writing had no length at all. It simply seemed to get wider and wider. He could not even say he had a manuscript, because editors know a *manuscript* has some principle of order and organization. The pages can be numbered consecutively. An index can be made. All he had were pages and pages. Maybe the typewriter had a will of its own, a plan not yet disclosed to him. He served it autistically; he was its motor, providing the muscle to keep it clicking.

"I'm trying to fill in the blanks about Bowman," he confessed miserably to Nancy.

"Maybe I can help with that," she said. Often these days she sounded like a widow. Bowman's widow. Whatever had happened that night on the boat, it had marked her profoundly, as if it were a larger experience than her fifteen years with Troy. Of course Jokaanen's death had burned the encounter into her mind like a brand.

"I'm *imagining* Bowman," Troy said. "He's out behind the Jap lines in my imagination. With Vachel. They're tracking down the killers. He throws Vachel the .44 . . ."

"Well . . . ," Clearly that sounded like crap to her. "I'm glad you're getting something on paper at last."

"I can't even stop it now. It keeps coming."

Still—on this Sunday morning of doves and grieving weather —he sat hunched in the basement in front of his typewriter and could not strike the keys. Rain dripped from the overhanging edge of the deck beyond his window. It dripped from blackened pines and the varied greens of oak sprouts in the underbrush, from Nancy's rosebushes and the silky brown heads of the tall grass. Doves that had come to feed on the last of the summer's blueberries made discouraged flights across the clearing toward the Bronsteins and sat with raindarkened feathers on sheltered branches. And all this demanded to be written about, as well as the rain that fell on Jokaanen's grave in a dripping German forest.

From the floor above he heard the voices of Nancy and Ursula. First they were quarreling about a mess of orange juice Ursula had spilled and left in the refrigerator; then their voices became liquid and confidential, as if they were saying womanly things he could not understand if, in fact, he could make out the words.

Presently he heard the sounds of two recorders. Nancy was teaching Ursula to play the melodies of folk songs. Nancy was not an expert on the recorder any more than she was expert at anything else. But she had the knack of squeezing a musical essence through her amateur attack. Presently, as Ursula caught on to the melody on her soprano instrument, Nancy put aside the alto and sang along. *Where do you come from? Where do you go? Where'd you come from, my cotton-eyed Joe?* The melody was a thread on which the vast morning was strung.

A bit later Nancy came halfway down the basement stairs. She crouched to get a view of him below the unpainted joists of the stairwell and said, "I'm taking the children to church."

"Church?"

"It's Sunday morning. It's raining."

Over the years in this house in the summer there had been many rainy Sunday mornings. Nancy had never come close to suggesting church as an option to meet the ennuis of these times. Yet, no explanation was needed, just as no complete explanation was possible. It had to do with Jokaanen's death of course, and the once-again bottled envy Nancy had expressed.

"Do you want to go with us?" she asked. "The children would like it if you did. Kevin won't feel right about going unless you come. He thought I was joking when I said he had to go."

"I can't."

"You *could.*"

"I can't break off what I'm writing at this point."

"You needn't be so grumpy about it. Of course you're writing. Have he and Vachel killed anyone yet? After all, that's probably a great idea."

"Killed who, though?"

"All the sonsofbitches that need killing," she said. Meditating this enormous slaughter she went off with the children to the Congregational church, which had only interested her before because of its beautiful, straightforward architecture.

He cranked a new sheet of paper into his black machine. With a crackle of drumfire he wrote: *Bowman fucked her into church.* As a beginning line for a novel it had a certain power, which was a plus, along with its impossible crudeness. Better save it for page two hundred and forty or maybe page nine hundred and forty.

Still, it was a hinge point in the design he was groping for so blindly. He rewrote it: *Bowman's penetration achieved one of those surprising conversions no amount of preaching could have achieved. Her obstinate agnosticism was gone in a rivulet of smoking lava. . . .* This was the derisive, fey, self-mocking style in which he used to write things for Margaret to pin up in the Cincinnati shrine. It, too, might have its uses if he put it in the right combination on the right pages of . . . whatever monstrous chimera he might someday glue together. Now he had no Margaret to write for, but Jokaanen instead, and her demands were on a larger scale.

In that hour while Nancy was in church Troy prayed, too. He punched at the typewriter keys with his knuckles. He was punching Bowman for screwing his wife, though it apparently had done her such a power of good. He tickled the keys with a finicking touch—and that was for Margaret who had fucked him back into writing. Oh, she had fucked him good in the end. He hammered away at Jan Savery for opening Pandora's box and letting Margaret out. Grateful to them all . . .

Grateful but in a frightened, even embittered way. They had put a surround on him, cut him off at the pass, hung albatrosses all over him and left him no occupation but this for the rest of his days, numbered and no doubt brief. He blessed them all with his curses while he kept typing furiously and the pages piled up beside him.

Nancy is your novel, Margaret crooned.

She is only *one* of my novels, he begged. Give me time.

I wouldn't give you the time of day, she said, sailing off her perch on a dune with a formation of fairies flying behind her.

She had a lovely face, the Lady of Shalott, wheezed old Jan with her dying breath.

Bowman said, *Semper fidelis. I'll be your hero.*

Well, maybe. Or maybe not. All he could agree on was that he had to find a hero somewhere in the vast accumulation of times and places he was obliged to sort and type through before he keeled over. Needle in the haystack. Let Bowman raise the dead, go to hell and bring back Jokaanen, disarm the nations, show a clean bill of health for Lazarus and the old fellow could claim the title.

Otherwise . . . we'll just have to wait and see who turns out to be the hero. All he knew was that the imagination required a hero and there would be one.

He had not heard Nancy actually leave the house with the children nor did he hear them return. In another of the moments of the summer which would seem more imaginary than real, Nancy was again on the basement steps. He suspected she had been watching him for some time before he became aware of her presence and looked around from his typewriter.

She had been to church all right. She was wearing her best summer dress. Her tanned arms and legs looked very handsome against the blue-flowered print.

"The divorce," she said brusquely. "Do you want it?" Divorce had not been mentioned since the night they got the news of Jokaanen. He had supposed the intention lapsed with the quieting of her feelings as the shock diminished.

"Is that what you thought about in church?"

"Yes or no? One syllable."

"How can I answer that way? If I could say everything in one syllable, why would I be writing all these pages? I guess you know I'm not really writing about Bowman. It is more about women. The way women are in these times. Women as I have known them. And you ask for one syllable!"

"There's no point if you can't be big about things."

"You don't have it straight. It's all over with that woman I had in Cincinnati. I'm not going to run off with her."

Nancy was not persuaded. She had lived too long with his vacillations.

He had to persuade her and now, at last, the truth seemed more useful than a fib. "I didn't dump her. She dumped me. For another man. Men."

Nancy believed him. Somehow it was the plural *men* that convinced her. For a minute he was afraid she would laugh and he could not have blamed her. She did not laugh. She only bobbed her head as if it served him right.

"I am also writing about that," he said with stiff dignity, "and about all sacred and profane love. Those are meaningful terms and they explain the screwy things that happen between all men and women. When I said I was writing about Bowman, that was just a sort of . . . shorthand to sum up the spirit of it, the central theme."

"If you had the divorce you would have more time for all this. It sounds like you had a lot to get out of you."

"Time . . . !" He was tempted. So tempted he dared not say any more just then.

"Yes, I thought about it all through church," she said. "People mustn't go on putting the cork in each other's bottles. He was right about that. We'll have to find another way. You say you're writing and I know you've got it in you to write. But you're not going to make it with me on your back, though I guess you're finally ready to go."

"I've got to do it," he said.

"So we get a divorce. Just write me a note on your typewriter when you're ready, and I'll pack. I want a divorce and don't you dare tell me I picked a silly time for it, when it won't do you any good with your floozy any more, because I've had all of that I mean to stand for. Don't blame *me* that she's laying it out for some new studs. If you'll just say 'Yes, divorce,' we'll call it even. We'll call it amicable."

He saw—as plain as day—that he was less desirable to her now that his Margaret option was gone.

Somewhere in the great multitude of pages he would have to get that into his book, too.

18

IT WAS astonishing how dearly he loved Nancy while he was writing about her. Great subject. Impossible woman.

He was writing about her quite a lot as the summer was dying unnoticed beyond the concrete walls of the basement where he had gone to earth. Among the disordered pages piling into the orange crate beneath his writing table, probably a third of them were consecrated to Nancy in her Greenwich Village days. How she was the raunchiest, bravest girl in her sorority at U of Nebraska and had come to study with Martha Graham before she went on to conquer New York. How she had driven poor Kunstler wild and forced him to defend his life with his fists. (You're right, Margaret. She threw Kunstler down that airshaft just as surely as if he had been a roach she found under her sink.) How furiously and righteously she had resented having to do her belly dance routines to support her loftier notions.

Now he imagined her sitting on a hill beside the Missouri River watching the fire truck arrive to save the houseboat she had set aflame. How she licked her lips and grinned! He imagined her back in the days when she had been homecoming queen of her high school and driven around in convertibles with boys named Beany and Larry who never got further than putting a finger in her. She was saving it all for the sick artists who waited for her in New York, for Kunstler and him and that emaciated, ballad-singing cowboy from Brooklyn who had gone on to a minor career as a protester in the Vietnam War. Kunstler believed she was putting out for the cowboy mornings when he was sick in bed with a sestina and that was among the things he had punched her for. Certainly she had done it, for she was a marvelous bitch in those days.

He remembered—no power of invention required on this— how bitterly she had rebuked him for wanting to watch her sometime when she was out entertaining with one of her "commercial" dance routines. At first he had thought she was shamming when she slipped away without telling him where she was booked to appear. (This was after they were already living together and swore to each other they had confessed everything, had no more secrets from each other.) "It's ugly, it's disgusting, and you know why I do it," she said. "As long as I'm bringing in my share of the rent, that's all that needs to be said about it."

So, once when she was booked for a two-week circuit through eastern Pennsylvania and New Jersey, he had rifled her little cardboard file of private correspondence and papers, read some mushy letters from Beany Coleman, then clerking in Nebraska City, and got the name of a club where she was going to dance in Trenton.

He was pretty well loaded before he slipped into the club before midnight. To tell the truth, even loaded he was scared of her finding him there, because she'd want to know how he learned where she'd be.

He sat at a table near the back wall with two foundry-men who had been there since nine, drinking beer. He ordered a marguerita but settled for bourbon on the rocks when the waitress seemed nonplussed. One of the foundry-men showed him the stumps of fingers on his left hand and wanted to tell him the whole story of how they had been lost and how much workman's compensation he got from the state for his mutilation. Troy said it was a damn shame, all right, but he wanted to listen to the floor show and watch what was going on on the stage across the room.

"Na," said the other foundryman. "Them's a coupla bums." He was referring to the comedians in straw hats who were telling about a woman named Mabel. "You waita Sugar Egypt come on. She grind it right downa the floor."

Sugar Egypt!

"Wull, this dumb jerk, see was supposa be running this fork lift, see and he had on maybe three, four boxes of sand, see. And I says, 'Who loada that for you?' I says. 'You're gonna lose it smash whole thing,' I says. I wanna help, see? But you know what the dumb sombitch did? So here I am with my hannin the chain drive on his fuckin fork lift and he still don't know I'm there, see? He's still got my glove in the fuckin chain drive an I'm sittin onna floor with no fingers, see?"

And there she was, with the clarinets and saxophones charming snakes right out of the Land of the Pyramids—Nancy in a black wig and purple chiffon. Across her forehead was a thick gold band ornamented with the head of an asp. Four inches below her navel a broader band of gold shimmered. And quivered. And shook.

"Grine it!" both foundrymen shouted. That seemed to be the appropriate show of appreciation, for all over the room men and their hearty women were shouting the same thing as Nancy began her undulations. Troy could not bring himself to join in. It seemed disrespectful.

It didn't matter. He was drawn in by the sheer, fierce inertia that swept them all. By what the poet calls the "fierce, undeniable attraction" of seeing his darling flex her nice knees as she began her long grind down to floor level. By the sight of her in the smoke under the spotlights that made the gold twinkle so—but also by something felt from the crowd, as if just then they all shared a common bloodstream and what was running through it was too warm to be endured.

What a sensation, that fusion with the blood of the crowd! As he wrote about it now, eyes fixed on the concrete blocks of his wall, trying to find the words that would make the gold belly-band contract and stretch, the arms of the crowd wave and the saxophones slobber—he trembled again with the promise of it all. He stopped writing and clapped his hands.

His mistake, he still felt, was only that he had gone to her dressing room later to tell her how great she had been. How much he approved. Naturally Nancy thought he had come to mock her with his superior tastes.

"Sugar Egypt!" he said worshipfully.

"You're drunk," she said.

He tried to lay hands on her, then and there. She called a friend (it was the old rooster comedian, still in his striped jacket and bow tie) to throw him out of the dressing room.

From that trip she returned to their apartment only to pick up her things, including her file of papers. "I suppose you read all my letters, too," she accused. "Pervert!"

"If you would listen, maybe we could finally get some things straight between us," he said. But he had little force to put into his persuasions. He had been drinking ever since she had him thrown out of the dressing room. "What you're doing has

250

poetry, strength, honesty. Why've you been always denying it?"

"Lies, lies, lies," she said. "I should have stayed with Kunstler. At least I knew he was a pervert."

He had let her go then because they both understood, beneath the heat of argument, that she wasn't going far. She only meant to discipline him for disobeying her. ("You sneaked in and saw me *that way,*" she said. "But I see you undressing all the time." "I'd be afraid to undress in front of you after that," she said. "I'd know what you're thinking." "You damn well know what I'm thinking all the time." "It's all right as long as it isn't perverted.")

Then she was only leaving him to take a sublet on Bleecker Street. She had the luck to find the apartment of a woman poet gone for the summer to a writers' colony in the Berkshires. When Troy showed up at the door of that apartment—not exactly hat in hand; they were in too deep by then to get out simply—they were quickly in bed together and almost as quickly in fundamental disagreement. Even about the apartment.

Nancy mooned over it because the poet lady had dolled it up with a woodburning wood stove and the canvases of her artist friends. He was charmed by what it must have been before the poetess took over, by the glamorous sweated mysteries of the immigrant poor who had lived there. To his lusting eye, Nancy belonged among those departed pasta-munchers the way she had belonged to the crowd in the night club in the garments of Sugar Egypt. She was *right* when she bathed in the oversized kitchen sink made in another century for laundering and dishwashing as well as bathing the bambinos. And in that apartment on summer evenings he could look up from screwing her on the floor (he grabbed her fresh from the sink) and see the rose-red fronts of the tenements across the street, the windows black, and be in the Old America she meant to flee.

The smell of bathwater steamy in the stifling apartment was a permanent touchstone for what he had *meant* to marry if he could.

Well, he had missed what he wanted most to take from her. Hence—this was all clear as day to him when it was too late to do anything about it—hence the dream world with Margaret, the even more impossible mooning about the tragic Jokaanen.

A pervert for sure. He loved them all for what they wouldn't willingly let him look upon. All of them peddling their ultimate and cherished virginities elsewhere, firing the Big O as Nancy had on Bowman's boat. Well, he would love them for that in the only way he could. By putting it sooner or later and all the time on paper.

So everyone was cheated and no one was cheated. Nancy had married him because he was supposed to be a writer. He had known that his drunkenness and poor health in those days were signs that he had already used up his little string as a writer. Bless her fond heart, Nancy had misunderstood it as evidence of his superiority in talent and sensibility. With the conserving instinct of Nebraska people gathering berries and stacking corncobs for the harsh times between summers, she took care of him when he was sickest and most desperate. He had spent five weeks in Bellevue before Nancy with a lawyer and a private practitioner had untangled the red tape to spring him.

And now—it served her right in all senses of that phrase, probably—he had hold of the string again. In poetic justice, he was a writer. If he couldn't be true to anything else, he had to be true to that.

On a bright Wednesday morning he called Dan Wiggs at Stoke & Bywater to tell him he was quitting. "I mean I *have* quit. As of now."

As befits the president of an institution of any size, Wiggs was never surprised by anything. He was just not very happy about the abruptness of Troy's leavetaking. "Well, you'll be in for a few months or weeks to clean up your desk. If you want to, we can talk it over more fully then. I don't know about finding money for a raise, though, if that's what—"

"No."

"Well, you'd be leaving a lot of loose ends."

"I can't help it."

"Mmmmmm."

"I'm in a crisis situation."

"Oh?"

"Midlife crisis." It was better than saying he was writing a series of novels that would culminate in the assassination of Gosta Haberman, alias Jokaanen Ober. Being a publisher, Wiggs had a very low opinion of writers altogether and had for years been quietly confident that Troy had "got that out of his system." Wiggs was a shrewd judge of character, but unprepared for miracles.

"The thing is, Troy, that Jan Savery has just told us she's quitting too. With both of you gone there could be a considerable mess in your department. Like with the Dangleburn matter. The fellow's been on the phone. Apparently he hadn't got your letter explaining our decision. You were supposed to wrap that up."

"Dan, the Dangleburn matter . . . That's one of the main reasons why I know it's time for me to get out. I'd lost my perspective. Was letting prejudices interfere with my judgment. I tried to make a good case, and I guess I convinced all of you. But on sober reflection, I think it would be good business to go ahead with his book."

This, at least, seemed to mollify Wiggs. He had wanted to publish that horror.

"Why did Jan quit? I don't hear anything up here. Health?"

"She's gone to Mexico to write poetry." Wiggs sighed. "Do you know how many practicing poets there are now in this country, not to mention Mexico. Hundreds of thousands. It's the deluge."

Confessing his move to Nancy was mandatory and there was no excuse for delay.

She nodded in silence when he told her. She got her chain saw and went to cut down two trees. When she returned to the house she said, "I've never understood your motivation."

"You were talking about divorce. I assumed you meant it. Even though we've talked about it before and nothing has come of it. But the primary thing is that I've got to write. I don't have that many years left, and so much is coming to me. I was thinking about our life in the Village and Tom Kunstler's suicide and that apartment you had on Bleecker Street that summer."

"So. Your novel really isn't about Bowman any more. Do you know what you're doing?"

"It is and it isn't about him. It's got a New Testament theme, in any case, and will end with a resurrection. Much father on."

The chain saw had not used up all her wrath. She said, "You *crook*. You've screwed me up again. Don't you know that divorces cost money?"

"If people can live together without marriage, I guess they can separate without a divorce. Divorce is bourgeois."

"And where do you think we're all going to live?"

"I suppose I'll stay here through the winter."

"Here? We certainly can't afford to keep up the mortgage on a summer house if we're splitting. Why don't you go live with this cunt in Cincinnati and let her support you? I had my turn at that, and I'm not doing it again until I see a finished manuscript."

"I told you once and I tell you again that the . . . person . . . is through with me, and I'm through with her. I told you not Cincinnati but Provincetown. I told you . . ."

"You didn't even tell me her name. If she's got one. Don't tell me again it's Rebecca West."

Caught! He had told himself there were no more surprises to come, but it surprised him how painful and hard it was to surrender the name that had been sacred and secret so long. "Margaret. Her name is Margaret Gill." He felt internal tissue balloon from his throat, a bit of gut exposed.

"Never heard of her. So now this Gillperson is up there ten miles away laying it out for a bunch of John Does, while you hide underground with your typewriter!" Her sneer was as merciless as the facts.

"I don't know if she's *laying it out*," Troy said. "I was not an eye witness and it's a mystery to me. All I know is she's living in The Deep Six, which is a gay whorehouse, and the men are getting some good out of her."

What Nancy made of this addition to her knowledge she did not say. In the spirit of divorce she kept her thoughts to herself. All he could be sure of was that the new information made her damn mad.

19

PASSING NEAR the phone he overheard this:

"Hello, hello. How are you Beany? This is Nancy Slater. Surprised? Nancy *Carson.* Yes, I *thought* you'd remember. How is all your family? And Mildred? Oh yes, Millicent . . . Well how *are* you?"

A considerable amount of long-distance phoning was going on. Troy understood that Nancy was making contact with people across the country she had not seen since college days, with men and women she had offended or forgotten, indiscriminately with those she still numbered as friends.

She was on the phone with those scattered legions we all have used up by a certain age. As far as Troy could make out, the results of her telephone campaign did not make her happy. The legions are not to be rallied for any practical cause, not even for reunions where the failed sentimentalities can be brandished one more time.

"Do you ever get to New York? Well, if you ever get to New York, don't *fail* to look me up. I'll be in the phone book. Yes, my name is Slater. s-l-a-t-e-r. I may go back to Carson. You know many women are in these days of liberation. How is Horst, by the way? Still with Provident Life?"

By these overheard communications Troy knew the Deluge was real. It had not smitten them for a single act or infidelity or even by the accumulation of grievances. It had come with stealth over the years. What seemed to be the storms had blown by overhead while grain by grain the soil had leached away from the foundations. Like most divorces, theirs had beginnings that predated the marriage, and the summer's toll counted less than the primal waste of years. Jokaanen's death, Ursula's accident in the riding ring, Margaret's flight into Phase Two—these were not primary realities, only the signal flags fluttering high on the mast while the ship took its time going down.

Divorce was coming, not because of his dalliance with Margaret Gill any more than because once he had snuck in to see Sugar Egypt do her belly dance. It was emerging like a rock that seems to rise because the tide is running out.

In the meantime it saddened him that none of the people she called on long distance phone appeared to accept her invitations to come dancing back into her life. Perhaps it needn't have saddened him. Perhaps her invitations weren't intended to be accepted in the circumstantial world. Like him, she was ordering and composing the vanished world. Building her ship of death, as the fellow put it. In the meantime, petty circumstances could be improvised day by day.

Circumstances like divorce or separation, that is. Just as he knew other things for sure now that had been uncertain speculations before, Troy knew that she had already divorced him.

He was not a part of her vital life any more, only of that life that consists of obligations and entanglements, bills and social commitments, hauling the garbage and taking the children to a drive-in movie—the firmest part of every marriage.

Such things continued without noticeable modulation. Some things were still fun. Some were not. As always and forever. The muffler fell off the Volvo and the police in Provincetown stopped Nancy to chide her for leaving it where it had fallen to litter their street. "If you'd taken care of it any time this summer when I mentioned it you'd have saved me being nice to the Pigs," she said. "Now you better get it fixed before I have to go back there again." But after she had finished this reasonable charge, she suddenly turned dark red and said, "Ah. That's what you mean by henpecking. I'm sorry. I could have got it fixed myself, of course." Speaking to him like a stranger, not like a wife.

In years past when they had been at points of talking divorce, sex had been better than usual. Hot emotions of any stripe are aphrodisical. This time not so. By unspoken consent there was no sex at all. They still slept in the same bed and used the same bathroom. Once when he was showering and she was washing her hands, he found her pensively studying his genitals, with a look of faint repulsion but mostly of dumb astonishment that she had ever had commerce with these grotesque attachments. And he was surprisingly shy of her lavish body. If he bumped against her in bed, he said, "Sorry"—making no big deal of it, merely uttering the formality appropriate for a light collision in the subway rush.

Out of her depths of meditation Nancy said to him one day, with resonant solemnity, "We've got to think of the children."

"Telling them?"

She snorted at his irresponsibility. "What's to tell? We don't have any plans. This is absurd. We don't have any plans! How can we make plans when you've gone away somewhere inside your head and sit in the basement all the time, doing whatever you do down there—listening to the bluejays bring you messages from beyond, I guess—and can't think of anything more constructive than to quit your job. Have you really quit, or was that just some more of your fantasy life? I mean we have to think of the children *so* we can make plans. Telling them whatever we tell them comes when we know what we're going to *do*. Labor Day approaches, and I suppose you could go back to your job and explain you just had a little mid-summer madness. You can't be *that* easy for them to replace after all these years, are you?"

"Sure," he said. "I could go back. I'm the one who knows where the bodies are buried in the office. I earn them more than they pay me. Everyone's replaceable, but it takes time. But, I may not be replaceable in what I have to do now. I can't quit. I'm not going back to the job, even to clean up my office."

There was a faint, momentary gleam of admiration in Nancy's eyes. She had seen him as a stranger and in that brief glimpse seen what he should have been as a husband—if there were any way to reconcile such impossible stretches. "You better turn out to be a damn good writer then," she said.

In the sense she meant, he might be a lousy writer. He had been in the business long enough to know quite a lot about the selling of books, and what he must accomplish, soon or late, had almost nothing to do with that. The connection was, in any case, a loose one between merit and sales. Sometimes they went together, sometimes not. As for his talents, what he had to do was no more dependent on talent than it was on the savvy that goes into deliberately constructing marketable books. It depended on work, time, and miracle—more on miracle, he was afraid, than on any talents or time he could be sure were his to use.

He had thought of the children. He had remembered a day earlier in the summer when he had gone blueberrying with

Ursula, and of that little excursion into the woods with his daughter he retrieved nothing as usable material for a story. It was only a sensation coupled with gossamer intuition. Suddenly he had felt the mild, uncanny *warmth* of the berries as he picked a cluster and cradled them in the palm of his hand, the warmth each little blue globe made from its season on earth. He knew as much about the way they lived as about how people lived. His intuition included the bare-shinned little girl crouched in the dappled sunlight just off his port shoulder: *she feels it too, knows who the berries are. . . .*

He and his child and the berries were in orgiastic, important communion. But what can be made of such fleeting stuff of truly epiphanal vision? It is no story by itself. He had to make something big enough to link the moth-wing irridescence with the gross revels imagined for Margaret and her black angels. Link moth-wing and itchy cunt to make the figure of a woman who could bear the necessary mermaid who died with the legendary Jokaanen.

Only a gambler would try. Only a damn fool would not try.

"Did you tell me the truth that there was nothing wrong with Vachel?" Kevin's question persisted. It was breathlessly ventured again from the conservative censorship he had imposed on himself when he learned that Miss Ober, who had been right here in the house, was really a bomb-throwing, gun-slinging terrorist, executed by figures of comic-book violence on the familiar road to Provincetown.

"Nothing *wrong*," Troy still maintained. "Just different from us."

"They all were," Kevin said, meaning all the Bowman troop. "Like even the day I went fishing with them. I can't remember it like something that happened. It was like being in a movie with them for just that long. The fish weren't real until I brought that one home and we ate it. Flying around with

Vachel, I couldn't tell if he saw what I saw or not."

"They're just people like us. What else could they be? But then Vachel has a lot in his background that makes him different from people you're used to. I think Vachel is *fine*. Just fine. Nothing wrong with him, the way you mean it, at all."

That was what he said, because when he thought of the children he couldn't go beyond wishing they would both believe as long as they could that everything and everyone was all right, within the terms they had to use at school.

But in his reckless imagination Troy shaped a scene which might be used far along in the work he had begun:

A senator is descending the steps of the nation's capitol in the full majesty and pomp of his well-barbered grandeur. The glory of his barbering shines out across the avenues and slums of the city and touches the mountain ridges as far as Tennessee, and he has opened his mouth for laughter and oration when he takes a round from a .44 Magnum. The roots of the tree of liberty are watered.

Vachel's handiwork.

But he could not save Kevin or Ursula by love or caution. The time he had believed he might was over. If they were to be saved—or him, or Nancy—something more radical was required. To be faithful to his little family, he had first to be faithful to the decision that would dissolve it.

Ah, that big, necessary, fateful decision had been made. The subordinate ones showed no signs of following in line. The corpses of their lives were already embalmed, it seemed, in habit and inertia.

"Well, what would you do if your poopsy-doll hadn't gone public?" Nancy raged. "You're not getting ready for a new life. You're just trying to sink us out of spite."

"Her name is Margaret," he said.

"To me she is your poopsy-doll. And if you need her, why

don't you go get her? Go get her and tell her Nancy is no longer an impediment. You must care something about her still, don't you?"

"I suppose I love her." What he meant to say was that in the change that had come over him, past and present tense had no useful distinction. Now he loved everyone he had ever loved, back to his eighth grade crush on one Pamela Stone. But love had ceased to be an appetite. He wanted to possess nothing that would stand in the way of his duty.

But he was not to be forgiven the difference between what he actually said and what he meant to say. Nancy took it as the starting gun for action.

Abruptly she broke off this meandering, if not circular, conversation. She went to shower and dress for the evening. He heard her tell the children she was going to Provincetown, and, no, they could not come with her. "It's mama's night out," she said.

He followed her to the car. "Isn't it all right if I go to Provincetown?" she asked, daring him to object.

"Sure, sure. I just wondered why."

"Probably to get laid," she said murderously. "There must be something to be said for it, or other people would have given it up, too."

The muffler had still not been replaced, and she thundered out of their driveway as if bearing down on some enormous prey, a Kamikaze in her dive.

All right, it was what he had asked for. He had bargained to be taken seriously as a writer. This was it. He went to the basement and cranked paper into his typewriter.

He heard nothing but the machinegun fire of the keys for what seemed a very long time. Pages of manuscript began to pile up on his left, and he fed the magazine from a ream of yellow sheets on his right. He knew he was thirsty and promised himself that as soon as he got to a stopping point he would permit himself to go up and mix a fine big drink. For the time being he only dried his mouth out worse with cigarette after cigarette.

"You really are writing, daddy." It was Ursula, on the basement stairs. Her note was nowhere near as reproachful as it might have been if she knew what all this clatter of typewriter keys was going to cost her in years to come.

"I'm going to bed," she said. "Kevin is already sound asleep."

"Good night, darling."

"It's past midnight. Mama's not home yet."

"That's all right," he said. "Don't wait up for her. You'll see her in the morning light. Sleep tight."

What he was writing for this evening was the approximately true story of a wife in midlife crisis, who goes to Provincetown in search of a dramatic way to cut the Gordian knot of her marriage. Before he brought it to the culminating action he had to sketch in a past that in perspective seemed more heroic than the present, and this had got him drawing more heavily on their days in Greenwich Village than might have been economical. How he had got Nancy away from Kunstler was a very long story in itself . . . and miles to go before you sleep, and. . . .

Typing steadily, he imagined Nancy's voice prompting him, "Whyn't you begin with the first time you went down on me in the shower when we lived on East Seventh Street? How's that for a surprise beginning to contrast with years of boredom? It surprised me at the time, I want you to know, and that was when I knew you loved me, to be candid. You always held it against me that I wasn't a virgin . . ."

Never!

"Well, that I'd lived with that neurotic Kunstler before I

found I preferred you. But the truth is—I tell you now for whatever good you can milk out of it for your work—that I was a virgin in that department. I thought you'd slipped on a bar of soap and maybe hurt your knees."

His editorial mind was trying to reject this as tasteless, but he wrote it in anyhow. Then he was up to the present time. He heard the fine, fierce needles of water in a motel shower in Provincetown, and the voice of Nancy saying to a young poet named Rupert, "Woops! Did you step on the soap? Are you hurt? Woops!"

He neither flinched nor laughed as he wrote this dialogue. He was a man of steel.

It was past two o'clock when he tiptoed upstairs and went to the liquor cabinet and refrigerator, fixing a drink. He had done well. What he had written was almost a love story. Now that love was not an appetite he could do justice to Nancy. The rush of the drink to his brain filled him with exhilaration. He remembered a poem of Baudelaire's about a decaying corpse encountered by lovers on a summer walk, and it seemed that like the poet he could promise his love he would preserve *la forme et l'essence divine de mes amours decomposés*. He could stand the smell.

To relax before he collapsed in bed he turned on the portable radio that Nancy liked to take to the beach to keep up on weather reports. News. In spite of the miniature volume the voice of the announcer was thrilling, and beamed straight at him.

What do you know? A jet carrying a delegation of U.S. and West German officials was hijacked from the Ankara airport. Headed for South Yemen. The announcer said. "In Rome the Jokaanen Ober Brigade claimed responsibility for the hijacking and demanded the release of fifty prisoners in West German jails and a ransom of twenty million dollars . . ."

Yes! He had known that Bowman and his men would not take this lying down. It was beginning!

"The Ober Brigade takes its name from the alleged terrorist assassinated gangland style two weeks ago south of Province-town, Mass . . ."

They were at it and he was with them, sleepless in the enormous night. Instead of going to bed, he went back down to his typewriter.

He must have passed out there, rather than giving up, be-cause he did not hear the thunderous, unmuffled Volvo when Nancy brought it into the lane. He woke in his chair when she hissed at him from the top of the basement stairs. "Still at your work, buddy? I figured this is where I would find you, and I hope you're satisfied."

He saw she was drunk, drunk as a lord. It was more her posture than her voice that gave him this idea. She stood with her fists resting on her hips, her head thrown back arrogantly. His dancer in her Viking pose. His woman satisfied at last.

"There's a present for you in the back seat of the car," she said. "I'm going to bed and don't bother to come join me. Now, don't say I ever cheated you on any count."

In the back seat of the Volvo, bound and gagged, he found Margaret Gill.

When he took the gag out of her mouth, her first words were, "My, she's a strong woman."

VI

20

NANCY SLATER knew when she opened her eyes that she was going to be badly hung over, but for once she didn't mind. Taking her orange juice to the deck, she found Margaret Gill sitting in their yellow chair talking to Ursula. Margaret looked fresh, as if she had slept well. Her hair was pinned off her neck and she had put on the gray cotton robe Nancy usually left hanging in the bathroom.

"Miss Gill is going to Italy, Greece, and Egypt," Ursula said. Like Dangleburn with his whales, Margaret had kindled the passion for travel in the little girl.

"What was the weather report?" Nancy growled. "Did anyone get the weather report on the morning news?" In their immediate vicinity the weather was munificent, a splendor of late August gold. But anything can change.

"She is going to Egypt because she has immortal longings," Ursula said.

"Miss Gill is staying with us until something is settled," Nancy said. She sat carefully on a plastic hassock and frowned at the taste of her orange juice.

"She says you tied her up to bring her here," Ursula said, wide-eyed with the wonder she reserved for fairy tales.

"Miss Gill is very imaginative. I thought you and Kevin would be over playing softball by now. Or is this field hockey day?"

"Kevin's already gone. Because of Jennifer," Ursula explained to Margaret. "He's got a commitment to Jennifer Minot."

"I'm sure you and Miss Gill have had a pleasant conversation, but it's time you went along. Did you wash your tennis shoes like I asked?"

It would have embarrassed Ursula too much to admit in front of a guest that she had come not to mind the smell of her tennis shoes, so she left without a reply.

Nancy said, "I hope you were as frank about everything as telling her I kidnapped you. I must have been drunk out of my skull, but you were so goddamn stubborn."

Margaret thought a while with her slender forefinger pushed to the tip of her nose. Nancy had tracked her from The Deep Six to the A-House and had lured her out for a drive on the beach under false pretenses. She must have had kidnapping or hanging in mind, else why was there rope handy in the car? Margaret asked, "What's that cat carrying?" Past the edge of the deck she had seen the Bronsteins' cat with something dangling helpless from its mouth.

"It's only a chipmunk."

"Alive?"

"He plays it either way. If it's alive, it won't be for very long. Me too. Look, orange juice is fine, but under the circumstances

270

I'm going to lace mine with vodka. Want some?"

Margaret declined. She felt perfect, thank you—riding the crest of life and too wise to tamper with perfection. When Nancy rejoined her she asked, "Where's your husband?"

"Troy? I thought you'd know, I told him it was free-throw time at the Slaters'. Didn't you sleep with him?"

"No. He put me in the guest room and rushed out. Hardly said a word. It made me happy to think he'd gone back to bed with you."

The vodka reaffirmed Nancy's sense of her true identity. "No more of that. I've used him up in that department and you're welcome I'm sure. The way people live around here in Truro, it's all right for you and him . . ." She did not mean to fall short of the example set by the Bowman ménage. If Elaine Bowman had shared her husband so generously, Nancy could do as much. There was nothing she couldn't do. When she had overpowered Margaret in the car, she had understood that rape also was among her options, but she had loftily let the opportunity pass.

Then, as Bronstein's cat gave a final snap to the chipmunk's spine, both of them heard the tentative sound of a typewriter beginning from under the deck. It seemed to be waking from a thin, exhausted sleep. It groped. It ceased. Then began again with a stronger rhythm.

"He's writing. He was writing all night. In the basement."

"I *knew* it," Margaret said. "I always promised I'd get him back to it."

"You?"

"I have great powers. I work through other people. Everyone does what I want them to do. I wanted Troy to write. Poor darling."

"*Something* got him going," Nancy said. She squinted against the bright morning sun. She rummaged under the hibachi and came out with an enormous pair of sunglasses that on her twitching face looked completely black. In the dark behind them she considered the mysteries of causality. "Pussy," she said. Someone had told her it was the great whip that drove Apollo's team. Bowman? Had Bowman said such a thing? Maybe Troy had said it, for Troy also was a writer and writers talked that way. They said some cute things. "We've certainly made him suffer."

"I told you he didn't need me any more," Margaret said. "I tried to tell him that in New York. That's why I'm free to go to Egypt with Mr. Parkinson."

"That old fag? What do you get out of it?"

"I tried to explain last night." Indeed she had. When Nancy drove her out to the beach at Race Point she had been expounding the marvels of old Parkinson. *While* he had been a gay among gays for nearly seventy years, this barren fact could not explain the richness of wisdom he had accumulated along the way. Like Tiresias, who had been both man and woman, Pierce Parkinson knew all that humans were supposed to learn about the sexual mysteries from courtship to parturition. As a youth he had known Maugham, Strachey, Dinesen and the Auden circle. He had once been the object of a moral parable by André Gide. If he had missed acquaintance with Oscar Wilde himself, yet he was a link with the great literary society that took the whole globe for its closet. Last night Margaret had come to the part of the explanation that likened Parkinson to Tiresias when—with a great cry of "Bullshit"—Nancy had pinioned her with her knee and begun to rope her wrists.

Now, taking the difference between drunkenness and sobriety into account, Margaret merely said, "Pierce not only knows all the artists who count, he's very rich."

"In your travels, find me a rich man," Nancy said. It was the kind of thing that girls of every age say to each other, the most banal and sisterly affirmation of the discontent that lives with them in the night and on the mornings after, the discontent by which they recognize their ultimate sympathy.

"You'll have to stay with Troy," Margaret said. "He needs you."

"The hell I will."

"That's why I sent him to sleep with you last night."

"The hell you did. I told you nix."

"I gave him the *impulse* to go to you."

"Wait . . . !" Through the parting fog of alcohol, Nancy was remembering something that must have happened, though it could just as well have been dreamed. "He *did* come rushing into our room. Maybe you did send him there. And I thought he had come to . . . to try to fool me again. And I said 'None of that'."

"He laughed like a maniac. No, he said. No. He had more than enough of women to last him a lifetime, but he wanted me to hear about how he was writing. You won't get this, because it has to do with people we were involved with this summer. The writer Bowman and—"

"Jokaanen Ober."

"Yes, you know about them from TV, and the tragedy. Well, he thinks he has an insight. Political, sexual, religious. All of that. They were big time people and their tragedy changed our heads. That's true. They're the reason I'm *going* to get the divorce. No joke. I may become a nun. Wouldn't that be a riot?

"Anyway, this Troy Slater is sitting on the bed beside me, spilling over again, telling me some rot about a quiff he saw across the airshaft on our wedding night, and he claims it was the same Jokaanen Ober. That she is some sort of charm or goddess to him who comes when he needs her and she is all he needs. And while he is telling me this—I guess I can admit it to *you*—he is getting a powerful erection. The damn fool! So when he explains how Jokaanen comes to him to help him write, he whips it out to show me. 'What am I supposed to do with that?' I said. 'Look,' he said, 'just look'. 'Go shove it in your typewriter', I said. And he said that's just what he meant to do."

Margaret nodded dreamily and excused herself to use the telephone.

The two women were listening moodily to the staccato of Troy's typewriter when they heard, in the lane, the purr of a huge and expensive automobile.

"Mr. Parkinson," Margaret murmured in explanation.

For she had made the necessary call to The Deep Six in Provincetown. Not too early. Not before she and Nancy had come to the sisterly agreement that no woman could or should have to put up with a writer.

He either went too far or not far enough. Was neither hero nor dependable stud, though by turns he imagined himself to be both. His imagination was always out of tune with the times, too early or too late. That's what being a writer is. Someone who is never on the mark when the gun goes off. Skeptical of eternity, throwing too wide a net to snare the day at hand.

Incapable, Margaret said compassionately, of either sacred or profane love. So she, for her part, was on her way home to exotic lands when Mr. Parkinson honked his Rolls Royce discreetly beside the Slaters' Volvo.

Nancy would have one more vodka and orange juice to prepare her to cope with lunch, the children's return from the playground, and the practicalities of ending a marriage.

"Just tell me—if you've read any of it—" Margaret said as she gathered herself for departure, "what's his novel actually about?"

"Haven't read a word. He comes to the surface now and then to babble something. See if you can figure it out. He says it is about the Old America. Kit Carson and his daughter Nancy. Shiloh. Bunker Hill. My apartment on Bleecker Street. The births of our children. Going pistol shooting with Bowman on Guadalcanal. A lot of crazy shit got into his mind this summer, and he thinks he's shuffling it into the rest that has happened, or might happen. No, I haven't seen a page. I just hear him going at it. For all I know he's down there hitting X's on his typewriter and pretending they express what he calls reality."

Then—while the great engine of the universe purred expensively in the lane—she asked, "Shall I call him up now? He'll want to say goodbye to you."

"No," Margaret said. "The one thing he can't tolerate is Mr. Parkinson. Let him imagine it."

Nancy, who did not need to imagine anything, walked out in the lane to see Margaret on her way. Nancy saw Mr. Parkinson's face—very pink with the pinkness of old age, indifferent to the sun that darkened the faces of most seasonal visitors to these holiday shores. He seemed perched very high behind the wheel of an absolutely actual Rolls Royce. Not a new model. An old Silver Cloud.

He seemed to her very gallant and spry as he sprang down to open the door for Margaret and be introduced to Nancy. His cunning old eyes twinkled mischievously in the slits of his lids.

Nancy held his hand a moment in her grip. "You remind me of someone," she said. "Do you know the writer Bowman? W.T. Bowman?"

"Never heard of him," Parkinson said with a resonant, ambiguous chuckle.

Then the doors of the fabulous vehicle were closed again, swinging with the weight and precision of doors on bank vaults. Feeling the pang of desertion, of missing what was rightly hers, yet wanting to be fair, Nancy called out, "Margaret, his novel will be partly about you."

"That will be good. Well, have a nice day," Margaret called back, waving good-by.